Roman Hawk

Contents

ROMAN HAWK ii
Dedication iii
Prologue 1
Chapter 1 6
Chapter 2 15
Chapter 3 24
Chapter 4 37
Chapter 5 52
Chapter 6 65
Chapter 7 80
Chapter 8 93
Chapter 9 106
Chapter 10 118
Chapter 11 131
Chapter 12 142
Chapter 13 154
Chapter 14 166
Chapter 15 179
Chapter 16 193
Chapter 17 206
Chapter 18 219
Chapter 19 231
Epilogue 238
The End 242
Author's Notes 243
People and places mentioned in the story. 245
Other books by Griff Hosker 248

ROMAN HAWK

Book 10 in the Sword of Cartimandua Series
By
Griff Hosker

Roman Hawk

Dedication

Thank you to all of you who have contacted me with comments about my books. I do appreciate all comments and advice. Thanks Rich- you are Drugi!!

Roman Hawk

Published by Sword Books Ltd 2014
Copyright © Griff Hosker First Edition

The author has asserted their moral right under the Copyright, Designs and Patents Act, 1988, to be identified as the author of this work.

All Rights reserved. No part of this publication may be reproduced, copied, stored in a retrieval system, or transmitted, in any form or by any means, without the prior written consent of the copyright holder, nor be otherwise circulated in any form of binding or cover other than that in which it is published and without a similar condition being imposed on the subsequent purchaser.

A CIP catalogue record for this title is available from the British Library.

Prologue

The Eudose lived in the dangerous waters off the Mare Germania and were a fierce tribe of Germanic warriors who raided and preyed on weaker communities. Many generations earlier they had fled the harsh winters, visited on them by the capricious gods, of the northern lake lands across the cold black northern sea. They had found a more benevolent climate in which they prospered and raised animals, the men fished and the women wove cloth. They believed that they had found a better land until the Suebi confederation of tribes began to edge further and further north moving dangerously close to their tiny toehold on Uiteland. The emerging Roman Empire was squeezing anyone who would not conform out of their newly conquered lands to the badlands further north.

Trygg Tryggvasson was the chief of the Tencteri tribe who lived on the eastern coast of the land of the Eudose. His father, who had been a wise warrior as well as a good warrior, had moved the clan from the mainland to the two islands they had fortified and protected. The land was a little poorer than on the mainland and they were severely overcrowded but they were safer and they could watch, from the security of their island fortresses, the privations suffered by others of their tribe who were attacked and enslaved by wave after wave of Suebi raiders, fleeing to easier lands than those in Germania. Every successive wave ended with the Suebi returning south and, inevitably some of the tribe would return to the mainland where for a few more years they would be prosperous- until the next invasion.

When Trygg became chief he made the decision that they would just stay on their islands where they were safe. Over the years they had become adept sailors and seaman, travelling vast distances in their dragon boats which could dart out and capture unwary traders or land at isolated villages to ransack and plunder. Consequently, the women and the old were often left alone for long periods without men to protect them. That task was left to the older warriors and those unable to fight. Sigambri was the shaman of the tribe, and one of the older and wiser heads amongst the ruling council. It had been at the first meeting, following Trygg's father death, that the young warrior put forward his ideas for the way the tribe would prosper.

Sigambri had not had much to do with the young Trygg. He had spent all of his time advising the old chief whose health had deteriorated rapidly in the months before he died. The shaman had become used to ruling the tribe and it had been a surprise when Trygg had convened the meeting. He noticed that the young warrior had filled out considerably over the past few years and the muscles rippled across his lean body. His hair showed where they had come from and flowed over his shoulders, like golden water. His blue eyes were an intense colour, marking him as different from others but it was his voice which was his most powerful weapon. When he spoke, men listened, and he was very persuasive. It was said that his skills were even greater with women, who longed for a son with the intense blue eyes. Trygg had been away for some time with the younger warriors; bringing back much treasure and slaves to enhance the prosperity of Hjarno-By. Sigambri listened with trepidation as he spoke, knowing that the young man would be persuasive and others would listen but it would take much to convince the old shaman whose way had worked for the old chief.

"The Suebi are spreading northwards again. Even as we journeyed home to this haven of Hjarno-By, we could see the burning farmsteads and fishing ports on the mainland. You will see them close to our land, again, and our brethren who sought a home there will soon be our slaves."

Sigambri stood up. "We know this, it is why we live on the island but why should we worry about the mainland?"

Trygg smiled; he knew that the opposition would come from the shaman. When families left the tribe to go to the mainland they paid for the shaman to intervene with the gods and bring them good fortune. It was a profitable enterprise. The fact that the payment only seemed to work for a short time was explained away by the wily shaman who told anyone who asked that the spell had to be renewed to keep it effective. Trygg would have to give the shaman something else to replace his lost revenue. "I do not want our people to go to the mainland where they will die or be enslaved. I want out people to stay with us where they will be safe and we can prosper." The shaman smiled, the young chief was easily defeated.

One member of the council, whose brother had gone to the mainland two years earlier with his family where they had been enslaved, spoke up. "But the land cannot support many of us. Apart from plentiful fish we only have the produce of our few animals. Why, there is little to hunt here and the men we send to the mainland are hunted and enslaved themselves."

Trygg took out a small bag which he jangled. "Do you hear that? It can be hunted but not eaten, it can be herded, but not milked, and it can be grown, but does not live." He knew he had all of them intrigued for his people loved riddles. He emptied out the gold and silver coins, all of which had the face of various Roman Emperors embossed upon them and they lay in a healthy pile on the table before the intrigued council.

Sigambri was almost disappointed. "Coins! Of what use are they to a people who need land? You cannot farm coins, you cannot milk coins. It is land that we need and the men to protect it." He smiled smugly, Trygg Tryggvasson was not the only one who could play with words.

Trygg almost asked about the irony of a shaman asking for such worthless coins but he let it pass. "We took these from Romans and those conquered by the Romans. They live in Gaul and they are all rich. With this gold we can buy better weapons and wood to build better boats and more of our young men can join us to raid their heartland." He leaned forwards, his eye evangelically zealous. "They are like young lambs with no sheepdog to protect them. The Romans who protect them live in stone forts and are unable to stop our raids. Once we have more warriors then we can settle, again on the mainland, but we will have slaves to work the land and build our walls so that we can be defended from the Suebi."

There was much nodding of heads. Sigambri stood up again. "And while you and the young men are all away who will protect the families who remain? Who will make the decisions for the people?"

Triumphantly he sat down, looking like the cat who has stolen the cream. Trygg spread his arms and gave his most disarming smile, the shaman had walked straight into his trap.

"Why you, of course, shaman. You will use your influence with the gods to protect us and, of course, we will make Hjarno-By into a fortress which cannot be assailed easily."

Sigambri had not considered that idea. He had felt certain that the young chief was attempting to alienate him in some way, to get rid of him, but it appeared that he was not. The old man had the vision to understand, in an instant, that he would have the power to become even richer and wield an even greater influence on the tribe. The wives of the men who were away making his money would be easy prey for his lascivious attentions. He even wondered why he had not thought of the plan himself. "We would need wood for the islands have little and we would need more ships."

Trygg had his man, bought and paid for. "We will buy the wood we need from the land of the lakes to the north or even take our young men to harvest the forests themselves." He held up the coins and let them tinkle from his hand like rain, "This is but one of the bags of coin we took and we brought many weapons which can be used by our young men but," his voice became even more commanding, "I want no more families to leave the island. The clan needs every warrior it can get." The nods of approbation, from all, including the shaman told the young chief that he had won. The first stage of his enlargement of the tribe and the creation of a secure base on the mainland had begun.

That was twenty years earlier and Trygg had been as good as his word, as had Sigambri. Trygg raided successfully and the fleet was gradually enlarged and the shaman ruled the islands. The two of them had made a powerful team and there were many young Trygg and Sigambri babies on the two islands and the mainland colony testimony to their endeavours. They had been so successful that they had managed to gain a foothold, with the building of their port of Orsen, on the mainland. It was better suited as a port than Hjarno-By for the water was deeper and afforded more protection during the harsh winter storms. Its security came from the citadel they had constructed, powerfully built over a long summer, it sat on a higher piece of ground which overlooked the harbour and it was manned by those older warriors who no longer went raiding. It had so successfully resisted the frequent invasions of the Suebi that they now went further west to find easier targets and the Eudose were left alone. For the first time in a generation, their numbers grew and the tribe prospered, as Trygg had promised. Although Sigambri had died some years earlier, his legacy lived on and Trygg used a council of shamans to run his fiefdom while he was away. The slaves they had captured were an asset, working the fields, hunting in the fine forests on the mainland and none of them able to escape for the only viable route to their homes lay through Suebi land and there they would be enslaved again. Trygg had a perfect organisation for his tribe and he was loved. All of their security and prosperity came from the chief and he could do no wrong. The gods did indeed smile upon him. Now that the Romans had built up their sea defences in Gaul he was adapting. He needed new sources of income and, on his last trip, he had found one, Britannia which was even richer and easier to pluck than Gaul had been. The next time they sailed, he and his ten boats would cross the short stretch of water to the east coast of Britannia where slaves, gold and jet were in abundance. Soon they would have two fortresses on the mainland!

Chapter 1

The five ships slipped slowly past the starkly steep cliffs which lined the east coast of Britannia. Although autumn with a chill cold wind blowing from their homeland in the east the Tencteri did not wear their cloaks as they rowed their dragon ships purposefully south. Their muscled bare arms were used to colder northern weather than this and the rhythm of rowing kept them warm. The two boys, Ormsson and Sigurd, scampered along the narrow aisle separating the rowers handing out dried fish and beakers of watered ale to keep up their energy. To the boys it was an adventure; their first raid in Britannia and they were both keen to impress Chief Trygg Tryggvasson. If they performed well on this voyage they would have the chance to return the following year as warriors. They enviously eyed the row of round shields which lined the sides of the ship; the chips and scars of each one a testament to a brave deed. The blades and axes, protected beneath the rowing benches by oiled sheepskins were the secret desire of both boys. To own a blade was to be a warrior and to own a blade of power was to be a hero.

The ships gently slowed and turned towards the sandy beach. The art of a good captain was to get the boat close enough in without ripping out its hull and yet close enough for the warriors to wade in through the surf. As the oars came up, almost as though by magic the boat came to a halt and then bobbed up and down on the tide. The rough anchors were thrown astern and then the warriors prepared themselves for the raid. Those lucky few with helmets, like the Chief and Snorri, donned the protection, whilst others, like Ormsson's father Orm and Lars, took their shield and slung it over their back before grabbing their weapon of choice. As the two boys fingered their slingshots they dreamed of the day when they too would go through this magnificent ritual.

As they assembled on the beach the chief summoned Orm and Sigurd. "Today you two will learn how to scout. Go with Harald Larsson. Watch and learn. This voyage will be his last as a scout and the next time he will be a warrior."

Eagerly they followed the youth who was only a little older than they but looked so assured. The bow he carried marked him as one of the few skilled archers in the tribe and the boys determined to learn its skills over the winter. The landing place was at the low point of the cliffs which were little more than a low grey scar across the green land and they swiftly headed south, up the sheep trail to the spongy turf at the top. Harald loped easily along with the rhythms of one who can keep the pace up for miles. The two boys sucked in the pain and gritted their teeth as they hurried after the scout. They watched as his eyes scanned left and right and then, surprisingly, upwards. Sigurd decided he would ask him later why he did that but as he only had enough breath to run he kept silent.

When Harald's hand came up they stopped, grateful for the rest but tensely aware that there was danger nearby. As Harald crawled forwards up the slight slope they emulated him exactly. He edged his head slowly over the grassy bank and, as they joined him, they saw the collection of huts and sheds which marked the Brigante settlement. Below them, the men hacked and chopped with axes and hammers at the rock of the cliff. Small boys and women waited with reed baskets to take away the black gold they had discovered. They were jet miners and, in this part of Britannia, were hewing the most valuable commodity the earth had, the black jet which was sought by kings, queens, witches and druids.

They slid back down the bank and Harald looked at the two boys. His scrutiny finally settled on Sigurd. "Run back to the warband and tell Chief Trygg that we have found the mines." Eagerly Sigurd set off and Orm, for a brief moment, hoped that his friend would fall and he would have the honour of being the messenger. Harald must have seen the look for he smiled and said, "You will have the honour on the next scout."

The fifty warriors waited below the skyline as Trygg and Snorri, without their helmets, peered over the sides to view the mines. "There are two paths one to the left and one to the right. The miners will only see us for the bottom half."

Trygg nodded, "You have done well and that is acceptable. Snorri, you take the right and I will take the left."

The peaceful miners and their families were no match for the fierce warriors. The men fought back bravely with their hammers and axes but it was to no avail. They did have their victories, albeit small, and Harald Larsson fell to an axe expertly hefted by the headman of the community who continued to fight against those who would deprive the people of their prosperity. He fell to the blade of Chief Trygg Tryggvasson. There was no honour in the blow for the miner, brave though he was had not been a warrior. The headman's death had not been in vain for it allowed many of women and children to escape the rapacious warriors eager for female flesh after a month at sea.

As the last miner was despatched they began to collect the valuable black ore. Trygg saw Sigurd and Ormsson looking sadly at Harald's body. "He is now in Valhalla and he is happy. Do not grieve for him. A warrior can ask no more than to die in combat with his sword in his hand. You two are now the scouts of the warband. Do not let me down."

The two boys immediately forgot their dead mentor and swelled with pride. They had taken the first steps to becoming a warrior.

Coriosopitum 122 A.D.

Emperor Hadrian gazed north to the road, built by one of Agricola's legions which cut like a gladius through the thick forests of northern Britannia. In the six weeks since he had arrived, he had seen how the weather in this part of the land could be as unpredictable as a woman's mind. The weary auxiliaries trudging back to the fortress had not been building the wall. They had not been aiding the Sixth Legion to construct the monumental structure which would serve as a reminder to the barbarians of the power of Rome whilst enabling taxes to be collected. They were working alongside the Second Gallic Mixed cohort defending the legionaries from barbarian attack. The Batavian auxiliaries had been repairing the devastating damage from an autumn rainstorm which had seen six uncia of water fall in less than two days. The wooden bridge, already damaged, had been swept away along with some of the legionaries working on the wall. It had made the river level rise so much, as water from the hills added to it, that it had flooded the two ditches which were intended as a deterrent to attack filling them with the mud and soil from the top of the wall. Capricious and unpredictable Mother Nature had undone the work of weeks. Had the cult of the Mother known they would have ascribed it to the power of the Mother, but they were all on Manavia and Mona plotting and planning more mayhem,

Hadrian turned to Governor Falco and Legate Demetrius, the two men the Emperor had given the task of building the ninety mile frontier. "Perhaps the gods do not want a wall here eh Julius?"

Julius Demetrius had served in Britannia for many years and knew the frontier well. He shook his head. "In all the time I have served here I have never known a storm like that one. I did not think there was so much rain in the world. "It had rained for well over a week, night and day. "It is just fortunate that we had some stone in place or the whole of the soil section would have been washed away and we would have had to start from the beginning once again."

The stone in question had been brought from Morbium to give a head start to the building program. The local quarries were closer but quarrying was difficult as the workers had to be protected from the constant attacks of the tribes. While the attacks themselves did not cause many casualties the delay was slowing down the building work dramatically. The Legate knew that the only way to catch up, after the autumn rains, was to bring more stone the forty miles from Morbium and the Dunum valley. "We will have to send to Morbium for more stone. At least there we can quarry in peace."

The Emperor was not convinced. In Dacia, he had used a whole legion to protect his builders and stone workers and succeeded in a much more ambitious building programme. The problem in Britannia was that he was building the limes with but three cohorts rather than one legion for the rest of the province was not yet totally subjugated. The south and east were largely pacified but the west and the north needed a whole legion each just to hold on to what they had. "How long will it take to bring the stone up here?" He could not understand why they could not use the local quarries.

"The problem, sir, is that it is now coming on to the winter and the roads, good as they are, will become difficult to negotiate as the autumn and winter approach. We need to bring as much as we can before the next moon. We will need to commandeer every wagon and draught vehicle and keep a constant line of wagons travelling up and down the road."

"Then see to it, Governor."

Falco's face fell at the size of the task. Julius smiled. It was as though because the Emperor had ordered it then it would be so. Julius knew that the Governor would have a difficult task ahead of him. "I think we need to use some of the cavalry to patrol the road. Although Morbium is safer than the Stanegate, we know from the rising earlier in the year that there are raiders, renegades and bandits as well as potential rebels in the area. Perhaps a couple of turmae of cavalry might deter any would be thieves."

Hadrian frowned. He knew from his discussions with the two Legates and the Centurion of the vexillation of the Sixth that the Second Sallustian Ala was vital to protect the legions working on the wall. In the weeks since he had arrived, the Emperor had seen at first hand how they were able to successfully keep a screen of horseman between the workers and the barbarians. The tribesmen seemed to outnumber the horsemen considerably. It confirmed Julius Demetrius' view that the barbarians respected and feared the cavalry. If almost a fifth of their complement were taken away would they be stretched too thinly? On the other hand, they needed the stone. He realised that this short visit to Britannia would have to be extended. He would only leave when there was a visible mark of his work on the landscape. "Very well Julius but only two turmae."

"Don't worry sir. Two will more than suffice and they can also patrol as far as the coast."

"In the name of the gods why? Surely the land to the east is pacified? I have seen no evidence of anything untoward yet." Was this another problem for the Emperor? In Rome Britannia was regarded as a conquered province- patently it was not so.

Julius nodded at Pompeius Falco. "As the Governor here will attest, we have had increasing raids from the lands adjacent to Germania. Now that the tribes have been subjugated there then the displaced tribes are seeking plunder in the adjacent territory. There are tribes there who are raiding the east coast of Britannia for slaves and plunder. The previous Governor knew about it but did nothing. It is not like the Irish raids, necessitating a cohort but it is having a debilitating effect on those who live on the coast. The Classis Britannica is at full stretch in other parts of the province and we need more help. If one turma goes to the coast and then returns to Morbium it will reassure the people and, hopefully, deter the barbarians."

"I have ordered the building of a series of signal stations around the coast but until they are built…" The Governor knew that the building programme was secondary to the wall and would not be completed this year.

Emperor Hadrian held up his hands. "Enough! I know there are more problems here than Rome realises but we have to start somewhere. I intend to build a port south of this river close to its mouth. The wall can then be anchored to that fort which, should be almost impossible to take. I will then order the building of some local ships to patrol the coast." He looked at each of them in turn. "Does that satisfy you?"

Grinning Julius said, "It does indeed sir but we will still need the turmae…"

"I give up. Will you two join me in the bathhouse? I feel the need to have a hot bath and massage."

"Yes sir but first I will send a message to the Prefect of the Second Sallustian to warn him of our requirements."

Livius looked up at Julius Longinus, the ala clerk, "Have the sentry bring me Decurions Marcus and Decius." Grumbling that he was too old to be a messenger boy the inky fingered clerk walked the few paces to pass the terse message on. "Just think Julius, when we make a stone fort you will have warmth and a hot bath."

"And when is that likely to be eh?" They both knew that their camp at Rocky Point was but temporary and a new stone one was planned but that was dependent upon the completion of the wall, for their fort would be built on the wall, and so far the legions were not making the progress they had hoped.

"It is early days Julius. By the spring we will be ready to lay the foundations."

"If we are still here. The barbarians are becoming even more cunning with their raids."

Livius had to agree. Even though they had cleared the sides of the roads and the camps for thirty and sometimes even forty paces the barbarians were still causing casualties. The previous week a despatch rider had been discovered not one hundred paces from the camp with his tongue and genitalia severed and his entrails hanging out of a sliced stomach bleeding his life from him. It had necessitated using half turma to protect the despatch riders which increased the load on the already overworked ala. "When will the new recruits and remounts arrive?"

Julius went to his lists and consulted them. "There should be some due to reach Morbium in the next few days and as for the horses, they are ready now."

"Good then when our two decurions arrive we shall kill two birds with one stone."

Longinus sniffed. "Huh. I suppose that means that the only decurion who can fill Septimus' pot adequately with decent meat will be leaving and that means porridge and bread for the winter."

"Cheer up Julius, you know what a magician Septimus is; he will make it taste palatable." Septimus had been a trooper until his skills as a cook had meant his promotion. Livius knew that good food made the men happier and happier troopers performed better.

The old man was spared any further discussion by the arrival of Decurions Marcus and Decius. As they stood before him Prefect Livius could not help but reflect on the changes wrought in the decurion he had known since birth. In the last two years, Decurion Marcus had held his dying stepbrother in his arms and had to bury his father. It was no wonder that, young man though he was, he was not yet thirty, his hair was showing flecks of grey and his face had a more careworn aspect than it had the previous year. Perhaps it was the weight of the sword which hung from his baldric. The Sword of Cartimandua was a powerful weapon but it exerted a huge influence on all around it.

There was an aura about the blade which affected the bearer and his protectors. More men had died defending the blade than was comfortable for the Prefect and yet, at crucial times, it had been the difference between victory and defeat. Indeed the Irish raiders led by Prince Faolan had one of their avowed objectives as the acquisition of the sword and that had nearly cost Marcus his life. Had the sword not been used then it might have resulted in an Irish victory.

Julius coughed discreetly and Livius smiled as he realised that the two young decurions had been awaiting his orders. "Sorry gentlemen. It must be being in old Julius' company which makes me act like an old man as well."

"Old man indeed!" The clerk began writing out the orders which he knew would be needed in a few moments.

"As you know we require stone for the building of the wall and I am afraid that the local quarries are suffering too many attacks. The Legate has decided that we will begin a non stop wagon train from Morbium to build up a supply of stone and cement to carry us through the winter. Your two turmae will be the escorts as you have more men. In addition the Legate wants the north bank of the Dunum patrolling to try to stop these raiders from the sea. That means that one of you will travel back up the road to Coriosopitum with the stone while the other rides to the coast and back. You will then exchange roles." He spread his arms apologetically. "I am trying to make the task less onerous and dull for you."

Marcus smiled. It was typical of his old friend that he would think about the orders he was giving. Having been a decurion himself Livius knew that the troopers needed variety or they would see what they expected to see. For himself, Marcus did not mind the mission for he would be able to see more of his family who lived close to the fort at Morbium and the Dunum. With Macro, his older brother, and Gaius his father killed in the last twelve months he now wanted to see his mother, and his brother's family as often as possible. Poor Metellus would be green with envy for Marcus would be able to visit Nanna, Metellus' new Brigante wife, at the horse farm close to Morbium. This would not be a duty he shirked; no Marcus would enjoy the respite from the non-stop fighting on the frontier.

"You will also bring back the remounts and the new recruits who are waiting in Morbium." He paused and looked at the two of them. "Any questions?" It was noticeable that Decius, one of the younger decurions, bit his lip as he pondered a question but then glanced at Marcus nervously.

Marcus looked at the map. "How long is the assignment?"

"You have until the new moon for by then the days will be becoming shorter and the roads less easy for wagons. If we cannot garner the stone we require in thirty days then the Emperor's wall will not be built."

"Good. Right sir we will be off then."

"Not without your orders you won't!" The clerks' authoritative voice made Decius start in surprise while Marcus and Livius just smiled.

"Anything you want bringing back from Morbium oh revered sage!"

Snorting at the sarcasm Julius handed over the two copies of orders. "Some more spices for Septimus would not come amiss and perhaps some more game."

Marcus marvelled that the pile of skin and bones that made up the clerk could consume so much food and yet not have an ounce of flesh on him. "I will bring you back some venison. There should still be a haunch hanging at the farm, it will be easier for your old teeth to chew."

"Cheeky young…" Livius saw the twinkle in Julius' eyes. The old man had, as they all had, been inordinately fond of the two brothers and with Macro dead, all that affection had been given to Marcus.

Chapter 2

When the two turmae arrived at Morbium they could see the effect the Emperor's presence was having. There was much more activity and auxiliaries were improving the defences of the fort. The ditch was being deepened and the fire zone from the walls increased. The rebellion the previous year had shown the vulnerability of this vital river crossing. It was the only place the Dunum had been bridged.

Prefect Marius Arvina was looking harassed as Marcus entered the Principia. "Good to see you Decurion. You will have to excuse the confusion. With the Governor up at Coriosopitum it is left to me to organise the distribution of the new auxiliary cohorts who are arriving daily. "He leaned back and smiled at the warrior who had helped to save his region from devastation by Irish raiders. The Batavians in the fort held the Second Sallustian Ala in the highest esteem. "What can I do for you?"

Decius handed over their orders and Marcus walked to the map on the wall. "There are problems with the construction wall and the Emperor needs more stone. " Prefect Arvina was a friend and Marcus felt he deserved a better explanation for he would have to organise his men to get the stone from the nearby quarries. Already over worked it would add considerably to their work load. "The barbarians are attacking the men who are quarrying and the builders." He pointed at the flooded fields just beyond the gates. "The recent rains have made work slower. We have been ordered to take all that you can provide for us and spend a month escorting wagons back and forth to the wall. In addition the Legate wants us to deter the pirates and raiders."

The Prefect put down the orders. "It would strike me that ships would be more effective."

Marcus nodded his agreement. "My thoughts too, but, apparently, we have to wait for next year for the ships to be built and until then my thirty men riding along the banks of the Dunum will have to suffice."

"I had hoped that the Emperor would have seen our dilemma, having lived at close hand and experienced life on the frontier." The Prefect quickly looked up at the two young men wondering if he had said too much and was relieved when they both smiled.

"Oh, the Emperor knows the situation. Having nearly been caught in an ambush by the Votadini he is acutely aware of the issues but, as Julius Demetrius told us, it is the money men in Rome who cause the problems. They believe that Britannia is conquered and want a return on Rome's investment. When the Emperor returns to Rome then expect more supplies, ships and men but until then, we will become the land borne Classis Britannica!"

"It will be good to have a mobile force close to us. I worry that my static little fort cannot react quickly enough to incursions. By the time we get there then the raiders have departed." He waved his arm at the flooded land which could be seen from the gates." With the extra rain, it means they can get as far as us if they choose. The winter is a dangerous time for the rain from the hills makes the valley more like a lake than a river. Even here the river nearly topped the bridge."

"I think, Prefect, that your bolt throwers would tear them to shreds if they ventured this far."

The Prefect chuckled, "Yes it would be nice to see the look on their faces as Greek Fire poured on to them. " They both knew the magic of both Greek Fire and bolt throwers when facing barbarians. They thought it dishonourable to fight from a distance. It was an edge the Romans did not want to lose. "Give my regards to your family. My patrols check in on them regularly. I think they see it as an outpost of this one."

"After the last raid and the death of my father, my brother increased the defences. He learned that we need stone walls and a double gate. By spring the walls should be stone for the whole of its circumference and the ditches make it look like a smaller version of Morbium."

The ride from the fort to the farm was a short one. The farm was south-east of the fort and far enough away not to be affected by the flood plain. There was a stream on his brother's land which afforded protection for three quarters of the perimeter and the last quarter had a formidable wall and gate. Much of the forest had been cleared to make grazing land for cattle while pigs were kept in large enclosures close to the main buildings. It was a prosperous farm, as Marcus told Decius whilst they rode down the muddy trail, "It is more a collection of farms than one enterprise but my brother manages it all."

"Are you not envious of your brother's riches?"

Marcus shook his head, "My brother does it because he loves it and it is for the family. Any riches we have are for the whole family and that includes those who work with us to till and harvest the land." He could see that Decius was having problems with the concept. "My mother is Brigante as are the people who work the land. She sees it as looking after the land. My mother adheres to the worship of the Mother."

Decius looked aghast. "No, not the corrupted and warped form of Morwenna and her cult, but the true Brigante version which works in harmony with the land, not using it as an evil power."

Ailis and Decius were delighted by the bonus of a visit from their warrior. They had all become far closer since the deaths of Macro and Gaius. The five orphans were also a welcome delight and distraction for the grandmother as they played with and entertained Decius' young son. Ailis noticed Marcus' look and smiled. "The Allfather works in strange ways. He took away two and gives us six."

"I would that he had left us the two as well."

Ailis shook her head. "Your father was marked for death. The harsh winter would have taken him and he would have died in a bed coughing out his life. Better to die with a blade in his hand as he lived. As for your brother, we all know that his mother marked him for death the day that he was born. At least he had more years to live the life he wanted and you know, son, that he always regarded you as his true brother. He had the times with you and I know they were special to him." She looked up in the sky, seeking the hawk that had begun to soar above the farm, "Which is why he watches over you still."

A cloud passed over Marcus' face. His brother was not with the Allfather and he had sworn an oath to protect his brother until he had redeemed himself. Whenever Marcus heard a hawk he knew that his brother was close at hand. He would rather his brother were with the Allfather, his father and Gaelwyn. He shivered for he did not like the supernatural and he changed the subject. "How is Nanna? We have to visit her to collect some remounts."

Decius laughed. "It is like having a female Cato. She works harder than any man I know and her workers always look exhausted and yet they love her. As for the horses, she is Cato's equal that is all I will say."

"That is good to know and Metellus will be pleased." Marcus had been privy to the courtship of his friend and the Brigante that he had rescued. Marcus felt a certain ownership when it came to Nanna, for he had been instrumental in saving her a second time when her wagon had been attacked by the Selgovae. "I will be visiting frequently for we are travelling in the valley of the Dunum for the next month."

Marcus blushed at the reaction from his family. He was not one given to fuss but all of them showered him with hugs and overt signs of affection. The warrior could not understand it and did not know the high regard the whole family had for this quiet unassuming warrior who was the embodiment of his father. Ailis could see, day by day, the son she had borne becoming the man she had married and it comforted her greatly. It was a circle of life and a sign that there was an Allfather, and he did have a plan, however convoluted and complex it might seem to the mortals who strove to exist in his dangerous world.

*

Marcus had decided to take the first consignment of stone on the wagons back to the frontier. The patrol along the Dunum was an easier task and Marcus knew that Decius was inexperienced; he could learn leadership with neither pressure from peers nor enemies. He would be a good officer but he needed time to develop those skills. He remembered how others, Cicero and Graccus amongst them, had not had the time to become good officers and had both been taken too soon. The journey north with the stone filled wagons was quite pleasant for the first twenty miles as they were still within Morbium's area of influence but, as they drew nearer to the border the old Explorate began to smell danger. The slow pace was too predictable and any barbarians waiting to attack them would have much time to prepare. His loyal turma, all oath brothers of the sword, recognised the signs and they too looked around for the danger.

Suibhne had been sent by King Lugubelenus to watch the Roman road. He had with him his own loyal warband. They were forty of the most experienced warriors in the tribe and all of them had lived close to the frontier all their lives. They knew every path and tree in the huge forest which lined both sides of the Roman road. They had been chosen for this task by the king himself and all felt honoured to have been chosen. All of them hated what the Romans had done; it was unnatural to cut straight lines through the holy forest and to use stone to do so was even worse. Stone was for monuments, for men to marvel at, not to plant their feet upon. The gods did not want man to leave his mark on the land and yet these Romans did just that, leaving their scar throughout the land. Days earlier, Suibhne had seen the wagons heading south, empty, and knew what it meant; they would be returning and when they did they would be full. He knew not what the Romans would bring, their needs baffled the simple tribesmen, but if he could stop it then it might persuade them to leave their land and to stop scarring it even more. Whatever was arriving on the wheeled wagons was valuable and if they prevented their arrival then the Romans would be weaker.

He had watched the empty wagons head south and knew when they would return and, when they did so, they would be full and heavily laden. They would have to move slowly, even on the stone roads. That was the time to hit them when they laboured up the hills to the fort at Coriosopitum. The rode rose for a long mile and then dropped easily down to the frontier fort. To create a trap he had had his men dislodge a line of stones across the road. It had taken them some time but he knew they had at least a day before the wagons returned. He then split his men into two even groups along both sides. They had learned how swift the cavalry could be, they would react quickly to any attack. All of the men with him were experts with slingshots. They had stolen skills and ideas from the Romans and now made smoother, rounder missiles which were more accurate and deadlier than the old stones which they had picked from lakes and streams. Now they made their own and they flew truer and hit harder.

As Marcus and his turma escorted the incredibly slow wagons he reflected that he knew this road now as well as any in the province. That did not make it any safer. When it had been first built it was secure enough for lone riders to use it safely. However since the demise of the Ninth and the problems on the Stanegate it had become a dangerous place. The sooner the wall was erected then the sooner they could control the barbarians. Marcus was in no doubt that they would still raid; from what he had understood from Julius and Livius the wall was a deterrent only. Men could still climb over it and then raid in the soft underbelly of Britannia. What they would not be able to do would be to bring horses which would make the ala's task that much easier; nor would they be able to steal horses, animals, goods and, most pertinent of all, slaves. They might get across the new wall but they would not be able to return the same way. He sighed to himself. All that was some way off and for the present, he and his turma would need eyes in the back of their heads and every sense attuned.

Just at that moment his new horse, Star, whinnied. He was a well-trained mount and did not make a sound unless there were strange horses nearby or something which made him wary. "Halt!" Marcus had learned to trust animals and their senses; it was better to arrive a little late but safe rather than on time with casualties and no stone.

His men were a really well-oiled team and they all stopped immediately and faced outwards with drawn weapons, their shields drawn up to protect themselves. The wagon drivers were neither well trained nor attentive and the command took a few moments to sink in and for them to react. Consequently, the first wagon rode on for a few more paces to the dislodged stones. The huge front wheels stuck in the new rut and the driver could not move it. Suddenly a barrage of slingshots rained down on the column but the warning of Star meant that the troopers were safe with their shields protecting them and, as they were facing the forest they made a narrower target for the Votadini.

"Half away!" Marcus' command told the troopers to split into two leaving one with the wagons whilst the other half sought out the enemy.

Suibhne knew that his ambush had failed in an instant. He had relied on being able to take out at least six of the horsemen and then he would have had parity of numbers given the superior weapons and armour of the horsemen. His men had not struck a single trooper. The odds he faced and the skill of the horsemen meant this encounter could only end one way, failure. He blew his horn and his men melted away. He had the satisfaction of knowing that they had killed three of the drovers and damaged a wagon; small victories but, as he had lost none in the brief encounter, he had a victory nonetheless. Marcus resisted his men's eagerness to chase through the forests after the fleeing warriors. They would be wasting their time and risking the wagons. They managed to move the wagon out of the rut and then replace the stones in the road so that the others successfully negotiated the obstacle.

When Marcus reported to Livius at the fort, having left his turma at Coriosopitum, the Prefect was concerned. "I think we had better put more men on the road patrol and less on the river patrol."

Marcus nodded. "It will be Decius on the next road patrol anyway and, as he will be bringing some of the new recruits and the remounts, I will just take ten of my turma. That should leave enough men to deal with another ambush."

"And I will have the Prefect at Coriosopitum have his men check the road. He won't thank me for it but he won't thank us if the fort becomes cut off!"

The two decurions met up again at the new home of Metellus and Nanna nestling close to the fort at Morbium and the old Brigante fortress of Stanwyck. Formerly belonging to Sergeant Cato, Marcus was astounded by the changes wrought in so short a time. Cato's tastes had been utilitarian and everything had been functional and drab. Nanna had swiftly transformed it into a colourful home with murals and friezes on what had been bare plaster walls. The furniture was more decorative and definitely comfortable. As with Ailis, the former captive would brook no slaves in her home but there were many servants for Nanna had been a woman of substance before her capture and the money she had hidden she used well. Metellus himself was not a poor man for the ala had become adept, over the years, at acquiring money and treasure. The two of them were, by local standards very rich. Nanna intended her home to be the grandest in the valley.

Nanna was obviously proud of her home and made the two decurions welcome. "Come in, come in! Bring in the troopers."

Marcus and Decius had looked at the sixty troopers and Marcus shook his head. "They will be happier in the barn for here they would worry about knocking over your statues and precious objects."

"They are not precious," was the lie she faced them with but Marcus had learned from Ailis and his sister in law that every object in a home, no matter how useless, was precious to a woman and that lump of pottery which was barely noticed by a man would become a rare and cherished item by the woman of the house. He noticed that she did not pursue the point but sent her steward to provide food and drink for the men.

"How is Metellus?"

The worry was not only in her voice but in her eyes. She knew how dangerous it was on the Stanegate. "He is safe. Metellus is a careful and thoughtful man, even more so since he became a married man. Fear not. He only has a few years to go before retirement and he will not throw his life away needlessly." He smiled at her and touched her hand, "He now has something to live for." As they relaxed with the watered wine Marcus brought up the real reason for their visit. "The horses, they are ready to be taken?"

Nanna loved horses and regarded them as her children. "We could do with another month to really school them…"

Marcus shook his head. "I am afraid that the Selgovae and the Votadini will not give us even one day and anyway the roads will become almost impassable in a month. The terrible rains we had in the last weeks have made the roads worse than they were."

Nodding her understanding Nanna asked innocently, "You will need more remounts in the spring?"

Marcus laughed, he liked this woman and she was so good for Metellus. "You need not fear for your business. You keep your stallions working and your mares in foal and we will use every horse you can breed. There are some recruits coming north soon and then more after the winter solstice. The numbers of the Gallic cohort and ourselves are below what they ought to be."

Smiling with relief she stood, "Good. Now you will both be staying in the house I take it. We have food for your men and it makes me feel safer to have all these brave young warriors around."

"We will Nanna but we will have to leave before dawn for I must take ten of my men to patrol the Dunum and Decius here has a wagon train, a horse herd and fifty recruits to march north!"

"Then we shall have a feast!" She might not be able to share her home with her husband, but his friends and comrades were the next best thing and it would give her a chance to practise her cooking skills on someone else.

Chapter 3

Marcus felt alive as he and his ten troopers rode east from Morbium along the trail north of the river. It felt like being an Explorate once more, just small patrol riding quickly through the valley. There were five or six small settlements dotted along the northern bank and they would be reassured by the presence of the turma. For the first time in a while, the turma could ride at their own speed and were not dictated to by slow-moving wagons or trudging infantry. Gnaeus, his new chosen man, rode just behind Marcus, keenly looking for any sign of danger. All of the turma were devoted to their decurion having taken the oath to defend the sword, but Gnaeus had been the chosen man of Marcus' brother Macro and felt he had something to make up to both of them, having failed to protect Macro when he needed protection. Gnaeus had served with the ala since the time the two brothers had been made up to decurion and he could not help but notice the difference in the two men. Where Macro had been reckless Marcus was deliberate and thoughtful, where Macro had been mercurial Marcus was cautious and yet both were excellent officers who led their men well. Gnaeus had noticed the change in Marcus since his brother's death. He seemed even calmer that he had been before and he loved life even more passionately. It seemed to the trooper, that the close brush with death and the loss of his brother had made him want to enjoy every precious moment he had been granted. Certainly Gnaeus was not worried that they would be surprised or ambushed, Marcus was too careful.

"Sir, are we going to take the river path?"
"No Gnaeus the rains will have made that treacherous." The same rains which had devastated the building of the wall had also flooded the Dunum. It had widened from a river of sixty paces to a lake of half a mile in places. "No we will ride the bluffs; it will take out all the bends in the river. We will head for Seolh Muba."
"Seolh Muba?"
"The mouth of the Dunum, the place where the seals bask on the mud flats."

"Do you think we will actually see any raiders?" Gnaeus was dubious about the value of the patrol. He felt they should have been on the frontier fighting the barbarians. He believed in what Rome was doing and hoped that the barbarians would, eventually, see it that way too. Pleasant though the ride was they were doing little good. "It seems to me it is the wrong season. The seas are wild at this time of year and it would take a brave or foolhardy captain to risk these waters."

"Perhaps you are right but we only have a month of this duty and then we will return to the Stanegate. It is not an arduous duty and I do not think it will involve too many risks. If we see a ship then we can report it and if we see any raiders we can follow. We are here as a deterrent only. " Marcus peered to the south where he knew the river flowed. The trees and branches before him obscured the view somewhat. He could identify little but as there were no masts to be seen he knew that there were no ships. "We will head for the woods between Oegels-dun and Eabrycg. That way we can cut out the mighty loops of the river."

Gnaeus nodded, the two settlements were palisaded and defended; it was unlikely that any raider could trouble them but at least they would be able to get some hot food when they reached them for the Brigante were always pleased to see the ala. Gnaeus grinned to himself, perhaps they would arrive just in time for a freshly brewed ale, the Allfather and Parcae would be on their side if that happened.

Trygg Tryggvasson turned to his lieutenant, Snorri. "I think this will be the last trip we take until the spring." The tall chief gestured to the wide floodwaters which made the Dunum less a river and more a lake. "We cannot go too close ashore, we do not know where the trees and rocks are and Odin would not like us to be beached here in this land of the Romans." He turned to look at the other five longships rowing in his wake. They had already made a successful raid on the coast and relieved many of the jet miners, who lived at the coast, of their bounty. The iron mines further north had yielded some fine iron ore which could easily be traded and the only thing they now required was a healthy boatload of slaves. They needed them to work the fields and to sell to their neighbours. However, Trygg had the novel idea of mating strong male slaves with healthy women to produce new warrior slaves for the future. Once they were weaned the young males could be trained in weapons and fighting. He had a vision of warriors who were totally devoted to the tribe without any family loyalty. Then he would be able to sail further afield, perhaps to the warmer waters further south and find new rich lands from which to take even more plunder. It was a long term plan but he was building an empire for his sons. He had heard that the mighty Roman Empire had begun with a small tribe living on seven hills. With Odin's help, some day, his descendants would rule a land as vast.

"Smoke ahead!" The lookout whose legs were curled precariously around the top of the mainmast pointed to the north bank of the river. They had passed one settlement but they had been seen and Trygg had no desire to lose men in a costly assault on a fortified town. He wanted easy pickings; he chose when he would fight a battle. He would pull ashore and approach this settlement across the land. With the fifty warriors behind him, he would easily be able to defeat an unwary village.

"Lower the sail! Ease her into the shore. Orm, keep a good lookout forrard, I don't want to run foul of any trees." The ships behind tacked in turn and soon they were twenty paces from the shore. "Lars, see what the bottom is like."

Orm stood on the prow. He took off his sword and jumped into the water. It was with a shock that he only landed up to his waist. Although he turned around with a sheepish look on his face Trygg knew that they had misjudged their approach and could have been grounded.

"Get the men ashore and then turn the ships around. Moor the ships in the middle of the river and keep watch for our return."

His men were well trained and had performed the same actions many times. They speedily spread through the woods. Without being told a party of ten became scouts and sentries to give early warning of danger. The one weakness of Trygg's methods was that he never scouted out a target beforehand. His argument was that it gave them the element of surprise but it could also work the other way. Two years ago they had tried to take a settlement in Germania Inferior not realising that a century of auxiliaries had been recently billeted there. It had cost the Tencteri chief too many men and he had switched to Britannia which appeared to be defended less diligently.

They found, to their relief, that the hill village was unprepared, being totally unaware of the proximity of the warband. The gates of the fort were open as people went about their daily work. The recent rains had damaged many of the crops and all the village were busy trying to save as much as they could before winter set in. Even ruined crops could feed desperately hungry animals. So when the raiders from the sea arrived, fully armed and forty paces from their walls it was a complete and devastating shock. The few men who stood up to the savage enemy were ruthlessly butchered, they were farmers not warriors. Trygg was interested in neither crops nor the paltry and worthless belongings of these poor people. He wanted their animals, their women and their children. They were all held in the same esteem by the Tencteri. When they had gathered them together they were tied in a long line and led off back down the river to the ships, a mile downstream. Trygg left the settlement as it was; he had learned that if you fired one then the neighbours would investigate. He preferred to slip in and out efficiently.

Marcus' sharp eyes were the first to spot the tops of the masts as they approached the woods. He knew that they could not be the Classis Britannica for he would have been informed that they were in the river. They could be traders but the wise decurion knew that was unlikely. He knew they would, in all probability, be raiders. There were two hamlets nearby, one upstream and one downstream. They were both about the same distance away, a meagre two to three miles.

"Gnaeus take three men and ride to Oegels-Dun, Drusus take three and ride to Eabrycg. I will watch here with the other two. See if they have been visited; if not then warn them that there may be sea pirates about. Return here as soon as you can." The two groups sped off riding back through the woods to travel on the carter's track which was faster going than the trail. By saving time Gnaeus missed spotting the warband who were closer to the river for Trygg was keen to be able to board his plunder on his ships as soon as he could. They passed each other like ships in a fog, both unaware how close they were to each other.

Marcus dismounted and signalled to the other two to do the same. They tied their horses to a tree and then, with bows drawn began to work their way from tree to tree through the woods down to the waterline. As was their practice, Marcus took the lead with the other two troopers on his left and right rear. It was effective and normally yielded results. This time it was both their undoing and the salvation of Marcus. The six scouts had heard the horses and hidden behind and up in the trees. One of the younger warriors, Halfdan, had climbed up into the branches to afford a better view and signalled to his five companions when he saw the three Romans descending the slope. He held up three fingers which was all the information that they needed.

The first that Marcus knew of the ambush was when Halfdan launched himself from the tree to land squarely on the decurions' shoulders. The horseman pitched forward and, although his armour and helmet saved him from serious injury, the bole of the tree striking him squarely on the temple rendered him unconscious. The two troopers who followed were not so fortunate for the five scouts made short work of them and they died where they stood, hacked by sword and axe. Halfdan turned Marcus' body over and, seeing the sword in the scabbard withdrew it. The others gasped at its beauty and as the young warrior turned it over in his hand he marvelled at its balance. He grinned at the others and, taking it in two hands raised it above his head to deliver the coup de grace to the Roman decurion.

"Stop!" Trygg's voice boomed out in the woods. Striding up to the surprised scout Trygg took the sword from him. "This is the sword of a chief, Halfdan. I claim this as mine." He noticed the crestfallen look on the man's face. "I shall reward you when we get home." He glanced down at the unconscious Roman, "And this looks to be one of their leaders. We will take him with us. Secure him and make sure he does not escape. Take their arms and armour; see if they have any gold or silver upon them and let us go. You may take your pick of their weapons. If there are three Romans here there will be others close by."

As soon as Gnaeus saw the ravaged and ransacked settlement he knew that Marcus had been correct and there were raiders loose on the river. His men soon reported back to him that no-one was left alive in the village. The warmth of the bodies and the remnants of prepared meals told Gnaeus that this attack had been recent. "Back to the decurion and the rest of the patrol. We may yet be able to catch them."

The tethered horses at the top of the bank gave Gnaeus pause for thought. He heard hoof beats thundering along the path and his patrol immediately drew their weapons. It was with some relief that they saw it was the other patrol.

"There are raiders, Gnaeus. Those at Eabrycg say they saw longships rowing up the river."

Gnaeus felt his heart sink to his feet. There had been no ships at the ravaged village which meant the raiders were here! "They have sacked Oegels-Dun. The decurion is down there somewhere. Be careful and keep your eyes peeled."

The eight troopers spread out in a half circle; Gnaeus followed the trail left by his comrades. The crows, already picking at the dead bodies of the two dead Romans, flew noisily away as they approached. It was obvious that the two troopers were dead but Gnaeus suddenly realised there was no sign of the decurion.

"Spread out and find the decurion. Marius, come with me." Kicking his horse on, he led Marius down to the river. They were just in time to see the five ships as they began to pull away from the shore. He glanced around for the sign of Marcus' body and he wondered where they had left it. With sudden clarity Gnaeus saw the unconscious decurion being hauled unceremoniously up the side of the last ship and even worse, he saw a tall warrior wielding the Sword of Cartimandua; the distinctive handle reflecting the light from its jewel-encrusted pommel. As an oath brother Gnaeus realised that he and his brethren had failed.

"Marius, take one of the men and bring the dead troopers to Eabrycg tell the rest to follow me. It will be a fruitless chase but I will trail these raiders until they reach the sea. Mayhap there will be a ship from the Classis Britannica at the mouth or they may put in again and we might yet save him." Marius' expression told Gnaeus that he was being overly optimistic but they both knew there was no other choice. They had to do all in their power to save the decurion.

Trygg Tryggvasson sat at the stern holding the newly acquired blade. He kept turning it over in his hand as he watched the Roman cavalry staring intently at him. He had not come across horses much before and, certainly, never in battle. They intrigued him for these warriors easily kept pace with the ships as they tacked and turned down the twisting Dunum. Perhaps he might investigate how to use them once he returned home. The tribes who ravaged his lands and had killed many of his tribe did not use horses. If he could, somehow, begin to use them then who knew what he and his emerging tribe might achieve?

He looked again at the blade. It was not Roman. That he could see quite clearly for they had other Roman blades captured in other raids. They were much shorter and broader. This was a long elegant blade with red, green and almost black jewels on the pommel. The grip was not only well made but well used. It was a blade which told a story, that he knew. He had spared the Roman's life because he wanted to know the story of the blade. If he was going to use it to lead his people in battle then he had to know who had made it and how he could invoke the spirit of the blade and its maker. It did not do to offend a magical blade. Some swords had spells and incantations attached to them; he would not use this blade until he knew from whence it came.

His eyes drifted to the unconscious form at his feet. They had been lucky to capture the warrior that was as certain as the tide and the sun; anyone who owned a blade such as this would be a worthy opponent in a fight and Trygg almost regretted not having the opportunity to win the blade through combat. He would use the Roman to help his tribe to become even greater for he knew that the Romans had some power which enabled them to claim such vast tracts of land. To the north of the Tencteri was cold and inhospitable and to the south was the Roman Empire. He would learn how they had managed to achieve that feat. The

Norns had determined that this warrior should live and Trygg had learned long ago not to upset the Gods and their minions.

"Open water and breakers ahead!"

As the motion of the ship became more noticeable Trygg stood to look at the land on both sides which was flat, wide and filled with mudflats. He and his men had escaped the Romans. The Norns' plan was unseen by Trygg but he had his own plan now. The warrior would breed him some slaves and teach them about horses, His helmet and armour showed that he was a chief amongst the Romans, although Trygg thought him to be a little young; he would enjoy discovering his story. He turned to raise his sword in salute to the Roman cavalry which had halted at the line of sand dunes. They too were warriors and faithful to their chief. Trygg admired that and it spoke well of the man at his feet. If his men valued him so much that they went, literally, to the ends of the earth, then he was a man worth speaking with. The leader of the Roman horsemen raised his own arm in salute. This time the raiders had won but Trygg knew it could have ended differently, Odin had been with them and they would give thanks and sacrifice at their feast when they returned to Hjarno-By. As a lonely hawk hovered above them Trygg raised his eyes and, shielding them with his hand, looked at the aerial hunter they tried to emulate. It was a sign from Odin that they were being watched. Its keening cry sounded high above the lapping waves on the boat as it bade farewell to the raiders.

Gnaeus knew that he had to visit the farm of Ailis and Marcus' brother, Decius, but he did not know how he would tell them his devastating news. Honour demanded that he do his duty but he also had the loyalty of an oath bother to consider. However, Ailis was like a grandmother to the young troopers and, having had so much tragedy lately, how would she take this devastating blow? His troopers had been silent as they rode back along the Dunum. They all felt the same shame that they had not protected the decurion; the fact that they had obeyed his orders was irrelevant, they had failed to fulfil their oath and would now have to redeem themselves.

"He is alive then?"

Gnaeus was astounded at the calmness of Ailis. "In truth, I know not but he was taken aboard the raider's ship and their leader has his sword."

Ailis nodded and closed her eyes. Her son was not dead, that she knew. Decius too appeared calm. "When the boats left did you see anything strange or untoward?"

Gnaeus looked confused; these were not the questions he was expecting. "The ships sailed out of the Dunum. The leader raised the Sword of Cartimandua, and we returned here."

"And nothing else?" Ailis' keen eyes bored into Gnaeus.

Desperately the young trooper tried to recall the images from the ship's departure to remember anything which appeared different. "There was a hawk hovering above that is all."

Ailis and Decius hugged each other. "Then all will be well for Macro watches over his brother still."

Suddenly Gnaeus remembered the moment the decurion had died and the hawk had first appeared. He had been so upset and concerned with his own role in the decurion's loss that he had forgotten the dying oath of his former decurion. Ailis was right; all would be well and, for the first time in half a day Gnaeus found himself smiling. The spirit that had been Gnaeus decurion now floated on the winds and hunted where he would; Marcus would have a protector; all they now needed was hope that he could be returned, alive.

The dangers of the frontier had been brought home to Emperor Hadrian when a party of Votadini had ambushed them close to the construction site of the new wall. Although the turma protecting the Emperor had driven them off, Julius had decided that they would increase the escort for the Emperor when he next inspected the progress of the wall. The two turmae of auxiliaries and the Praetorian escort made a formidable sight as they inspected the first section of the wall which had been completed with stone facing. Although the top was, as yet, unfinished, it was now faced with stone and there were regular and well-made stone steps to reach the top. It could be defended now and was a visual and imposing statement to the barbarians that Rome had made their mark in the land. To the Roman builders it was a clear boundary, to the barbarians it was an insult to the land it scarred.

"It is a good choice for defending this line, Julius." The Emperor looked at the legionaries who were busily working away like a colony of ants. The auxiliaries, under Prefect Vibius, had taken to dividing their forces between building and guarding their lines to speed up the process. The Emperor nodded to the Prefect who was labouring away with his men. "This strategy seems to work. When I visit the other vexillations I will encourage the practice. It will make construction a little quicker."

"You are leaving this section then sir?"

"Yes, Julius. We will call in at Rocky Point to say farewell to the Prefect and I will join Governor Falco in the east. I want you to stay here and make sure the work carries on at the same speed."

Julius looked at the skies doubtfully; once again rain clouds filled the air and there appeared to be the threat of more rain. "In winter sir, the cement will not set in the cold. We cannot expect the same progress that we have made so far. And remember sir, here the days are much shorter. When it comes to the winter solstice the sun will begin to set almost as soon as it has risen."

Hadrian had come to realise that Britannia was totally different from Italy; they actually had winter in this northern outpost with frosts and snows, thick ice and fogs so thick that a man could not see the hand before him. It was as though the gods had made a different land here in the wild northern outlands. "I know Julius but when it is too cold for cement and digging the men can line the top with stone ready for the cement. We will let neither the barbarians nor the weather slow us down."

Julius felt proud to be a Roman, even the barbarians had to admire the spirit of Rome and its doughty warriors toiled despite the weather and despite the attacks of the barbarians. Whilst the tribes would be hunkered down for the winter, the Roman machine carried on grinding away. The soldiers on the wall would not stop for the snow, ice and cold; they would build and patrol regardless of the weather. He knew the Emperor was correct, the sooner they finished the wall the safer the frontier would be and it made sense to keep the legionaries busy; if they were not working they would be gambling and more likely to get into trouble. If they were working they would be too tired to do anything but eat and sleep. At least the auxiliaries were kept constantly busy patrolling and scouting.

The large party of mounted and armed men headed west to Rocky Point. As they entered the gates, bristling with sentries, Julius sensed something was amiss. The normally cheerful troopers looked down in the mouth. There was an air of despondency he had not seen before. He wondered if they had not managed to go hunting and augment their diet. The Second Sallustian Ala ate well and that usually kept their spirits up. It was normally a pleasure to come to this outpost and the Emperor himself had valued the time he had spent amongst the cheerful and industrious horsemen; this day it was though there had been a death. As they dismounted Hadrian turned to Julius. "I will join you in a moment, I just want to say farewell to the cook here."

Julius smiled. The trooper who had become the cook for the ala was a magician with the food and the Emperor, whilst not a gourmand enjoyed the meals and had taken every opportunity to join the ala to eat with them. As he had admitted to the Legate, he liked the atmosphere in the camp where there was an air of optimism and camaraderie he wished other troops and forts could emulate. He strode towards the kitchen area and, to anyone watching who did not know he was the Emperor, he would have appeared as just another officer going about his duties.

Entering the ala office, Julius sensed the mood of gloom and depression was even greater than outside and both Livius and Julius Longinus, the ala clerk, looked greyer and older than they had the previous week. "What is wrong Livius? You both look as though some disaster has occurred."

When Livius looked up a spark of anger flashed across his face before the Prefect controlled it, Julius Demetrius was not only his superior he was a friend and he did not deserve scorn. "Decurion Marcus has been taken by raiders from across the Mare Germania. He is now a slave."

Julius slumped into the chair. First Macro had died and now Marcus, his adopted brother, had been taken. He could now understand the mood in the camp. The two were the Romulus and Remus of this unit, they were its heart and the sword was its soul. "Where did this happen?"

"On the Dunum. He was with two other troopers when they were surprised by barbarians; five boat loads." He paused and looked meaningfully at the Legate, the pain in his eyes reflecting the pain he felt in his heart. "They have the sword."

Julius shook his head; it was bad enough that Marcus had been taken but if word got out that the symbol of the Brigante people had been taken then the whole of the north of Britannia could be filled with unrest. Many of the Brigante tribe accepted Roman rule because a descendant of the Brigante royal family wielded the weapon. Already the younger warriors had rebelled but the loss of the sword could be the spark to ignite the frontier and rekindle the fires of rebellion and freedom from Roman rule.

Neither man heard the door quietly open. Julius had always been a positive person, an optimist who looked for a light in the darkest room and he sought to lessen the pain in the Prefect's face. "At least we have the stone now and the frontier will be safer."

Livius' face filled with a fierce anger which Julius Longinus, the clerk, had never seen before. "Well that makes everything fine then doesn't it? You may have gained your stone, Legate, but the ala and I have lost our heart and, you know, I don't think the wall is worth it!" He spat the words out and his pretence of stoicism crumbled like frozen cement.

The Emperor's quiet voice made them both jump. "That is not a comment I thought I would hear from a Prefect in the Roman army. You had better explain yourself."

Julius saw the look on Livius' face and, before his friend could get himself into trouble, he interceded. "The Prefect has just lost a Decurion on the Dunum, sir. Decurion Marcus and the Sword of Cartimandua. He is naturally upset."

A soldier himself, the Emperor could understand Livius' views but not his words. "I am sorry for your loss as I am sorry when the Empire loses any of its warriors who die for their country but understand this Prefect, there is no greater priority than the building of this wall and even if every man in your command dies then that would be a price worth paying to secure the safety and security of the Empire. Is that clear?"

Even as Livius stood and said, "Sir, yes sir." He realised that he was just a pawn to be used by the Emperor. His men were there to be used and sacrificed for the greater good of the Empire. Just because he had fought alongside the Emperor in Surrentum he had felt that there was a bond between them, as there was with the men of the ala. Now he saw that that had been an illusion; the Emperor's first thoughts were always with the Empire and neither the ala nor he was important to him, merely a useful tool. It would change the way that Livius commanded from that moment on. Perhaps his brother and his uncle had been correct, perhaps Britannia did need a British ruler; someone who cared for the land and its people. For him, it was the family of the ala which was important and he believed that the security of the Empire would benefit from that family, obviously, the Emperor did not share his views. As soon as he could he would discuss with Julius and the decurions what they could do about the lost decurion because Livius was certain about one thing, they would not forget his friend and the living embodiment of the ala nor would he let him die as a slave across the sea. Something would be done. He knew not what it would be but they would do something. He would not leave his young decurion to end his days as a slave in the lands to the east.

Julius glanced over his shoulder to his young acolyte. He had taken a huge risk with his outburst and the Senator was politician enough to know that Emperor Hadrian, good man though he was would not forget the display of disloyalty. He did agree with Livius that something should be done but the Legate knew that it would have to be something created away from the Emperor's hearing and knowledge or it might jeopardise not only the Prefect's future but also his life. As the gates slammed shut behind the departing Imperial column Julius began to formulate an idea which, if he could bring it off, would be the only chance young Marcus had to be rescued. He had known the boy since birth and he knew that he was a strong character from good stock. He hoped that he would be coping with the horror of capture and slavery.

Chapter 4

Marcus knew he was on a ship before he even opened his eyes; having spent almost two days below decks on The Swan the previous year, he recognised the gentle rocking motion of a ship at sea. He was immediately aware that he could not move his arms for he could feel the ropes biting into them and, lying there rolling across the deck with the surge of the sea he began to piece together what had happened. The last thing he remembered was being knocked from his horse and hitting the ground and then blackness. Before then he had seen the masts of the ships. He had been captured; that much was obvious. He had blundered into an ambush and he was immediately angry with himself. As an Explorate, he had been trained to assess the risks and dangers of potential ambushes. He had become complacent and paid the price. What of his two companions; the two young troopers who had followed him through the woods? He would have to wait until he opened his eyes to discover what had happened to them but lying in the darkness he used his other senses, those of smell and hearing, to work out what was going on around him. The language he heard was neither Latin nor Brigante but it did sound vaguely Germanic and one or two of the words were familiar. At least it was not the Hibernians. His first fear when he saw the masts of the ships was that the Hibernians had come to finish off what they started with his brother. He knew that he was not heading into the clutches of the witches and the Irish and that thought gave him some comfort. He assumed that he was heading east, towards the lands as yet unconquered by Rome. He could hear the noise of wood rubbing on wood; he was on a ship propelled by oars. He could smell the sea but it was intermingled with the sour smell of men who have not bathed in a long time. They were barbarians then. Finally, as his ears became attuned to the sounds around him he heard sounds from further away, the sound of gulls and the surf hitting the bow and then, very distinctly he heard it, the sound of a hawk, high above. He felt comforted for his brother was nearby, Macro was watching him. He could begin to plan to escape; he had hope again.

"That hawk has followed us from the Dunum. Should I try to shoot it with an arrow?"

Trygg looked at the warrior, standing next to the steersman, "Snorri, we have no one on this ship who could hit it. The only man who might stand a chance is Drugi the hunter, and he is on the island. Besides, it is a fine bird and I hope to see it hunt. If it follows us home then we may try to capture it. Drugi would be the man for that." Trygg looked at the recumbent form at his feet. "I hope this Roman does not die on us, I have many questions. The Norns have done well to give us such a rich treasure."

Snorri looked at Marcus and snorted, "I cannot see where the treasure is there. We captured him easily enough."

Trygg shook his head. "Look at the sword, look at the armour. Look at his muscles and his scars. They all lead to one inescapable truth, this is a warrior and a warrior who has fought in many battles. Odin and the Norns conspired to bring him to us. Had one of his men been felled rather than this their leader and chief then he would have fought hard to survive; we might have lost many warriors trying to take him and his sword. No, he has been brought to us for a purpose. I will wait until I have spoken with him to find out why."

Snorri still looked dubious. "If he is so great a warrior, will he not escape as soon as we reach our land?"

Trygg laughed and pointed to the sea. "And where would he go? Even if he were to flee from our island fortress and swim to the mainland, would he survive the Germans? No the only way he could escape is by sea and we control the seaways. Fear not Snorri, I am not worried about his escape. I do have some ideas about how we may use this warrior, this gift from the gods. There is a woman from Britannia who, I fancy, would produce healthy offspring with this warrior. Once he has accepted his fate he will become one of us then we will have someone who can teach us to ride, teach us about the Romans, their language and ideas and, most importantly, how to fight the Romans."

"Fight them? I thought we just raided their land. We have not fought them. They are like ants they are so numerous. How could we defeat them in their large numbers?" Snorri had heard of the numbers who fought in Roman armies and he could not comprehend the numbers. For him an army was a hundred warriors; he had heard that the Romans fielded thousands. He was still uncertain about the veracity of that for he had yet to see so many men in one place.

"No, we have not fought them because I knew we would not win and yet as a warrior, I felt ashamed when we fled. I would like to have met them blade to blade but look at his." He picked up Marcus' armour which had been stripped from his body. "I think that it would take a fine sword or a good axe blow to pierce this and what of the helmet? How many of our men have helmets? And even fewer have armour. No Snorri, we take on the Romans when we have arms and armour which can defeat them and then that will be a glorious day when we meet them blade to blade."

Snorri was caught up in the rhetoric and found he was grinning like a child. "Soon we will have more men and more ships. Why we will even defeat the Suebi who crawl over our land like evil little cockroaches."

Trygg's face darkened. It galled him that they lived in fear from their neighbours. Before they defeated the Romans they would drive the Germans from the mainland and send them back to their own lands. That was why he had brought back the Roman for the Germans had been defeated by the Romans and this warrior would show them how.

Marcus was picked up bodily once the fleet began to turn east again to round the peninsula which jutted out into the cold black sea. Chief Trygg was not going to risk him being swept overboard and he had two men haul him upright. His plan to remain as though unconscious was thwarted when Snorri hurled the bucket of icy salt water onto him and his reflexes suddenly opened his eyes. The man with the bucket grinned and Marcus saw for the first time that they were all the blond haired giants from the north he had expected. He glanced around and saw that he was the only prisoner on the deck; had his men perished or escaped? He hoped the latter. Behind the man with the bucket, steering the ship was a huge warrior with a long beard and moustache. His hair was plaited and Marcus saw the shining torc which marked him as a chief. Although wearing no armour he looked to be a powerful warrior with a well-muscled body. As

Marcus looked him up and down, assessing him as a future opponent his heart sank when he saw, strapped to his waist was the sword of Cartimandua. He had hoped, vainly as it turned out, that he had lost the blade in Britannia and one of his men had recovered the symbol which inspired his men. Now his spirits fell to their lowest point as he began to appreciate the disaster which had befallen him. He pulled at his hands to try to break his bonds for he had a foolish idea to grab the warrior and throw them both over the side, better to lose the sword to the sea than to a barbarian. Something in his movement alerted the man with the bucket for he suddenly tugged hard on the rope tied to his leg and Marcus crashed heavily to the floor. He had been tethered well by his captors who were used to slave raids and ensuring their victims did not escape. The Allfather had to have another plan for him and, resigned he sank to the floor. He heard them speaking but the only word he recognised was 'Roman'.

"See Snorri. The Roman warrior might be tied but he wants to fight and he struggles to escape his bonds even though he is alone. We were lucky. Feed him but shorten the tether. I fear he would try to fight with us all if we gave him the chance." Before he had captured this Roman he had wondered about them as warriors for they had short hair and neither beards nor moustache. To the Tencteri that was for women or those who chose to live as women. He also smelled of a woman and did not have the manly smell of his warriors and yet when he had stood and faced him he had had the dangerous look of a wild boar cornered and yet willing to sell its life dearly. He would bear watching, this horseman of Rome.

Marcus was on his feet as the fleet edged into Orsen Fjord. He had seen glimpses of land as they had rounded the coast into this unknown sea but he had seen neither another boat nor a single human save for his captors. It was as though the five barbarian ships had left this world and entered another world, unknown to Marcus. He had eaten all that they had given him and he had drunk whenever offered. He cared not that the fish was rancid nor that the drink smelled old, he had to survive and that meant keeping up his strength. He surreptitiously exercised, lifting himself on his feet and hands when no-one was watching. He did not want his muscles to become soft.

He stood on tiptoes to peer as far as he could see. The two islands of Alro and Hjarno were close both to each other and the mainland making navigation and entry difficult. The decurion noticed the concentration on all of the crew. Despite its familiarity, they treated the passage with caution. His military mind took in the fact that any ship which passed the island would have to pass whatever defences the people had. Already the Roman was thinking of escape. If they had brought him back to kill him then so be it, then Allfather had willed it but if he was spared, he would do all in his power and move heaven and earth to regain the sword and return to Britannia. As they approached the wooden jetty he realised that escape was a long way off. The port he could see lay at the end of a long finger of land, obviously an old sand bar which had been built up by the barbarians to provide a natural breakwater; it also afforded protection for any ships sheltering in the harbour. The village was a little way away from the port but was only the height of a child above the surrounding land. The soldier living in Marcus' brain told him that it was the water which was the major defence. If auxiliaries landed on the island then they would be able to scale the miniscule walls easily, the problem would be landing them on the island.

The return of the chief was a major event on Hjarno and hundreds of people lined the jetty and the walls to scream and shout their welcomes. Anxious women looked for husbands, fathers and brothers; sometimes they did not return. They were all desperate for the glimpse of hair or hand which would tell them that this time their prayers had been answered. The lack of young men on the island told Marcus that most of the warriors were aboard the five ships he could see. He watched the chief, for in the past four days he had seen everyone defer to the tall leader and he knew that the blond-haired warrior with the torc was the leader, as he signalled the other ships in first. It marked him as an astute leader for it combined generosity in allowing others to be reunited with their families first with a political acumen which gave him the most number of people to cheer him ashore.

As the other ships disembarked their cargo, Marcus could see that it had been successful and there were many women and children and animals. When he saw no men led ashore he knew that his troopers were dead. These barbarians would have had their weapons and armour as trophies. He mourned inside for them, saying a prayer to the Allfather to welcome them. He wondered when he would be leaving the ship and he glanced up at his guard; the man with the rope had rarely strayed far from his side. Marcus had deduced that his name was Snorri. He had picked up other words but he had kept that a secret from his captors.

The crew began to leave and with them the precious cargo they had captured, the coins and the boxes of jet. Marcus felt himself being tugged by Snorri and he contemplated pulling back to give his minder a soaking but relented, he would have to be subservient, for a while, at least. He saw everyone staring at him as he was led down the gangway. He tried to work out what their looks meant. He would have been surprised to discover that it was two things, the fact that he was a man and that he had no facial hair which marked him out as a new freak worthy of interest.

Trygg felt proud as his people roared his name over and over again. He stood on the top of the gangplank and pulled his new sword from its scabbard. One of his men had oiled and polished it for hours so that when he drew it the sunset caught the blade and reflected the rays making it appear to flame in Trygg's hand. "Once again we have returned with riches beyond our wildest dreams and our people will prosper but Odin has given us two greater prizes. See this mystical blade which Odin has given to me to smite our enemies and behold we have a Roman and not just any Roman but one of their chiefs. From him we will learn much. Tonight we celebrate and tomorrow we plan our future, a future of greatness for the Tencteri will soon be the most powerful clan of the Eudose and we will rule all of Uiteland and we will drive the Suebi back to their holes!"

Marcus had no idea what the leader, he now knew was called Trygg, had said, but the effect was astounding and every face was raised to him as though he were the Emperor himself. As he was led through the throng, some of whom poked him, not maliciously, but out of curiosity, he could see that they all looked different to the people of Britannia. Some of them had the red hair of the Caledonii and Pictii but most were blue-eyed and blond. They were also bigger in stature than the people at home. Marcus himself was bigger than most of the people in Stanwyck and Morbium but here he would be average.

Once they entered the stockade Marcus found himself in a different world. The people who had captured him used neither round houses nor stone buildings but long halls which looked like upturned boats; they had a high roof and a hole to allow the smoke to escape. He was led to one which was next to the largest of the halls. Marcus was intrigued by the guards standing at the large double doors. Snorri led him into a large high room and the only light came from the huge fire in the centre. The women and children who were in the hall were obviously not of the tribe for they looked like peoples from Britannia and other lands. Their emaciated forms and hollow eyes confirmed that they were indeed slaves. As his eyes became accustomed to the light he saw that there were large rings bedded into the wall and Snorri led him to one. Unlike the ropes which had hitherto bound him, these were iron shackles and Marcus found himself shackled by the leg to the wall. He could move eight or so paces from the wall but no more. Snorri checked the security of the ring and, grinning at Marcus' discomfort, left after first gently slapping him on the cheeks. The Roman decurion became accustomed to the gloom in his little corner of the great hall and he saw that the eyes which looked at him were dulled and lacking curiosity. He did not know it then but it was only the unique nature of his age and sex which afforded him a second glance for he was in the hall of the thralls, the place of the slaves.

He knew there was little point in making a break for freedom in daylight and the fact that the slaves were herded outside soon after his arrival confirmed that it was still daylight. He was left almost alone. Whilst the ships had been arriving they had been kept apart, they were not of the tribe and were a commodity, like the pigs and hens they kept. In the far corner were three women with nursing babies and another woman covered by a blanket. As none looked as though they were going to speak to him any time soon he began to examine the inside of the hall. It had a much higher roof than a roundhouse and the curve of the timbers would have made it impossible for him to climb the walls and escape through the turf which lined the top of the hall. That left the door as his only exit. He could see there would be a problem of the two guards who stood with spears and shields at the huge doors. He had to assume that they would either lock the doors at night or leave the guards there to prevent the slaves escaping. If it was just the guards then he would have a chance. All he would need would be a weapon of some description. As he moved his arms the iron shackles rattled not only was it noisy it told him that he could not just walk away. He would have to find a way of escaping the iron bonds which bound him to this prison. Unless they let him out in the day he would find it hard to acquire the tools he would need.

    He began to feel depressed, even though he was an optimist he could not see a way out of this web. He was trapped like a fly on the spider's web and this web was in a land he did not know. He was doomed to die in a foreign land far from his family, his friends and his men. Suddenly he sat upright. They had spared him for a reason. Perhaps they wanted him to torture or humiliate in some public way. He remembered that his namesake, the Prefect Marcus, had been captured by the witch Fainch and imprisoned in a wicker cage to be burnt alive. It could be that the people who had captured him had the same practice. Some peoples believed that human sacrifice produced good fortune for their clan, perhaps he was to be a sacrifice. He could think of no other reason for his capture. He wondered, if that were the case, why they had fed him on the voyage across, why they had not treated him with cruelty for they had taken pains to protect him from the cold and see to his bodily needs. He shook his head. He would have to wait and see their purpose but he would also watch and observe for escape would come. He had been an Explorate and had more skills than these people could conceive.

    He dozed a little, more induced by mental exhaustion than physical tiredness. He was awoken by rough hands lifting him to his feet. Two armed warriors took him by the arms, whilst a third held on to his metal shackle and led him into the light. He found the light of the sunset too bright and tried to shade his eyes with his hand. The tight grip of the guards prevented it and he had to squeeze his eyes shut and he stumbled across the open space between the halls. As he stubbed his toe on a step he looked down and saw that he was climbing the steps of the huge hall which he had seen close by the one in which he had been imprisoned. Here the two guards were dressed in fine armour and each had a double-handed axe next to him. The warrior in Marcus recognised them as elite fighters who would be dangerous adversaries in a fight. Once again the hall had no windows but this one had bowls filled with oil which burned brightly on the tables in the middle. This added to the light from the fires, which were halfway down on either side, making this hall seem to sparkle and glow. At the end was a raised dais and there seated on a fine chair was Trygg. Next to him sat a beautiful woman of about the same age who also wore a torc and Marcus assumed that was the wife of the chief. To one side stood Snorri now dressed in much finer clothes that those on the voyage and, for the first time, Marcus could see that he too was a chief of some description and, from the sword by his side, a warrior. The only other person on the dais was a female slave at the foot of the dais.

Once again, when he was forced to his knees next to the slave he heard Trygg speak but once again he could not understand a word. There was a pause and then the slave began to speak to him.

"The chief of this tribe, Trygg Tryggvasson welcomes you to Hjarno-By and asks, what is your name?"

Marcus looked at her in amazement. She had spoken Latin. "Who are you?"

The terrified look in her eyes was echoed by her words. "Just answer my questions or we will be punished."

The terror in her words made him nod. "I am Decurion Marcus Gaius Aurelius of the Second Sallustian ala of Pannonians."

She translated and Trygg asked her a question which she then answered. Marcus wondered what had been said for Trygg turned and smiled at Snorri who shrugged. Under her breath, she said, "He wanted to know what you did. I said a cavalryman." The chief then spoke at some length and the slave turned to him. "The chief said that this is your new home and you will be a slave of the Tencteri. He urged you not to attempt to escape for if you do they will cut off your toes. A second attempt will cost you your left hand," she spread her arms out, "and I think you can work out the rest. You will be taught our language and then you will teach the Tencteri about horses and the Romans. If you work well then you will not be shackled and you will be allowed to move around the island freely."

Marcus looked up at the chief, almost for the first time. He had seen many barbarian leaders but, hitherto they had all seemed cruel, unthinking barbarians. This one appeared different and in that lay danger for Marcus, it was an unknown factor, a thinking barbarian.

The chief spoke again and she translated once more. "The chief wants to know if you understand."

"Tell him, yes." Marcus was desperate to question the young slave but he knew that he could not do so in the hall.

The chief seemed pleased with the answer but then took out the sword and spoke again to the slave. "The chief wishes to know about the sword which was yours and is now his."

Marcus could feel his face reddening and filling with anger and he was also acutely aware of the close inspection Trygg was giving him. "Tell him that the sword belongs to my family and is a sword sacred to the Brigante tribe. It is the Sword of Cartimandua." He paused as she translated. As soon as she stopped speaking he began again. "Tell him I will happily fight him for the right to bear the weapon." She looked at Marcus and shook her head. "Tell him!"

When she told him Marcus noticed that the chief nodded, as though to himself, whilst his men burst out laughing and began jeering the Roman. Trygg allowed it for a few moments and then held up his hands for silence. He spoke again.

"The chief says that he had the measure of you when he captured you. You are a brave man and a worthy warrior, as would any man would be who wielded such a weapon. He asks why he should fight you for it when he already owns it and you, a slave, can own nothing?" The men began cheering and banging their beakers on the table. Trygg smiled at his men and sheathed the sword before he continued. "Besides he would gain no honour from killing a slave."

He spoke again as Marcus reddened. The female slave spoke quietly to the decurion as though to calm him. "The king asks which part of Britannia does the sword come from?"

Sighing Marcus began, "The sword comes from the land south of the Dunum, close to my home. I hold the sword through my father and my mother who is a descendant of the last Queen of the Brigante, Cartimandua."

When the girl had finished translating the King spoke with those around him. They kept looking at Marcus and pointing. The decurion did not enjoy the examination. He knew that they were impressed, both with the sword and Marcus' lineage. The chief spoke again to the slave.

The girl stood and Marcus felt himself jerked to his feet. The girl took his arm and said quietly, "We are dismissed. We can talk in the hall."

Marcus was torn between trying to invoke a confrontation and talking to the girl about their predicament. The Metellus side of his mind overcame the Macro side and he nodded. They left to the jeers of the warriors who continued their feasting. It had become very dark and very cold during the interview in the hall and Marcus could feel himself shivering. The girl did not seem to mind the cold and he wondered how she had come to be there. The guards on the door did not enter the hall and merely dropped the bar on the door as they entered. One of Marcus' questions was answered; he would be locked in and guarded each night but at least he would not be shackled. If he could discover a way out of the hall then escape was possible...

The girl led him to a corner of the hall where there was a bearskin and she sat down. "Sit here Decurion."

"What is your name and how came you here?"

"First, I will get you some warm milk for you are cold."

She rose to go to the pan which was laid by the fire. "I am all right. I do not need it."

"But I need you to be well for as long as you are alive my life is better." Enigmatically she walked over to the pan leaving Marcus wondering at her words. Her face looked young but her actions and her words seemed like those of a grown woman. The Parcae had woven a serious web around Marcus this time. When she returned with the beaker she watched as he drank it all down.

It tasted good to Marcus and he recognised honey as well as some other indistinct taste. If he had been offered a drink in Britannia by some strange girl he would have refused fearing poison but, somehow, the girl seemed to inspire confidence.

She inspected the beaker when he had drunk and then said. "Good. For you must not become ill. My name is Frann. I know you, for my home was on the road from Morbium to Eboracum and I saw you and your men as you patrolled the road. I recognised the Sword of Cartimandua when the chief brandished it. I was captured in a raid five summers ago when I had seen but ten springs. My father spoke well of you and your family for he had served with your father. He taught me how to speak as a Roman for he was proud to serve with Marcus' Horse and my mother was Brigante."

Marcus knew the answer to his question before he asked it but he went ahead anyway. "And your family where are they now?"

"My father was killed in the raid defending us. My mother suffered a blow to the head and did not survive the crossing. My sister lived until last year." She looked for the question which she had thought he would ask and when he did not, answered it anyway. "She was older than I and…" She drank some of the honeyed milk from her own beaker.

"Why did you say that I should not become ill? What is it to you?"

"I was taken as a slave as you were but have you not noticed that you are the only man in this hall?"

Marcus looked around again and saw that even the boys who were in the hall were less than ten summers old. "I wondered but then I did not know what the chief wanted of me. Now I do."

"The older women work the fields, preserve the fish and tend the halls. The boys look after the animals and the girls… we are there to be used by the men. My sister became ill after she was taken too many times last year and she bled. That is how many of the girls die. There are few of us who become grown women." She shrugged, "At least I have seen none in my seven summers in this place. As long as you live I am safe for the chief has said I am not to be taken until he has learned all he can from you."

There was a silence as Marcus took that information in. It slowly sank in that he now had a responsibility to the girl. He could not escape without taking her for he would not allow her to be raped to death like her sister. The Parcae had woven their spells well. "So that is how you were chosen to be with me because you spoke the language."

She nodded, "As soon as I saw you I felt hope soar in my heart." She leaned in to him. "Can I tell you something?" Marcus nodded, intrigued by this resourceful young woman, for she was no longer a child or even a girl. "I knew you would come for yesterday when I was picking seaweed on the beach I heard a bird and when I looked up I saw a hawk such as we have on the Dunum and he was circling above me. When I saw the bird I knew that someone would come. As soon as you arrived I told the shaman that I could speak your words and I was chosen." She smiled a cheeky smile, which suddenly made her look her age. "I made sure I beat the other girls to offer those services and I give thanks to the hawk."

Marcus closed his eyes and nodded. "Now I know that the Allfather is looking over us and this has all been intended." The girl looked at him curiously. "My brother died last year and he took a death oath to protect me. As his spirit left this earth we saw a hawk and I heard it as I was taken over the sea. The hawk is my brother's spirit and now I have hope."

"I am glad that you were brought here for now I too have hope." She pulled the bearskin over them. "If you want to take me…" Marcus recoiled. The girl looked appalled. "Am I too ugly? I can…"

Marcus shook his head. "No, you are beautiful. You are lovely but you are not an object to be used. There may come a time when we…there will come a time but we will choose the time and the place because we wish it to happen and it will not be a coupling in a barn with others listening and watching."

She moved her head back to look more closely at him. "You have never had a woman have you?"

Marcus thought that it was a good thing that it was dark for he felt himself reddening. "That does not matter. Your father served with my father; I do not think that either of them would want me to take you here in this hall."

She shrugged and snuggled in next to him. "If you change your mind... but we will need to be close for it is very cold in the night here and we need each other's warmth." As she cuddled in to him Marcus wondered if he had been too hasty with his words for he felt a stirring in his loins he had not felt before but he then thought back to his mother, Ailis, and how she had been a slave used by others and how his father had waited until they could be married and Metellus, his mentor, had also waited with Nanna the other Brigante slave. He sighed as he heard the gentle breathing of the sleeping girl; he had been brought up too well with too much honour.

The next day and the ones which followed were a pleasant interlude for the Roman decurion. Trygg had had warm clothes provided for Marcus and insisted that the girl spend every waking hour teaching him their language. It was on the third day that Marcus noticed a sadness which seemed to hang about the girl. "What is the matter Frann? Am I not learning quickly enough?" Marcus had been really trying to learn the language, partly to please Frann but also so that he would know what the barbarians were saying.

There was a wry smile on the old face of the young girl. "You are learning too well for once you can speak to them why would they need me for you? I would go back to being..."

Marcus was horrified. He had not thought it through. "I will learn slowly then, so that I can never speak their words and will always need you."

"That would not work. They would blame me and there are other girls. Lars would love that to happen and then he could get his hands on me."

"Lars?"

She gestured subtly with her head to a huge bear of a man who lurched past. Marcus had noticed him giving them both queer looks. He had a huge scar running down his face, through a whitened dead eye, and finishing near his mouth giving a strange lopsided grin making look like a simpleton. It was a frightening appearance. "My father did that to him when they attacked us, before he killed my father. He was the one who killed my sister and he swore he would do the same to me."

"I will tell this chief that if he does not let you stay with me I will not tell him what he wants to know."

"But they would then torture you."

"That would be preferable to what he would do to you."

"You would do that for me?"

"I would." Marcus sounded defiant but he wondered how long he would hold out. He hoped it would be until his death but he was not certain.

"Thank you for that but it would do no good for they would just torture me to get you to talk." She kissed him on the cheek, "And I know that you would."

With a sinking heart, Marcus could see no way out of the dilemma. At the same time, a thought wormed its way into his consciousness. If the Allfather had saved him so far and the Parcae brought him together with Frann then it must be for a purpose. He needed to hold fast and keep faith. He was convinced that they would both escape this trap. Then just as quickly as the hope rushed into him it was taken away as he remembered the other deity who liked to play with men's minds, suppose Morwenna and the Mother were toying with him and giving him false hope. Suppose they had brought him here to take away not only the sword and his freedom but the bright young girl who had leapt into his life.

Chapter 5

Marcus stood before Trygg in the main hall. The only other people who were there were Frann, Snorri and a young shaman, Karl Sigambrisson. Frann stood just behind Marcus and Trygg addressed her over Marcus' head. "Let us see what you have taught this young Roman, slave."

"She has taught words Chief Trygg." The words sounded awkward and he still did not have all the words he needed but Trygg was impressed.

"You have all our words, Roman?"

"Not yet. Have some."

Trygg nodded. "Then you stay slave in case he does not understand. Tell me, Roman, how do you ride the horse?"

Marcus looked up at the chief as though he had not understood and the chief repeated his question. "I understand words but not meaning. I sit on the back of horse and ride."

Trygg looked amazed. "You do not fall off?"

"When I first learn yes but then becomes easy."

"How old were you when you learned?" Marcus had not learned numbers yet so he held up three fingers. "That is young." The Chief looked to be running the idea through his head. "So our sons could learn?" He pointed to the two boys who were standing close to the Chief. They looked to be about ten or twelve years old. Marcus nodded. "And could we? The warriors, could we learn?" Marcus did not have the words but he rocked his hand back and forth suggesting that it was a possibility. "We will get some horses and we will see."

The chief turned to Snorri. "Send for Drugi and have him capture some horses for us." Marcus understood all the words but he kept his face impassive. If they had horses then they had the chance to escape. Despite what Frann had said about the German tribe which were between them and the Empire, Marcus spied a kind of hope and that was enough.

Trygg turned again to Marcus. "Now Roman, how do you Romans fight?"

For the first time since he had arrived at Hjarno-By, Marcus grinned. "We fight well. Better than Tencteri." He had wanted to say barbarian but he did not know the word.

"Brave talk from a slave who was captured so easily."

"There were few of us. I have fought others like Tencteri and I have never lost. I have led my men against," he held up his two hands, "that times the number of our men and we won."

Trygg could detect from the voice that this was not bravado. He was coming to understand how this warrior had had such a fine weapon. He was a warrior and now, it seemed, a mighty leader. "You Romans, do you fight in lines?"

Marcus had a problem. He did not know how much they knew and he did not want to give them information which might result in Roman deaths. On the other hand, if they thought he was lying or hiding something then it would go badly for the two of them. Having seen the numbers of the Tencteri and the weaponry he did not think that an insight into Roman tactics would help them. Besides other tribes knew the Roman way of war and still lost.

"Foot soldiers fight together," he pulled Frann next to him so that their shoulders touched, "this close. Men on horses, "he moved her arm's length away, "this far."

Trygg smiled. He liked this young Roman. "You were a horseman?"

"I am a horseman."

Trygg stood and walked down to Marcus. He was taller than Marcus and about the same breadth. Not for the first time, Marcus thought of Macro. He would have been both taller and broader than the chief. They would have liked each other for Marcus did not dislike this chief. He had not been unkind and he could see a thoughtful, albeit barbaric side to the blond-haired giant.

Trygg wanted to see into Marcus' eyes, to see the lie if it were there. "Would you fight for Tencteri?"

The question took the shaman, Frann and Marcus by surprise. "Against Romans?" Marcus asked the question to allow the time to think of an appropriate and acceptable answer.

"No not against Romans, against the enemies of Tencteri."

"Germans?" Trygg nodded. Marcus could see no dishonour in fighting the enemies of Rome, especially as it would afford him more opportunities to flee. "Then yes!"

Trygg clasped him by the forearm. "Good, I like you Roman and I will enjoy fighting alongside you. When we have horses we will talk again." He looked down at Frann. "You have done well." The two Brigante braced themselves for the words they were dreading that she had finished her task. "You will continue to look after him until," he patted her stomach, "until the baby you will grow is too big."

Marcus left the hall stunned. He had been asked to fight for the barbarians and to produce a child. He could almost hear old Gaelwyn laughing at the irony.

First Spear Vibius felt strangely relieved when it began to snow. Although the work on the wall did not halt it meant that the barbarians were less likely to attack for the snow meant the auxiliaries returned to their guard duty rather than helping the legionaries with the construction. He left his senior centurion in charge and rode to Rocky Point. He had had little chance to speak with Livius since Marcus had been abducted. It was a fear all soldiers had; it was one thing to die on a battlefield, or to be wounded, for in both cases your comrades could honour you or look after you but to be a prisoner meant you were alone and if you died your body would be discarded like yesterday's rubbish and your spirit would wander for eternity looking for a place to settle. Vibius shivered with the thought.

Although the sentry at the gate recognised the Gaul he checked the password and halted him. Prefect Sallustius could be a martinet when it came to security. As he rode through the gate Vibius, like Julius Demetrius before him, noticed the gloomy and dispirited atmosphere. The sentry outside the Principia stamped his feet together, rapped his spear on the wooden floor and shouted, "First Spear Second Gallic Cohort."

"Come in Vibius."

When First Spear saw Livius he was taken aback. In the few weeks since Marcus' abduction, the Prefect had aged considerably. The few flecks of grey were now a sea and the increased numbers of lines on his face reflected his tormented mental state.

"Sit down. It is good to see you. How goes the wall?" Livius managed a wan smile, so forced that it shocked Vibius even more.

"Fuck the wall, sir. What has happened here? The place is like a cemetery with the dead still walking. This isn't the Second Sallustian any more."

Livius looked up, seemingly surprised that the question had been asked. "But did you not hear Vibius? Marcus has been taken by raiders from the east."

"Much as I like the boy, and I do, he is just one man. He is not the whole ala is he? By all the furies in Hades, he might not even be dead! Have you thought of that?"

Livius' face fell as though he had been slapped. "Not dead?" Over in the corner of the office, Julius Longinus looked up, a slight smile on his face. He had wanted to talk to the Prefect as the Gaul had done but their relationship was a different one. This might be just the conversation to stir some life into the Prefect and the ala.

Vibius sat down and poured himself a drink from the amphora on the office table, it was half empty a sure sign that the Prefect was drinking more than usual. After a mouthful, his face took on the expression of someone who has just sucked a lemon. It was even worse than that, the Prefect was not drinking too much wine, he was not drinking! "Water! Have you no beer or even wine?"

"I'll get you some, centurion." Julius bobbed out of the Principia.

"When we fought in Germania this happened more times than I care to remember. The only time the barbarians killed their captive soldiers was when they wanted to show us what they had done. If they had wanted to kill him they would have done it where your men could have seen. You told me that your lads were at the Dunum estuary when the ships left and one of them waved?"

"Yes, it was Marcus' chosen man, Gnaeus."

"And they followed them all the way down the river?" Livius nodded. "Well if they didn't kill him then why would they take him all the way back to their own land? It is at least a seven day's sail." Julius came in with some beer in a jug and a beaker. He took a mouthful. "By all the gods this tastes like gnat's piss. I will bring you a barrel of my latest brew. That'll cheer up your lads." Julius couldn't help liking the coarse Gaul. He was known as brewer, someone who loved ale and since he had been at the wall had brewed up barrels of ale for his own consumption. As far as Julius knew this was the first offer he had made to give the stuff away.

"But we thought he was lost."

"Don't get me wrong, it will not be a barrel of laughs for the lad. He will be a slave. They will not treat him well but believe me, somewhere across the Mare Germania, in some little port Marcus is a prisoner but he is alive."

Later, when he was alone, Livius mulled the words of First Spear Vibius over and over in his mind. How could he have been such a fool? Of course, Marcus was still alive! Every fibre of Livius' being told him that. As he rode into Coriosopitum for the conference called by Legate Demetrius, the Prefect thought how best to exploit that information. He had mentioned it neither to the officers nor the men, for he did not wish to raise their hopes unnecessarily but there had to be something that they could do. Riding through the gates of the stone fort of Coriosopitum Livius remembered that he had neither seen nor spoken to the Legate since he had snapped at him and then been admonished by the Emperor. He did not regret the words but he regretted that he had offended the Legate. Treasonous though the thoughts were, he did not care what the Emperor thought, for he did not know Marcus and he did not know the ala but Julius did and he would have been as distraught as he had been. He wondered how he could begin to mend those particular bridges.

He was the last to arrive but noticed that Vibius had saved a seat for him. Centurion Quintus Broccus gave him a sympathetic half-smile as he came in. The other Prefects and centurions also nodded their acknowledgement. Livius had served on the frontier longer than anyone apart from the Prefect of Coriosopitum; all of the other senior leaders held him in high regard but they all noticed the change in him in the last weeks. Those who were newer put it down to the stresses and strains of frontier command but his older colleagues knew the real reason; it didn't help, they could do nothing to ease his pain.

Julius had a map on the wall and a pointer which he used to illustrate his comments. "Gentlemen, welcome. For those who are new to the province and have only served further south, I must warn you of a particular phenomenon here in northern Britannia. We are about to experience days which are but a few hours old when the nights seem to last forever. It will become so cold that those precious pieces of manhood we hold dear will flee to the warmer confines of our insides for protection." Apart from Livius and the Prefect at Coriosopitum the others looked confused. "I mention this because it means that we have less daylight in which to work and the enemy have more hours of darkness to cause mischief." He let the idea permeate through their minds and the implications of that fact. "We are not yet behind schedule but neither the Emperor nor his engineers have experienced Britannia in winter and until they do they will expect the progress they planned. I know this will not happen but I should warn you, the Emperor will." He looked at Livius and nodded. "The other problem is related to the cavalry. We do have grain for their horses but they need fodder. Once the snow is on the ground they can patrol less. I tell you this so you do not think that Prefect Sallustius and his men are sitting in their camps enjoying themselves in the warm whilst you and your men freeze in the snow. It means that the auxiliary foot will have to shoulder even more of the burden. Now as to the work plans of the next few weeks…"

After Julius had outlined the plans they all said their goodbyes. "Er Livius if you have a moment."

When they had all left Livius just jumped in. "Can I apologise for my outburst when you and the Emperor visited. I know that you were as upset as I was and I had no right to embarrass you like that in front of the Emperor."

Julius shook his head, he had totally understood the outburst although he regretted that the Emperor had heard it and would think less of the Prefect. "Do not worry about that. I explained to the Emperor the situation and he understood your reaction, he didn't agree with it, but he understood it. I am more worried about you and your men than my feelings. I have been receiving reports about them."

"What that they are not doing their duty?" Livius face filled with anger.

The Legate held his arms out to calm down Livius. "No, no, nothing like that. No one is impugning the honour of your men. Rather it is to do with their state of mind. The reports suggest that they are despondent and depressed. And we both know what that can do to the efficiency of an ala."

There was a silence in the office. The only sounds which could be heard were those from the fort, footsteps on the ramparts, challenges at the gate, the rattle of horse harness. "You are right Julius and that is my fault."

"No Livius the depression is not your fault but the lack of a cure is. The men look up to you, use Cassius, Metellus and Rufius. You must inspire your men."

The idea which had been growing in Livius' mind on the ride over took form. "There is one thing sir." Julius raised his eyebrow at the formality but let it slip. "Vibius has persuaded me that Marcus may still be alive. If he is then I would like to find him."

"Is that all?" Livius shrugged. "You want me to let you go… well I don't actually know where, to find one man who may or may not be alive?"

"Hear me out sir. We know that they were blond-haired and came from the east or the northeast. If the Classis Britannica could stop ships and find out where the raiders took their slaves…" even as he said it Livius knew how ridiculous it sounded.

Julius,, however,, began to think. The fleet was too busy just managing the seas without trying to find a needle in a haystack. On the other hand one ship, a civilian ship could visit the ports where the raiders lived as a trader and ask questions about slaves.

"Sorry,, sir. It was a stupid idea. It just struck me that it might just be the kind of hope which would put the spark back into my men."

Julius stood up, excitedly, and went to the other map on the wall, the one of the Empire. "We have The Swan, remember. If she sailed, here, just north of the last Roman port she could sail up here, around this peninsula asking questions and trading. The other ports further north are less well known but we could start in the south and, who knows, they could find some intelligence which might lead to discovering his whereabouts."

Livius joined him at the map. "Isn't that putting old Hercules at risk? Not to mention your ship."

"To be honest I think that the old man misses the excitement, he enjoyed our last two adventures and it could make money for me. There are Roman goods we could trade for timber and amber. It could be profitable."

"One more suggestion sir. As you said the next couple of months are quiet ones for my ala. I would like to accompany The Swan."

Julius shook his head violently. "Out of the question, you are far too valuable running an ala and a mixed cohort as you do. No, not you, but you could send a decurion and a trooper. Metellus or Rufius perhaps?"

"Not Metellus, he is just married and I would not like Nanna harassing me. It would have to be Rufius. Yes, Rufius, for he was close to Marcus and Macro. When can you get The Swan here then sir?"

"She is due in Eboracum at the end of the week with some goods for me. I will meet her there and arrange it. Send Rufius and the trooper down to the new fort at the mouth of the Tinea and we will meet them there."

In the three weeks since he had arrived in Hjarno-By, Marcus had changed dramatically. His hair had quickly grown as had his beard. Wearing the leggings and tunic of the Tencteri with a deerskin over his shoulder he would have been indistinguishable from the other men but for his lack of weapons. He no longer moved like a soldier of Rome; he was more casual in his gait and his back was less stiff. But it was in his demeanour that he had changed the most. He was much calmer and philosophical about his incarceration than when he had arrived. If he had analysed why he would not have had to look beyond Frann and her influence upon him. His first foray into the nightly coupling with Frann had been a revelation. Before he had experienced it himself he had only heard the boastings of his troopers and some of the other decurions. It had seemed somehow, a furtive and grubby experience with much fumbling, groping and, to hear them something of a mess at the end. Perhaps because he was so gentle, unlike the men who had taken her before, Frann responded in a gentle yet considerate manner. She knew what to do whereas the virgin decurion didn't and she guided and helped; she was a teacher and she was a patient teacher. Now, after three weeks they had both found how to pleasure each other and to do so even in the hall filled with others. Because Marcus was the only male slave the only other groping beneath the bearskins were those between women desperate for some love and comfort from any source. The girls who were taken by the warriors were always removed to the warrior hall. Frann always looked sad when the tearful girls returned as she remembered the horror of her visits and the fearsome drunken warriors who regarded the girls not as human beings but lower animals to be used and discarded. Whenever they returned to the slave hall she nestled and cuddled even tighter than before and her eyes filled with gratitude. Marcus had saved her from that nightmare, at least for a while.

    He could now converse quite well, understanding most words and able to communicate effectively. When Trygg had asked him about the training of Roman soldiers Marcus had explained about the wooden rudius. "Your warriors do not practise with real weapons? They use bits of wood?" Trygg had sounded incredulous until Marcus had had the carpenter make two to his specific directions.

    "Here are two rudii. Feel one."

    "It is heavier than a sword."

    "Yes, and it hurts when you strike." Marcus looked directly at the chief. "When your warriors train with real weapons do you get injuries?"

    Trygg laughed, "Of course. It is what makes them warriors."

    "But sometimes they are hurt so badly they cannot fight again nor go on a raid…?"

Trygg looked with interest at the wooden sword. "Yes, but does that not happen with your training?"

Marcus shook his head, "No, the worst that would happen would be a few bruises or a bloody nose." He took a deep breath. "Would you like to try a bout with me?"

Snorri gasped and stepped forward, his sword halfway out of its scabbard. "No Snorri. Do you think he can kill me with a piece of wood? If he can then he should be chief of the Tencteri not I." He saw at the eager look on Marcus' face as he looked at his sword. But I will take temptation away from him." He removed the sword of Cartimandua and handed it to a servant. "Take this to my hall."

Taking the wooden sword he faced Marcus who smiled at the poor stance. "One thing chief; we have a rule that you strike no head blows for they could be fatal."

Trygg smiled and gestured to Snorri. "See Snorri. He warns me of the dangers." Suddenly he launched himself at Marcus who had been expecting such a move. Stepping forward with his left leg he half turned his body so that Trygg crashed passed him and he hit the flat of the rudius hard into the midriff of Trygg who collapsed on the ground, struggling to catch his breath. Snorri ran forward but the chief held up his hand and when his breath returned said, "No Snorri, I am but winded."

Marcus gave an apologetic smile. "Sorry Chief Trygg but the training took over and I just reacted to your attack."

"I can see now why you wished to fight me for the sword. I would have rushed in like that. I see you stand differently to me why?"

"You balance on the balls of your feet and you keep your shoulders low. Let your enemy do the work for you and tire himself out. Try it." Trygg adopted the same pose. "Now do not use the sword like a club. Hold the blade so that it points upwards and use it to stab. If you have a sharp point it will go through leather and only iron will stop it. If your enemy has armour, then go for the legs. It slows a man down and makes him move less well."

The two practised until Trygg was too tired to lift his arm. "Why is it that you are not out of breath, and I am ready to fall to the floor? This wooden sword seems to weigh as much as an anvil. You can still lift your weapon and yet I am like a baby unable to move it any more."

"Training. We do this for an hour every morning, sometimes more. My brother, who was a much better warrior than I am would train for three hours every day."

"And he is better than you?"

"He was, he died last year."

"I would like to meet the man who could beat the man who could beat you."

"It was no man. It was a witch." It was as though thunder sounded. Both Snorri and Trygg made the sign against evil.

"Thank you for today Roman. Every day I learn more about you and about myself."

Marcus had been called upon to give others a lesson with the rudius. Snorri had eventually learned a grudging respect for the Roman after he had nearly had both wrists broken. The one warrior Marcus wanted to fight, and to hurt, Lars the rapist, never came near the lessons, making his hatred of Marcus obvious to all.

One morning, when the snow was lying crisply on the ground, Frann and Marcus were led to the jetty. "Come Roman. We are going to the mainland to meet Drugi."

Marcus could feel the excitement coursing through his body. Although it was an icily cold morning he felt expectantly hot. He had not forgotten his plan to escape but, as he needed to take Frann with him, he wanted a safe and secure plan. This took him back to his Explorate days. Observation and deduction were key skills taught to him when he was young. All the training from Gaelwyn and Rufius would be used as he harnessed every sense and skill he possessed. He had already worked out that it would be easier for them to leave from the west coast of the mainland for that would be a shorter journey but he had no concept of how the land to the west of their island lay. He was also excited because Drugi was getting horses for them and that, too, was a major part of his escape plan. Once on the back of a horse, Marcus felt that he had no equal. The only flaw would be Frann for if she was with child it would make flight difficult, almost impossible and he had no idea of her skills, if any, as a rider. He could only hope that coming from the northern horse country, she had been familiar with horses.

Trygg had only brought a handful of men with him and Snorri was not amongst them. Marcus took that to be a sign that Snorri was not as suspicious of him as he had been for the warrior had been a little friendlier since the Roman had been teaching them how to fight Roman style. The boat they boarded at the jetty was tiny in comparison to the long dragon ship which had brought them from Britannia. There were six oars and then just enough room for Trygg and Marcus. Frann was left at the jetty. Marcus knew that his improved language skills meant that she did not need to come and he also suspected that, as it was the first time he had left the island refuge, they were ensuring he could not flee, at least not with Frann.

As Trygg steered the small boat west Marcus was able to examine the fjord in more detail. It was a perfect place to defend for their two islands effectively blocked a swift entrance and exit. A rope could easily be used to block all three channels as they were not wide although he assumed there must be a deep channel for the ships to use. He now understood why the defences were so small; they did not need to withstand a siege or a frontal attack if a huge force came they could easily retreat to the citadel and harass any attacking ships from the islands. He would have to leave across the mainland and he peered west to view the land. The harbour they were heading for was at the end of a smaller fjord and he could see, just above the jetty a walled citadel with much more prominent defences. It reminded him of the stronghold in Manavia but this one was much closer to the harbour. He would not see many hills and the land was flatter than Britannia. What he did notice, however, was the number of trees. It was as heavily forested as north of the Stanegate. That in itself was useful.

Trygg had noticed how the Roman was using his eyes and taking everything in. He would have to be careful with this horseman of Rome for he had shown much intelligence in the time he had been there. Already Trygg had learned much from his captive but the chief of the Tencteri was no fool, the warrior staring at the land would escape if he could. Trygg had hoped to tie him to him through loyalty and he had not given up on that but he felt certain that the Roman had already tied himself to the Brigante slave and that would act as an anchor; he would not be able to leave quickly. The trip to the mainland was not only to look at the horses which his slave, Drugi, had acquired it was also a test for Snorri and twenty warriors had been sent over the previous day in case the Roman tried to escape.

"This is Orsen, our citadel. It is new, Roman and I would be grateful if you would look at its defences to see how they may be improved." The chief pointed to the south. "The Suebi attack us constantly. This is why we built our stronghold so that we could have a toehold on the mainland. When we have seen the horses we will walk the walls."

"I will help you for you do not fight Romans but when I return to my people you should be aware Chief Trygg that I will know of your weaknesses."

Trygg laughed. He liked this young Roman and his honesty. "I think we are safe then Roman for, unless you are like the hawk and can fly, you will end your days on Hjarno."

As Trygg tacked the boat towards the jetty Marcus noticed an enormous man standing at the end of the jetty. He was not only tall he was broad but the most noticeable thing about him was the total lack of hair on his head and his bald pate seemed to gleam like a beacon in the morning light. "Who or what is that?"

"That, my young Roman, is another special slave, that is Drugi who comes from further east than a man can travel in a month but he is the best man I know to both hunt and to care for animals. That is Drugi the Hunter. He comes from the land of the Wends."

Chapter 6

Drugi had been captured, not by the Tencteri but by slavers from further east. He came from the land far to the east, at the end of the dark sea and close to the land of the ice. He came from the land of the Wends, themselves a fierce nomadic people who lived by following the herds which crossed their land. He had been sold from one seller to the next until he was brought to the slave markets and bought by a captain who needed a nimble boy. Drugi proved not to be that boy for he was a boy of the land and he had proved a poor sailor. When the captain had pulled in to Hjarno-By he had been more than glad to trade the young slave of ten summers for a barrel of dried herring. Trygg had seen something in the boy which he liked. As the boy grew, his prodigious size became a real talking point in the village not only because he seemed to grow daily but also his skills as someone who could work with animals which soon marked him out. He was able to control even the wildest dog and control the most truculent pig. He could train hunting birds and he could trap any animal which walked. Even before they had built their port Trygg would take Drugi with his warriors to go hunting on the mainland. One of the reasons Trygg had built his fortress was to afford Drugi more opportunity to hunt for his warriors grew to crave the delicacies he hunted. The slave's aversion to the sea, the kindness shown by Trygg and his relative freedom all meant that Drugi behaved very much as a freeman would and did not miss what he had only experienced for the first three or four years of his life.

The huge bull of a man easily caught the rope thrown by one of the rowers and he held the boat steady with his enormous hands. As Trygg stepped ashore he bowed slightly to the Chief of the tribe but Marcus noticed that his eyes took in everything and appraised Marcus quickly and effectively. The huge slave intrigued Marcus who could not see any guards. Why did the man not escape? It worried him slightly for it suggested that escape, even on the mainland side, was impossible.

"Drugi. You have the horses?"

"Yes, Chief Trygg. I apologise for the time it took but I had to hunt deep in the forest and one of the ones I collected was wilder than any beast I had seen before." He glanced mischievously at Marcus. "Is this the one who would ride?"

"Yes, Drugi this is Marcus, the horseman of Rome."

Drugi scrutinised Marcus up and down and appeared to examine every uncia of him. Marcus felt exposed and embarrassed. "I could take my clothes off if you want to see if I have a tail!"

Drugi laughed. "I have never seen a Roman before. You do not look different. How have your people conquered most of the world?"

Marcus relaxed a little as he realised there had been no malice in the examination, merely curiosity. "I was born close to the coast on the island called Britannia. I was not born in Rome. Rome is not a people, it is an idea."

Trygg nodded. "That is interesting Roman, we will talk more, later. Now come, Drugi, I wish to go hunting with you once we have seen how this Roman rides."

Marcus could not help glancing up at the walls of the citadel as they passed. His curiosity was piqued. It would be a valuable exercise for his mind to see how to improve the defences, especially when he returned to Rocky Point to report to the Legate. Even as he thought it the decurion wondered just when that would be for it seemed a long way off but he was still an officer in the Auxilia of the Imperial Roman Army and until he ceased breathing, he would continue to behave as one.

"I have built a fence to keep the horses contained. It is close to the walls."

"Have you built a shelter for them?"

Drugi looked around in surprise at Marcus' question. "A shelter? But they are wild animals. They are not cows or pigs."

Marcus smiled. "The pigs you keep were wild; you hunted them did you not? Now you have pigs that are domesticated and peaceful. If a horse is kept like a wild animal it will behave as a wild horse. If you wish to ride them then they must be trained and treated as any domestic beast."

Drugi looked again at the Roman. It had made sense. He had enjoyed capturing the horses for he had not done so before.

It had taken him many days to track them and then lay the traps. Sadly two had died in his traps and he had had to change the way he hunted them. Drugi was not a cruel man and loved animals but he would hunt and kill them easily understanding that Mother Earth and Odin put them there for the benefit of man. He always invoked the spirits and the gods of the woods before he hunted and he was always rewarded but it was good to learn something new. He would talk more with this Roman.

Marcus heard the horses whinny as they approached and he felt his heart race as his blood coursed more quickly through his body. For the first time in weeks, he was close to a horse again. The hunter had done well. There were three small ponies, a mare and a stallion. He could see that the stallion was wild as it paced around the sturdily built enclosure. Drugi had made it high enough so that it could not escape but it would take some controlling. Marcus glanced at the slave and noticed the questioning look on the man's face. He did not think that Marcus would be able to ride him. Marcus had a secret, he had been taught about horses by the best, Sergeant Cato, and he would need every trick he had ever been taught to ride this one but he knew, in his heart, that he would be able to do so.

He turned to the chief who was looking somewhat fearfully at the beast. "You will need saddles if your men are to ride them."

"Saddles?"

"Yes, like seats for the back of the horses and you need reins, something to control them." He looked around and found a length of rope. As his hand went to Drugi's belt to get the knife which was stuck in it, the six bodyguards' hands went to their weapons but Trygg held up his hand to restrain them. Marcus sliced a hunk off the rope and returned the blade to the smiling Drugi. The Roman was interesting, he had not known how close to death he had been. Marcus was, in fact, not in the land of the Tencteri, he was back on Cato's stud farm. He was thinking the problem of managing a horse through and no-one else existed. He was Marcus Aurelius, the horse trainer of the Second Sallustian again.

As he approached the corral he began to fashion the rope reins as he had been taught years ago. The movements were second nature and he was not even conscious of their performance. He did not notice the amusement on the faces of the men watching him as the stallion snorted and stamped angrily in the enclosure. The first thing he did, once his reins were fashioned was to climb on the top rail and sit there just two paces from the horse. The black beast looked at him, nostrils flaring and forefeet stamping. He began humming a song Gaelwyn had taught him as a child and as he did he slid over closer to the horse. He was close enough to touch the animal but he did not. He laid the rope reins, still held in his right hand, over the mane of the horse and it shook it off. Marcus repeated the action a number of times, patiently until it tired of its action and sniffed the rope which was closest to Marcus' hand. He slid a little closer so that the horse could if it so chose, bite him. Despite his confidence, Marcus was ready to roll backwards off the rail in an instant. He began to talk to the horse using the Brigante words taught to him by Gaelwyn. "You are a fine animal and a noble beast. You do me honour by allowing me so close." He held out his hand to the black stallion. It moved its head back but Marcus left his hand where it was and the horse, eventually, sniffed it and seemed to accept it. "When I ride you I will not own you. We will be as one, part of the Great Spirit and we will be greater together than we are apart." He slid off the rail to stand close to the horse. His left hand stroked the mane whilst his right hand remained on its muzzle. He put his mouth close to the horse's nostrils and breathed into them. "I give you my breath so that you know who I am. I give you my words that we might become friends. I give you my heart as I take yours."

 Drugi looked on in amazement. He had never seen anyone do what the Roman had done. "This one is special Chief Trygg. I was sure the horse would bite him the moment he could."

 "I know faithful hunter. I saw the mark of the gods in his eyes."

 They watched as Marcus slid the reins over the mouth of the horse and then he untied its halter from the rail. Drugi and Trygg held their breath at this moment in time, frozen still in the chill air of the Uiteland morning. Marcus' breath and the stallions were steaming in the icy air but the horse's hooves were not moving, for the first time since they had approached.

Holding on to the reins in one hand and clutching a hank of mane in the other the Roman decurion slid effortlessly on to the back of the horse. The horse bucked but years of experience and superb balance enabled Marcus to stay on and he leaned forward to speak to the horse. "I am not a heavy burden and when you have eaten of the treats I will prepare for you then you will become the mightiest horse in the land. Now we will ride." As he kicked his heels in to the flanks of the horse he said, "Walk!"

To the astonishment of all who watched the horse began to walk around the corral; even more amazing was that the ponies all followed and Marcus rode around the enclosure. Kicking again he shouted, "Trot!" The horse responded immediately and Marcus rode around the enclosure until he was satisfied. He returned to the halter and, sliding off, retied it to the rail. He nuzzled the horse and spoke into its ear, "You are now Cato and, while I live in your land, you will be my horse."

He climbed over the rail and walked back to the eight men who stood with open mouths, "He is a good horse and the others will be trained much more easily for he is the master and they will follow."

Drugi picked Marcus up in a bear hug. "You must teach me your skill for Drugi is the master of all animals but, Roman, you are the master of horse."

Trygg looked at the horse longingly. Marcus knew that, having seen the horse ridden he would be able to emulate the Roman. "Could I ride the beast?"

"Not yet for he is not trained. It will not take long to train them but if you were going to ride him we would have to…" Marcus struggled for the word geld. It was where he needed Frann. In the end, he had to mime cutting off his own testicles.

Trygg looked horrified. "I would need those cut from me?"

Marcus laughed, "No, the horse."

Trygg looked relieved while Drugi hid the smile. "That would make him tame?"

"Yes. Most of the horses we ride have it done to them."

Drugi walked over to stroke the mane of the horse. "It would be a shame, Chief Trygg, for we could breed fine horses from this magnificent beast."

"But I would not be able to ride him."

"In time you would but it would not be this year. I have been riding since I was small and it took me many years to progress to such animals."

Trygg seemed satisfied. "Good. You will stay here with Drugi and train these mounts, and the others which Drugi will capture."

Marcus could see from Drugi's face that capturing the horses had been more difficult than the chief imagined. "I would stay here on the mainland?"

"Yes Drugi has his own hut and you could share."

"And Frann...?"

Trygg's face darkened. "She is a slave. You can speak our words now of what use would she be?"

"I still struggle with some words and besides she comforts me at night."

"Do not forget Roman that you are a slave as is Frann. She will continue to be one."

Marcus knew that he was taking a risk but he couldn't allow Frann to go back to the slave hall and the attention of Lars. "It may be that if I do not have my comfort then I may not train the beasts as well as I should."

Drugi took a step back as Trygg moved threateningly towards Marcus. "Do not try to trade with me or threaten me. If you do not train the beasts to my satisfaction then you are no use to me and you will be punished."

"If I cannot have Frann then you have punished me already." Marcus did not flinch from the stare of the chief. His men's hands were already going to their weapons, anticipating the order to kill him.

Suddenly the threatening silence was broken by the scream of a hawk above them in the sky. They all looked up. Marcus knew that it was Macro and he smiled. Drugi saw the look and wondered what it meant. Trygg's face was calmer when he looked back at Marcus. "We came here to hunt. We will hunt and the matter of Frann is forgotten, you will not mention it again."

Marcus knew that it was not forgotten but he would bide his time. He did not think that Lars would do anything until he knew that the king had sent Marcus to the mainland. They set off in a line with Drugi at the front. He had a bow and a quiver whilst the others had spears. Marcus was, not surprisingly, the only one who was unarmed and he felt almost naked. Trygg gestured for one of his warriors to follow Marcus who had obviously become a threat once more.

As they trotted through the forest Marcus began to run through his options. He could now escape. He knew that. He had a horse and it would have been simple enough to ride off as soon as Cato had obeyed him. He had stayed for Frann. If he could not save Frann then he could, at least, save himself. As quickly as the thought came into his head he dismissed it; he could not desert the girl who had helped him and, if he was honest with himself, she meant as much to him as his mother had meant to his father.

Once they entered the woods Drugi took over and all of them, Trygg included, obeyed his every signal and gesture. Marcus watched him and saw in him many of the habits and traits he had seen in Gaelwyn. He was a consummate hunter and, for such a big man, moved surprisingly quietly. He held up his hand and then seemed to sniff the air. Having ascertained where the wind was coming from he then went on all fours to examine the ground. Once he was satisfied he led them off but this time in a different direction. When Marcus reached the place Drugi had stopped he knelt down and saw the hoof prints and the spoor. It was deer. He was prevented from further examination by a spear being rapped into his back. He had to remember that he was just a slave, he was not on a hunting expedition with his brothers and great uncle. There were no shackles to be seen but he was bound to the warrior behind.

The whole line was moving swiftly and quietly. Drugi held up his hand and then gestured for them to spread out in a semi-circle. Trygg pointed to Marcus to stand behind the line and for Marcus' guard to stand behind him. Marcus knew that he was most definitely being watched and that told him that he was not trusted. He smiled to himself; they were right not to trust him because the moment the opportunity came he would fly and, having been captured once, he would make sure that they would not succeed a second time. Marcus watched in amazement as Drugi climbed with fluent grace up the tree and he sat astride a large branch with his legs dangling. For a large framed man he was remarkably agile, quick and, most important whilst hunting, silent. Marcus had a professional interest as Drugi notched an arrow to his bow; the bow was a short hunting bow and Marcus' own, back at Rocky Point, could easily outdistance the short-range weapon. The decurion was desperate for a closer look but he had to try to peer through the line of warriors; it was not easy. His hunter's eye caught a movement that the warriors did not see nor notice and the flash of russet brown told him that Drugi had spotted a deer. The scent of the hunters was being blown away from the prey so that it grazed contentedly on the piece of grass it had uncovered. Drugi and the hunters would have all the time they needed to make a successful kill.

The wild boar was an old tusker. He liked to sleep more than he had when he was younger which was how the line of hunters had missed him. Drugi had been concentrating totally on the trail of the deer herd he was following otherwise he would have picked up the smell himself. When they had spread out into a semi-circle the warrior on the right had disturbed the sleeping monster. Waking unnaturally from its sleep the boar smelled man. Man meant only one thing, he was being hunted and the old tusker had become old by not waiting to be attacked but attack himself. Marcus saw a shadow on the ground and looked up to see the hawk flying above- Macro! He looked around, the presence of his brother's spirit meant danger. Just as Drugi released his arrow the boar leapt from its lair. The warrior closest to the animal stood no chance and its long tusks ripped into his unprotected groin. The next warrior in line watched in horror as his companion's entrails cascaded down to the frosty floor like a multi-coloured waterfall. He tried to turn and run but fell, his spear tumbling from his hand. The old boar saw the recumbent warrior and raced towards his body. Marcus knew exactly what to do. The spear was not a boar spear nor could he throw it for the boar would be able to rip the man apart even with a spear sticking in it. His only chance was to attract its attention. Picking up the spear he leapt at the boar roaring out a wild primaeval scream. The beast heard him and turned remarkably quickly to face this new threat. It spun around and pounced ferociously at the figure it could see coming towards it.

Marcus was aware of time almost slowing. He could hear the dying man's death groan and the screams of fear from the fallen warrior. He could also detect Drugi trying to turn for a shot with his bow and Trygg trying to pull the sword from his scabbard. Most of all he could see the huge wild pig leaping at him. He dropped the end of the spear to the ground and fell to one knee. As he expected the boar took off to try to rip off his face. Marcus followed the beast's snout with the end of the spear and, moving his head to one side thrust forwards with a stabbing motion and he felt the spearhead sink into the beast's throat; as it did so he threw himself backwards and the surprised animal found itself flying upside down through the air. The spear was torn from Marcus' grasp and the animal crashed to the ground behind him. Before it could rise to its feet Drugi hit it with an arrow and Trygg hacked at its head with the razor-sharp sword of Cartimandua.

Marcus sprang to his feet and raced to the dying animal; as he took the spear from its throat he twisted it and the animal lay still. Looking skywards he spied the hawk and he raised it in salute. Only Drugi saw the action and he stored the information for a later date. The warriors all went to the dying warrior who was attacked first and as they reached him his body gave a dying spasm and he lay still. They stood in a circle around Marcus, the admiration clearly visible in their faces. Even though he was a slave he had behaved with more skill and honour than any of them. The man, who had fallen, whose life Marcus had saved, clasped him by the arm. "I owe you a life."

Marcus understood the debt and nodded. He was too shaken to speak. He knew that Gaelwyn would have been both proud and disgusted that Marcus had risked his life for someone who had been so afraid. He had drilled into Marcus the need for caution around wild pigs and bravery when they attacked. Drugi reached the pig and, with a sharp knife cut into its belly. He put his hand in and ripped out the heart. He walked over to Marcus and proffered the still-warm organ, still oozing blood. Marcus took it and bit out a chunk from it. It was then offered to Trygg who did the same, Drugi, and finally, the other hunters all followed suit to take the animal's bravery into their own bodies and become more powerful themselves.

There was an unbearable silence as no-one knew quite what to say. Finally, Drugi shook his head. "I can see that I will have to improve my skills. I kill a fawn with an arrow and feel proud of myself and this young Roman takes on the king of the forest with but a spear." He slapped Marcus on the shoulders, almost knocking him over. "At least we eat well tonight thanks to you." He examined Marcus and his eye flicked to the sky where the hawk still circled in the thermals, "There is more to you than meets the eye, Roman."

Trygg nodded, slapping Marcus on the back. "I am sure there must be some Tencteri blood in you! Come let us take these glorious kills back to the boat."

When they reached the boat Marcus went to board but Trygg stopped him. "You have a task to perform Roman. You have horses to train."

Marcus squared up to Trygg, "And Frann?"

Again Trygg's face darkened. "Are you threatening again?"

Drugi interrupted. "Without wishing to interfere, Chief Trygg, it would be easier for the two of us if we had a slave to clean and feed us and I am sure that the Roman will work harder if he has such an incentive."

Trygg could see that this was a way out without any loss of face. "You would make a good counsellor Drugi. And Roman, we all owe you a debt for the bravery you showed today and therefore I will accede to this reasonable request from Drugi. Your woman will come back with the boat but do not make a habit of challenging me for I have seen you fight. I would not fight you, I would have you executed!" The threat was serious and Marcus knew it.

"Just one more thing Chief Trygg." Drugi groaned and rolled his eyes to the heavens. Trygg's hand went to the pommel of his sword. Marcus smiled, disarmingly, "The saddles, the bridles and the reins for the horses. I do not need them to ride but you and your riders will."

There was a collective sigh of relief. "Tomorrow I will bring the smith, the carpenter and the tanner over. Try to have something to show them." Trygg wagged his finger in Marcus' face. "Some spirit watches over you Roman for others who have done as you have and spoken as you did are now dead."

The two slaves trudged back up the hill to Drugi's hut. Marcus looked up at the sky; it was two hours until night time. "Have you an axe?"

Drugi looked at him in alarm. "Why would you need an axe?"

"To build a shelter for the horses. It will be a cold night tonight and may snow. I would like a blanket for them if we have any."

"We have them for us but not for the beasts."

Marcus nodded. "Then when Frann arrives she can make them." He paused and looked sincerely into Drugi's face. "Thank you for what you said Drugi, it has saved three lives."

"Three?"

"Frann's, mine and of course Chief Trygg for he would have died first."

As Marcus strode off to collect his wood Drugi shook his head. He had no doubt that Marcus had truly meant what he had said. He would enjoy talking to this Roman slave. He had lived alone for too long and it looked like his life was going to become more interesting.

Drugi had just finished preparing the squirrel stew when Marcus returned. It was well past dark and Drugi had wondered if the slave had run. He would have been surprised if he had run for he seemed to care for the slave, Frann. Drugi could not understand ownership. He owned nothing. The bow he used was just a tool and he owed nothing to it. The most valuable object which the slave possessed was his skill as a hunter. When the Roman shivered his way into the cosy hut Drugi could see that he looked exhausted, and a little blue. "Finished?"

"Aye. They have a shelter which will give protection from the north wind. They are watered and I found some grass. We must find them better food. Were we back in Britannia I would have given them some of my ration of oats as a treat but I have not seen any here."

"Oh we have it but we reserve that for the tribe, not wild animals."

As he took the proffered bowl of steaming and delicious smelling stew Marcus shook his head. "Then that is where you are wrong. The moment we put a fence around them they are no longer wild and they are our responsibility." He shrugged. "As a horseman, I feed my horse before I feed myself for my mount can get me out of trouble quicker than I get us into it."

Drugi could see that Marcus, tired though he was, was nervous and he kept glancing at the rough door. "Do not worry Roman, if Chief Trygg says he will send the woman he will send her."

"But it is dark now, why is she not here?"

Almost in answer, they heard the crunch of feet on crisp, freshly frozen snow and Marcus leapt to his feet. The door opened and a relieved looking Frann stood there, a tiny pink face framed by a huge wolf skin. As they embraced Drugi said, diplomatically, "I will just check on the animals."

Marcus did not contradict him even though he had just returned from that duty. "Were you safe today?"

"I was but the whole village is filled with news of your bravery, how you saved Gurt and the chief."

Marcus shrugged modestly, "I saved myself." He waved his arm around the hut. "Will you be comfortable with this?"

Frann smiled and giggled. "We have had bigger audiences before than the hunter and besides Drugi is the kindest man I have ever known. Or he was until I met you." Drugi came in and she disengaged herself. "I will make our bed over there if that is all right with you hunter?"

"Wherever you wish. I am honoured that the two of you share my home."

While Frann organised the sleeping arrangements Drugi prepared the food for her. They all ate for a while in companionable silence. After they had eaten Frann went to the bearskin and covered herself. Although he was tempted to join her and enjoy the warmth and comfort of her body, Marcus wanted to know more about this man with whom he would be living for the foreseeable future and he needed to know the measure of the man. Leaning back against the wooden box which housed Drugi's hunting weapons Marcus looked at the huge hunter. "Why have you never escaped?" He waved a hand vaguely towards the west. "There are neither chains nor bars to hold you here."

"I quite like it here. This is my home; the only home I have ever really known. I was taken when I was a child and my first masters were cruel. My people were the Rugii clan of the Wends and we lived by the sea. It was a band of Cherusci who captured me and they were not good masters. When I was sold to the Frisii I was almost dead and the Frisii, although not cruel had little use for me. It was Trygg's father who bought me eventually and found a use for me. I hunt and I live by myself. I am content."

"Do you not miss your family?"

He looked sad and stared into the fire. "They were all killed, either in the raid or later on the journey west. I was so young I can barely remember them." Marcus could not imagine a life where you did not remember your parents and then he thought of Macro whose father was killed when the boy was barely weaned and whose mother had tried to kill him, twice. Drugi shook himself. "What I do miss is the taste of the wondrous Kielbasa; the food of my childhood."

"What is Kielbasa?"

"A wonderful sausage made with pork and other ingredients. As big as a man's dick."

Marcus laughed. "Some men had longer dicks than others Drugi."

Drugi looked seriously at Marcus and then glanced between his legs. "The Rugii are all big men. As big as my dick then Roman!"

"A hearty meal indeed."

The irony was wasted on Drugi. "What I wouldn't give for one of those. It is food fit for Kings, no , food fit for gods!"

"Do you know what goes into them?"

"Pork, bread, the lights of a pig and spices."

"Well why not make one yourself?"

"We cannot get the spices."

"Then you must ask Trygg to ask at the ports for Roman ships and Phoenician ships trade them all the time." Drugi looked confused. "They are light to carry but valuable and Rome has the trade routes to the east. We can get hold of them from

Eboracum. They are expensive but you do not need much to make the taste of the meat change."

Drugi's face lit up. "You have brought light into my life Roman. I will indeed ask for such a boon. I am glad that you were captured."

"You will understand if I do not share your sentiments."

"You want to escape?"

"Of course."

"Then why have you not left now on the horse. I would not stop you."

"You wouldn't?" Drugi shook his head. "Well I will but for the moment I cannot."

"The girl?"

Marcus glanced over and saw, from the regular breathing beneath the skin, that Frann was asleep. "The girl. But I also need a plan. I could go through the Suebi lines and fight my way to the Roman lines but she would need a ship."

"Then you have a problem for the Suebi control all of the ports in the west and the only other port I know of, in the east, is here."

"I will find a way. I have to return to Britannia."

They both lay down and covered themselves with their bearskins; Drugi also had a fine wolf pelt to ensure his whole body was warm. Marcus felt warmer as he cuddled closer to the sleeping Frann. Unconsciously, in her sleep she moved even closer to him. There was a silence only punctuated by the spitting of the resin from the logs on the fire. "The hawk. Do you control it?"

Marcus felt a sudden shiver run down his spine as though a chill had just entered the hut. "What do you know of the hawk?"

"I know that it is close to you for it showed me where to find the black stallion. I had not seen it before and I had thought to capture it and train it for it is a fine hawk and a good hunter. I watched each day as it killed. It is the best hunter in the forest, apart from me, of course." Marcus remained silent. "When it warned you of the boar and you saluted it then I knew there was a bond. What is the bond Roman? Tell me hunter to hunter, for as well as a being a warrior and a horseman I know that you are a fine hunter."

Marcus spoke quietly and told the story of Macro from his birth to his death and of his death oath."So, Roman, you have a weregeld with your brother." He nodded in the dark. "It is good to have a protector and I am glad that I did not try to capture the hawk."

Marcus laughed. "In that, you would have failed for even when he was mortally wounded my brother found the strength to return to me and swear an oath."

"An oath on the sword which now hangs from Trygg's baldric."

"Just so."

The fire crackled and outside a hunting owl hooted. "Then I too will make an oath for, while I will never leave this place, you should return home, with your woman and with your sword. When you are ready to return to your own land then Drugi will help you."

"But why would you do that? You barely know me."

"I know that you are the only other man I have ever met who cares and understands animals as I do and that makes us brothers and today I saw you risk your life for someone who cared not for you. That makes you worthy of life and more than that a life which you choose." Marcus did not know what to say and lay in the silence wondering about Macro, the Allfather and the Parcae who were making the whole world, it seemed, work for him. "Of course I have no idea how you will achieve your escape but it will be interesting to watch. Life is not dull around you, Marcus, Horseman of Rome."

Chapter 7

Livius stood with Rufius and Gnaeus as they watched The Swan tack into the newly built port at the mouth of the Tinea. The bastion anchoring the wall at its eastern end was precariously perched atop a low cliff and looked as though a high tide could wash it away. It was, however, a statement that Rome was clearly marking its northern border with a substantial stone-built fort and port. Neither Rufius nor Gnaeus had needed any persuasion to join the quest and were both eager. Livius looked at them both seriously. "This is more than dangerous, it may even be suicidal. You do not have to go. If you go you are volunteers and we cannot come to your aid should you find trouble over there." He looked intently at the two young men; one of them was a close friend and the other one of the brightest prospects amongst the troopers. They were both valuable members of the ala. "I want you both to return safely. If it is without Marcus then so be it. It is the Allfather's will but be careful."

Rufius laughed, "Yes mother."

"The Legate does not want to lose either Hercules or Furax in this rescue. Do not jeopardise those civilians just to get Marcus. Do not take any unnecessary risks." He glanced from one to the other. Rufius looked much older than Gnaeus who seemed to the Prefect to be little more than a boy. "Rufius you still have the letters from Emperor Trajan?" Rufius nodded and patted his satchel. "You will be outside Roman territory but use them when you are in Imperial land."

"Letters, from the Emperor?" Gnaeus spoke quietly to Rufius as Livius went to the jetty to greet the Legate who was giving his final instructions to Hercules.

"I have a letter from the Emperor authorising my actions and I am a frumentari."

If Rufius had slapped Gnaeus in the face he could not have had a bigger reaction. "I had better watch my step then."

"I tell you this not to impress you but to impress upon you the danger we will be in. I have done this before when I served as an Explorate. We had to operate amongst the enemy far from friends. You will be doing the same. Where we are going no-one is our friend and we will need to watch each other's backs constantly."

Gnaeus wondered at his decision to volunteer and then he remembered two things, the oath he swore to the sword and then the sight of the barbarian waving at him. His honour demanded that he go.

The Legate waved to the three of them as the trader gently nudged the wooden jetty, bouncing up and down on the waves and the tide. Hercules appeared, "You two ladies had better get aboard quickly for the tide is turning and I don't want to end up on those rocks."

The two men threw their bags aboard. Julius Demetrius clasped Rufius' arm. "Bring him back but, just as important, bring back yourselves and my ship. I care deeply for those two." He nodded at the old man and the street urchin he had rescued from the Lupanar.

"We will." They jumped over the side of the ship and stood in silence watching the land disappear in the flurry of sleet, rain and snow. It disappeared far faster than Gnaeus expected and he looked up, a little warily, as the darkness enfolded them and the sailing ship's bow bit down into the choppy sea. His reverie was broken by Hercules' voice. "The Legate said we should sail east but there is a bloody big bit east. Could you refine that and give me a better direction than east?"

Rufius looked at Gnaeus. "Gnaeus here saw the ships and he said they had dragon prows and the men were blond. That is right Gnaeus?"

"That's right." In the cold dark of night on a black empty sea heading into the unknown, that seemed perilously little to go on.

"That means east by northeast then. We will try Uiteland first. It is a peninsula."

Gnaeus looked blankly at Rufius who laughed. "Like a long island attached to the land. It means that Hercules can sail around it. What is our story then?" Both Romans were dressed in civilian clothes and looked just like the other sailors. They had not shaved for a few days and looked much less reputable already.

"We act just what we purport to be, traders. We have some jet, which explains why we have been to Britannia and, just in case anyone notices that we are a bit Roman, some lemons and spices." He pointed at Gnaeus. "We are relying on you spotting either the men or the ships. That will be just the start for it is unlikely they will have kept him at the port. He will, if we are lucky, have been sold on."

"And if we are not lucky then what?" The question almost stuck in Gnaeus' throat.

"Then Marcus will be dead!"

By the time of the winter solstice, the impossibly long nights and the ridiculously short days, Marcus had finally trained Cato so that the beast was calmer in the enclosure. This made the ponies easier to control and he had those rein trained quickly. Trygg came, with his sons, to see the ponies and they even managed a circuit of the enclosure whilst their ponies were led by Marcus. The falls that they had suffered, confirmed Marcus' opinion that they needed saddles. Chief Trygg had spoken quietly to Marcus as his sons had fed the ponies some oats which Frann had managed to procure. "I see that you were right about the skills and the saddles. I did wonder if you were using that as an excuse."

Marcus looked directly at the chief. "I do not speak falsehoods, Chief Trygg." He gave a wry smile. "In fact, I believe you find my honesty a little disconcerting at times."

Chief Trygg laughed. "It is true that others who spoke to me as you have done would have lost their heads already but I believe that the sisters who weave our fate, the Norns, have woven a web with you and me in it. It is not for me to break the spell."

Marcus felt a shiver for the Norns sounded too much Morwenna and her Mother cult for comfort. He changed the subject. "How are the bridles and saddles coming along?"

"Good. It is a quiet time for the tanner and carpenter and they enjoyed the challenge. Within a few days, they will be ready. And how is life with my hunter, Drugi? He looks happy enough."

"We get on well and he seems to like having Frann around. He certainly enjoys her cooking and we have much in common for we are both slaves."

"You are slaves but not as others," the stern look he gave to the Roman left Marcus in no doubt that he had been afforded special treatment and that he would need to reciprocate with his advice and help on all things military. He looked off to Hjarno-By. "You were right about Lars, Roman. He does feel anger to the woman. You were wise to keep her close but she is still a slave. Until she has a child Lars could rightfully claim the right to take her and I could do nothing about it. Nor would I want to."

The tone in his voice and the expression on his face told Marcus that he should make Fran pregnant as soon as possible. Marcus felt like saying that they were trying every night but instead asked a question about Drugi. "Drugi is happy here and he is a content man but he yearns for some of the sausages he ate as a child in the land of the Wends. Frann could make them but she needs some spices; the ones which come from the east. I know that Phoenicians trade them. Do you get traders here for it would make his heart happy for a fond remembrance of his childhood if we could make the treat for him?"

"You are a strange man Roman. Many other men would have thought only of themselves but you think about the woman and the other slave. Yes, I will ask the harbour master to ask visiting ships about the spices. We get a few traders here but none from the south." Trygg wandered over to inspect the horses which appeared contented as they ate from the bags which Marcus had fashioned about the rails enclosing the beasts. "The animals, even to my untrained eye appear to be healthier than they were."

Marcus nodded. "They are being treated as domestic animals now not wild and as man profits from care and husbandry so do the animals." He pointed to the bags. "The food, tied away from the ground is warmer and is nutritious. There is little grazing hereabouts and they need to supplement their food. They are doing well and will improve over the winter."

"But we need more."

"We need more. Drugi and I will be going out in the next few days to capture as many as we can. The short cold days mean that they have to forage further afield for their food and they are weaker, easier to capture."

"Good."

Although Marcus was used to the cool Britannic winters he had never been as cold as when he and Drugi set off through the forests to try to capture horses. The wind whipped all the way from the east and the icy sea it crossed merely added to its icy hold on the land. He was glad that he was living with Drugi for the hunter had many pelts and Frann had made a leather jerkin and breeks to be worn beneath the bear skin cloak he affected. He also wore a hat made from squirrel skins but he could do nothing about his cold hands as he needed his fingers free for the bow he carried and the ropes, wrapped around his shoulders that they would use to catch their prey.

For a big man, Drugi kept up a healthy pace and, allied to his familiarity with the land, meant that they were soon in the part of the forest where Drugi knew there were horses. As he had said, before they set off, it was easier for two men to capture horses than one. They had developed a system of signs which meant that they needed few words. They both spied the hoof prints and steaming dung at the same time. The horses were near. Drugi gestured for Marcus to move left. As he did so he unslung the first rope and then slung his bow across his shoulders. He eased the noose into a loop ready, should they suddenly spot one. Their aim was to gather a small herd but if they had to capture them one by one then they would do so.

Marcus saw the five horses grazing on some moss on the north side of a tree. They looked, to Marcus' eyes, emaciated and thin. There were three mares and two-year-old foals; a perfect start to their hunt, if they could be secured. Marcus watched as Drugi assessed the wind. They had both known that the horses could not smell them but it was good to be certain. Drugi tied one end of his first rope to a tree and walked towards Marcus. The Roman did the same and walked towards Drugi. When they met they had a half-circle which, hopefully, would halt the horses when they bolted. The two hunters then retraced their steps to go around the herd. One they smelled the humans they would move away, into the barrier, or so the two slaves hoped. Marcus identified the horse he would rope first. Neither man would bother with the foals for they would stay close to their mothers and the dominant female was closest to Drugi. As they edged ever closer Marcus saw similarities between the foals and Cato. If this was his stallion's herd then life would be much simpler. Could the Parcae be making life easier for him? Or was it Macro? Marcus suddenly knew that it was Macro's doing and that gave him all the confidence he needed.

The dominant mare lifted her head; she had their scent but was having trouble identifying it. Marcus and Drugi had been close to their ponies and Cato that morning and Marcus knew that horse scent would be on them. The delay gave them the edge and they both stepped forwards their ropes looping over their heads to strike the two mares. The third looked around in confusion and Drugi tied his first rope to a tree and then tried to rope the second. Marcus, not as practised as Drugi was slower but he had his foal caught at the same time as Drugi. The third foal pressed himself close to his mother making his capture simple. Marcus had brought some of the oats Frann had acquired and he held them to the dominant female. At the same time he began to keen to her. "Come now pet, we aren't going to hurt you. We will take you where it is warm and your master awaits. Come here pet, eat the oats." His soothing voice calmed the mare and she was so hungry that she ate the oats greedily. Marcus repeated the words and the feeding with the others and they were soon calm.

As they led them back to the citadel Drugi shook his head. "What are those words you use Roman? Are they witchcraft? Are they magic?"

Marcus laughed, "No Drugi they are just the words I spoke as a child, Brigante. You could use Tencteri words it does not matter as long as the tone is soothing and the movements slow."

"Ah. I will try that. It is good to learn, even if one is old." He looked curiously at Marcus. "The commands you use with the horse, Cato isn't it? They are in your language not Eudose." There was a twinkle in the hunter's eye. He had seen through Marcus' ploy.

Marcus had the good grace to nod. "True they are in my language. It is just a way for me to keep control and make myself indispensable. I can teach you the words if you like."

It was now the turn of Drugi to look embarrassed. "I have learned them already and they do work."

The two men laughed. For the first time since Gaelwyn had died, Marcus felt close to someone who was not his brother and it felt good to be able to relax and enjoy life. It was a shock to Marcus that this life as a slave was not only bearable but pleasant. He and Frann had a good life, he was working with horses. He and Drugi enjoyed hunting and Trygg and his bodyguards treated him with respect after the boar incident. But in his heart, he knew that he could never be as happy here as Drugi was and he would have to return to Britannia but he could not see how that was possible. He looked up in the sky but there was no hawk; there would be a way, he knew that.

Rufius and Gnaeus unpacked the crate which they had brought with them. Hercules was steering but Furax joined them. This was the first day since they had set sail that the weather had been benign enough to allow them to work on the deck.

"What is it Rufius?"

"A surprise in case we encounter a dire emergency." Rufius winked at Gnaeus and the two men began to put together the strange contraption.

When they were halfway through Furax clapped his hands in excitement. "It is a bolt thrower. The ships used them in Manavia. Can I have a go?"

Hercules' voice sounded behind them, he had left the steering to the First Mate and come to observe the war machine. "It is not a toy Furax. It is a deadly weapon and if we have to use it then we will have failed to complete our task as we should, discreetly and secretly." The old captain had not been happy about its inclusion but, as the Legate had pointed out, they were going to the dens of pirates and that increased their risk of having to fight. He was happier about the extra men recruited in Eboracum by the Legate. They were all ex-soldiers signed on for one voyage only. As there was less work available in the winter months there had been many takers especially as many of them had served with the auxilia and looked forward to a little action, albeit on a ship. Below decks, there were more weapons for the extra crew to use. As the cargo they carried was small there was no overcrowding.

Once the machine was built they placed it at the bow in line with the bowsprit. It meant that they could aim easily and yet the machine could be covered with a tarpaulin to disguise it. Furax helped them to tie its feet securely so that it did not move whilst at sea, in battle, they could loosen them to allow it to traverse. Rufius looked at Gnaeus and grinned, they were like children with a new toy. "I think we should try it out eh Gnaeus?"

Furax squealed in delight and Hercules stomped off, mumbling about too many children being on his ship. Gnaeus cranked back the handle as Rufius fitted one of their precious bolts. "Let us try the maximum power and see how far it goes." Gnaeus kept on winding back as Rufius elevated the front to its maximum. "Well, that is ready." Both men could feel that Furax was almost bursting and Gnaeus nodded. "Well Furax would you like to see how far it goes?"

"Yes please Rufius."

"All you have to do is to release this catch here, just pull it and the bolt will fly." The boy stepped forward and nervously approached the machine which suddenly seemed both enormous and deadly. He looked up at Rufius and then touched the catch. With a whoosh and a sharp crack, the bolt was hurled forwards. The whole crew watched in amazement is it arced into the air for what seemed like the longest time and then slowly dipped down towards the horizon and the white flecked waves.

Furax clapped while Rufius said to Gnaeus. "That went further than I anticipated. "He turned to the First Mate. "Throw out a rope let's see how far it went."

One of the sailors quickly put a knot in a rope and threw the end over. He then fed it out over the stern of the ship. The boat went forwards swiftly but still, they did not reach the bolt, finally, just as the sailor called out, "No more rope!" Furax pointed to the red feathers on the bolt which could be seen four hundred paces in front of the ship.

"That is over half a mile," said an astonished Furax.

"And the ones with the metal barbs go even further. Let's get this covered up and secured." Furax looked disappointed.

"Sorry, Furax, but we have a limited number of bolts and we can't replace them." Rufius was happier now that they had something to warn away any pirate who wished to pick the easy prize that was The Swan.

The next day the lookout spotted land and the tension on the ship became palpable. They were approaching a coastline where Rome did not rule. To the south, fifty or so miles away, was the mighty river which marked the end of Roman expansion. The people whom they encountered now could be pirates or barbarians intent on taking an unwary ship; this was no longer the land of Pax Romana. Hercules had confided to Rufius that he had never sailed into a port which was not Roman; he had neither charts nor ideas where the ports were. Furax had been tasked with keeping a map which could be used by other sailors but for The Swan, they were on the edge of a precipice and they had no idea how big was the drop. Hercules shortened the sail to reduce their headway and a man at the bows leaned over to watch for rocks.

"It is an island. No sign of life."

Hercules steered to the north of the island and behind it they could see the coast line of the mainland stretching away north, to the end of the world. "Smoke to the nor east!" The voice from the lookout drifted down to them and Hercules put the tiller over. It might be a farmhouse or it could be a port, but it signified people and that was the start of their quest.

While it was not a port it was certainly a settlement. They could see small coastal fishing boats pulled up along the shoreline and the ten large huts all emanated smoke suggesting that they were all occupied. As they edged in, they noticed the men emerge from the buildings and Furax's sharp eyes spotted that they were armed. Hercules ordered the sail lowered and the anchor dropped when they were fifty paces from the shore. The fact that the boats were drawn up on the beach meant that it was unlikely that there were rocks but Hercules did not want to be stranded on a lee shore. The small rowing boat was lowered into the water and two ex-soldiers climbed down into it while Rufius and Gnaeus prepared themselves to meet the villagers.

Hercules came over to them. "Remember lads we are looking to trade. Don't even think about mentioning pirates, raiders or slaves. We will save that for a port. All you need to do is to find a port."

They lowered themselves into the boat. They had brought some pottery to trade, for the Roman province of Britannia produced high quality pottery which would be valuable in the lands beyond the frontier. The two ex-soldiers pulled hard on the oars and the boat went swiftly through the surging surf. Rufius kept his eye on the men on the beach. Although the men were armed they did not appear to be threatening; he had had plenty of experience at gauging danger and he sensed that this was not a dangerous situation. Perhaps the small number of men in the boat reassured them. Rufius had a smattering of a number of tongues and he hoped that they would find a common one. They had decided, back in the Principia at Rocky Point, that the last thing they would do would be to speak Latin. If any barbarian spoke it they would claim to know but a few words.

The two sailors jumped out when they reached the surf and held the boat against the waves. Rufius climbed out first, leaving Gnaeus with their merchandise. The leader of the welcoming party stepped forward. Rufius held both hands out to show that he had no weapons and came in peace. He tapped his own chest. "Gaelwyn! Brigante." The old scout's name came easily to Rufius and he did not want to be caught out in a stupid lie.

The man tapped his own chest and said, "Cnut." He pointed at the ship with a questioning look on his face.

In answer, Rufius signalled to Gnaeus to bring out the merchandise. The young trooper waded out with the pot in his hands. Rufius held it to Cnut. "We are traders. We are here to find new markets."

He had no idea if Cnut had understood but he must have gleaned some information for he shouted something over his shoulder, the words were lost on the wind, but an older man came forwards and spoke to Rufius. "I am Carl and I speak your language. I was a sailor for many years."

Relieved beyond measure Rufius showed him the bowl. "We are from Britannia and we are trying to find new markets for our goods. We would like to trade with the people of this land."

The two villagers spoke a few words and then turned the bowl around. "It is a fine bowl. Perhaps too fine for us. We are but poor fishermen. What could we trade with you?"

Rufius recognised the lie but went along with it. "What have you that you do not need?"

The man smiled and picked up some of the sand, he let it trickle through his fingers, "Sand!"

Rufius dutifully laughed. "Have you any dried fish?" They did not need fish but he had to start somewhere. When Cnut had Rufius' words translated he grinned and nodded. Again, he shouted over his shoulder and four of the men went up the beach. "Where is the nearest big village?"

The older villager pointed north. "Meldorf, a day up the coast. They have a jetty and they trade." He leaned forwards. "And they are peaceful. You know? They are not pirates."

"Thank you for that. We are peaceful and we do not wish to lose our cargo to pirates."

The man nodded and said something to Cnut who smiled sympathetically. "This side of the coast is safe but if you round the north coast to the dark sea then beware for there are dragon ships. They have oars and are swifter than you."

Cnut's men had brought enough fish to feed the ala but Rufius would have been a poor trader to refuse any. "We will call again in the spring and, as a token of our friendship will you take this?" From his satchel, he took out a delicately carved fish. One of the troopers who had a skill with carving had spent a week carving small items out of some jet they had acquired in their raid on Manavia.

Cnut's face lit up at the precious gift. Rufius reasoned that it would probably be the most valuable item in the whole settlement. He took it and clasped Rufius' arm. The older villager translated his words. "He says, Gaelwyn of the Brigante that you are a friend and will be welcome here again."

"Dried fish!" Hercules was disappointed in the trading skills of Rufius. "Next time I will send Furax. He is much more skilled at trading than a horseman. Dried fish indeed! You may not have noticed Rufius that there is a sea out there with fresh fish!"

Rufius sighed and shook his head. "The purpose is not to make a profit but to find Marcus."

Hercules was not convinced. "If we are traders then we must play the part. Fortunately, you have found us a port which means I can do the trading and you can ask the questions."

Meldorf was a very small port but it did at least have a jetty. There were not only fishing boats, which were drawn up on the beach but also small traders most of which were smaller than The Swan. The only berth they could find was at the end of the jetty which was covered in a glistening film of hoar frost. Leaving the First Mate in charge Hercules, Rufius, Gnaeus and Furax all headed towards the glowing buildings at the end of the wooden structure. Furax carried a leather bag which contained another of the pots. There were fewer of the usual idlers on the jetty as the wind was blowing hard and it was not a pleasant place to stand. Rufius walked up to one of the men and spoke. "We are traders. Do you have a harbourmaster?"

They looked blankly at them but one of them pointed to a large hall lying close to the end of the jetty. They nodded their thanks and headed towards it. The door opened as they approached and a well dressed but corpulent man appeared. He gestured for them to enter. When they were inside they felt the heat immediately. As their eyes became accustomed to the gloom, for there was only the light from a solitary fire, they could see that there were many men and they were all drinking or eating. Rufius surmised that it was a communal building. The man spoke to him in the same language as Cnut had done. "I am Gaelwyn, a Brigante trader and this is my captain, Hercules."

To the relief of all of them, the man understood them. "Welcome, I am the headman of the village, Harald Haraldsson. Welcome to Meldorf. We welcome all traders here. How did you hear of us for you are the first Brigante who have sailed here?"

"We met some fisher folk, at Cnut's village."

There was immediate relief and sympathy on the headman's face. "Ah Cnut, they are a poor people, you will find better goods to trade here. What sort of goods do you have?" Like a market magician Furax took out the pot with a flourish and he handed it to Harald. "A fine pot. You can always tell quality. You Brigantes do make good pots."

"Tell me Harald Haraldsson, if Brigante ships do not call here how is it that you can speak our language so well?"

"Ah that is easy. We have many Brigante slaves." Perhaps Gnaeus was not as good an actor as Rufius for his face darkened and the headman went on quickly. "Oh do not misunderstand me we do not take slaves, we buy them at the markets." When Gnaeus, after a sharp dig in the ribs from Rufius smiled, the headman continued. "They are good workers and I found it easier to learn the language. Well, how many of these do you have?"

Hercules spoke for the first time. "We have a healthy consignment but we do not know what you have to trade with us yet. What do you have which is as valuable as this pot?"

The two men wandered to a nearby table where Harald ordered some beer. Rufius, Gnaeus and Furax split up to eavesdrop on conversations and gather as much information as they could.

Later that night, as they rode at anchor, away from the jetty, they compared notes and they all had the same information. The pirates and raiders all lived on the east coast of Uiteland. They also discovered that the slave markets were also there but there had been none for three months and one was due. After trading some of the pots for some amber and timber Hercules had decided to anchor in the roads. As he had said to Rufius, "That Harald seemed pleasant enough but I wouldn't put a bit of theft past him. Besides we have the information we need."

"We do indeed; we have to go to the very place Cnut warned us not to go, into the lair of the pirates."

Chapter 8

Marcus had been tending to the horses making sure that the new acquisitions were as comfortable as the original ones. Cato had pranced around the enlarged enclosure whinnying, stamping his hooves and, generally, showing off. The stallion was now used to Marcus and he made for him as soon as he came in sight. Part of that was due to the fact that Frann had found some old wrinkled apples and carrots and Marcus had been giving them as a treat. The sons of Trygg had managed to stay on the backs of the ponies now that they had saddles and reins. A cynical person would have said that Marcus had done that to ingratiate himself with the family but he had done it because he enjoyed teaching people to ride. He had however made himself indispensable to the family and Trygg's sons were his biggest allies; they listened with rapt attention to every utterance from their Roman slave. He had still to discover a way to escape his trap, it was a honeyed trap, but it was a trap nonetheless. The winter solstice had been fourteen days earlier and the days, while not any warmer were slightly longer. The door of the hut was open and he saw Drugi and Frann awaiting him. They both had a happy look on their faces and Drugi kept glancing Marcus' way while speaking to Frann; he wondered what their conversation was about. However, Marcus was pleased that they got on so well. It made the domestic arrangements work well.

"What are you two gossiping about? I think Frann is a bad influence on you; you are becoming an old woman."

Frann affected an outraged expression. "And you are calling me an old woman?"

"No, what I meant was…"

Drugi laughed, his whole body rippling with waves of guffaws. "Oh, the two of you… you do make me laugh. If this is what it is like to be a family, perhaps I should get one."

Frann walked up to Marcus and took him by the hand. "Speaking of families…"

Marcus had not the first idea to what she was referring and he looked at her with a blank expression on his face. Drugi put his arm around Marcus' shoulder. "You know, Roman, for an intelligent man you are sometimes slower than a snail. You are to be a father, Frann is with child."

Drugi left the two of them embracing. He would need to let Trygg know so that Lars could be warned off at long last. Both Drugi and Marcus had had to watch for the increasing visits of the scarred rapist who took every opportunity to come by the horses and the hut. Others came by to look at the new addition to the tribe but Marcus and Drugi knew the real reason. Lars' visits were deliberately threatening and the leering lascivious looks he threw Frann's way made Marcus want to strike out at the hulking brute. It had angered Drugi to see Frann cowering in fear inside the hut. But they were slaves and no matter what Lars did they could not retaliate; to strike a warrior would have resulted in a severe punishment, possible death. Marcus and Drugi knew that their value was outweighed by the honour of the warriors.

That night, as they lay in the hut Drugi brought up the unpleasant truth they had both avoided. "This alters your chances of escape now Marcus."

"I know."

"Escape?" Frann had not known of this and it both surprised and excited her.

"I had planned to escape with you on Cato and ride to the west coast and find a boat." His voice drifted off as he realised how ridiculous that sounded.

Frann was appalled. "Go! Go now! I will hold you back and you can escape."

"Do you think I could leave you here? No, we will go together. It may take longer than I would have hoped but you and my child will return to the land of Brigante and I will return with the Sword of Cartimandua."

Frann hugged Marcus whilst Drugi looked over to the island of Hjarno-By. "I would like to see how you can do so with the sword which is now about the Chief's waist and spends each night close by."

Marcus shrugged. "If I knew how I could do it I would have done so but I will find a way."

When Trygg discovered the news it was as though his own son had found an heir. "This is great news my Roman. You will become a great warrior leading my horsemen against the Suebi."

Marcus hated deceiving Trygg who had only shown him support and kindness. He would desert him in a moment. Marcus' training of the Tencteri had gone well. None had managed to beat him with the rudius nor had any managed to outshoot him with a bow. Marcus knew that Drugi could shoot far better, but Drugi was a slave. Two or three of the warriors had also shown that they could ride although the sons of Trygg were far better. Marcus was torn; he knew he should return but he felt a strange allegiance to the Tencteri and its dynamic king. He had not seen the hawk for a while and he just awaited the next message from the Parcae and Macro.

The snows had not fallen for a few days and there had been a slight thaw when the Suebi suddenly attacked, an unexpected foray in the depths of winter. Marcus and Drugi were feeding the horses when the hawk appeared. Both men looked to the skies and then to each other. The strident cries of the hunting bird alerted them both.

Drugi looked at Marcus. "It is your brother. What does it portend?"

"It cannot be good." Marcus glanced over to the pregnant wife who stood by the door of the hut. Could he ignore a warning such as this? And yet it was the cry of a hawk! He felt a pain in the chest. "Let us take Frann and the horses into the citadel and ask the commander to keep a watch."

Drugi looked at the Roman he now called friend and nodded. Marcus slipped a halter on Cato as Drugi opened the gate of the enclosure. As he led the stallion out, closely followed by the other horses and ponies, Marcus shouted to Frann. "Gather our belongings we are heading for the citadel." Frann knew Marcus and she knew Drugi; more importantly, she trusted both of them. She did not know why there was such urgency but she knew that it was not trivial and she gathered the essentials they would need.

The guards at the gate looked in alarm as the horses and the slave family entered the gate. The headman strode up to Drugi. "What means this?"

"There may be danger. Sound the alarm."

Were it anyone other than Drugi and the Roman the headman might have faltered but Drugi was a legend and the

Roman had saved the king. He turned to the sentry. "Sound the alarm. Close the gates."

The sentries all looked towards the forest but could see nothing. As silence descended the headman looked at Drugi. Was he the victim of some enormous prank? Suddenly one of the sentries shouted, "Suebi!" and they all looked out to see a horde of Suebi warriors hurtling out of the forest towards them. It was the first time Marcus had seen these fierce warriors who seemed to have a yellowish hue to their faces and loped along like some kind of animal. The bristling weapons showed no uniformity but the war hammers, axes and swords were familiar to Marcus. Some of the curved blades were new to Marcus and he mentally began to prepare himself for combat.

Although the ditches had been deepened and lillia strewn Marcus knew that the garrison could not withstand an assault. He turned to Frann. "Find somewhere to hide." To Drugi he said, "Get every archer on this wall and have the women boil up kettles of water."

The headman next to Drugi looked as though he was going to burst into tears. "There are too many. Where is the chief?"

Marcus pointed to the island. "That is where he is with the warriors. We need his help."

"I will go myself!" Grateful for the chance to escape the headman ran off towards the gate closest to the port and fled to safety. Marcus shook his head. He had seen other senior offices panic in the same situation. He turned to the sentry next to him. "Tell the men to keep their heads down and not to fire until ordered." Such was the authority in his voice and the reputation that he had gained that the sentry obeyed instantly. Drugi reappeared suddenly with a dozen men with bows. Marcus unslung his bow. "We are going to be the difference between the Suebi winning and the Tencteri surviving. I want us to hit every warrior that we see. Aim for the gut and keep firing until your arm drops or you run out of arrows." As the thirteen archers went to the ramparts Marcus yelled, "Bring the boiling water to the ramparts and await my command." In the distance, Marcus could hear the screams of the Suebi as they raced towards, what they considered a soft target. In the east Marcus could hear the noise as Trygg tried to embark warriors who, an hour earlier, had been drunk. Marcus knew that they had a long hour. "Without turning his head he shouted, "Drugi, if I fall, stop them from breaching the wall. If we keep them on the other side then we have a chance. We need to hold on until the warriors can reinforce us."

Marcus heard Drugi's voice shout, "The hawk has not screamed; you will live."

The other archers and sentries looked at each other. Loki was ruling the world and madness prevailed when slaves commanded and talked of hawks that spoke. The Suebi were confident. Their scouts had reported that the warriors in Hjarno-By were drunk once the sun set and there were barely fifty warriors in the citadel. By dawn they would have reclaimed the mainland and captured many slaves; their chief knew that the Tencteri would never retake the citadel once they had captured it and they would not lose their lands again.

"Ready! Loose!" The arrows fell like rain on the Suebi. Few had helmets and even fewer had armour. Still, they came, a sea of bloodthirsty barbarians hurdling the bodies of the dead, eager to capture the ripe captives of the Tencteri. There were not enough arrows to thin their ranks too much and they were warriors. A few Tencteri would not be the same as fighting the Roman legions. Marcus could see that they would reach the ditch and his arm ached as once again he pulled back the bow and let fly another messenger of death. His one consolation was that his men had suffered no casualties as yet. They were almost firing at point blank range as the Suebi hit the ditch and the lillia. The shock and surprise were audible as they fell into the deadly traps. Soon the ditch was filled with bodies and the Suebi reached the ridiculously small ramparts. He screamed above the noise. "To the ramparts, pour the kettles of boiling water on them."

He drew the sword he had taken from the headman; it did not feel comfortable in his hand but it was a weapon, even though it was not the Sword of Cartimandua. He hacked down on the first, bare head which appeared before him and suddenly he felt calm; he was once more in Britannia and he was fighting his enemies. The screams of scalded men filled his ears as he hacked and slashed at any face which dared to appear before him. He knew that Drugi and his archers were still fighting when the man who tried to hack at his unprotected back fell with a flurry of arrows embedded like the tail feathers of a pheasant in his back. Suddenly, there were no more Germans before him and he could see the surviving Suebi fleeing south. They had won. He knew not how, but, against the odds, they had succeeded. He glanced around and saw the mounds of bodies who had fallen either in the ditch or around his feet. In the distance, he could see the boats drawing up at the jetty and disgorging Trygg and his warriors. The Suebi had decided that they could not fight the Tencteri whilst the citadel remained free.

He slumped to his knees, exhausted. He did not feel anything other than relief that the mother of his child was safe. Drugi came to him and looked at the bodies all bearing the marks of a blade, they were the ones killed by Marcus alone. "That, Roman, was impressive. If Trygg was an honourable man he would grant you your freedom and send you and your lady home for you have saved his land this day."

By the time Trygg arrived at the gates, Marcus and Drugi were there to greet him. The chief grasped him in his arms. "Thank Odin that you did what you did. But for you, we would have lost all that we had won. If it had been left to this wretch all would have died." Marcus glanced down to the bound figure of the former headman. "Tomorrow he dies and we listen to you, Roman, and make our town safer."

The Swan struggled around the northern shore of Uiteland. The winds were not favourable and the sailors had to endure storms with sleet and snow as sharp as needles. The fact that the channels were narrow and they had to spend long hours on the deck taking in and reefing the sails, only to unfurl them a short time later, did nothing to help their situation. No-one was warm despite the furs they buried themselves in when not on deck. All of them were relieved when they finally edged into the calmer waters of the dark sea. Here there were small lumps of ice floating on the icy, almost black, water; not being enough to damage a ship but a warning that they were in strange waters. Hercules rubbed his salt rimed chin. "I tell you Furax, I will never complain about the Mare Nostrum again. This is indeed, the edge of the world."

Part of his worry was that they would soon be amongst ships which preyed on others for a living. Their only hope was that they make a successful visit to a port and actually trade. The whole crew, Rufius and Gnaeus included, were nervous as the trader edged its way around the headland to the smoke which came from their first port. Hercules was tacking carefully but every sailor was on deck ready to unfurl the sails and flee as quickly as possible should danger threaten. It was with some relief that they saw the six longships drawn up on the beach. Their crews were not in a hunting mood. The jetty, although that was a rather grand name for some planks of wood thirty paces long, had no posts for them to tie up and so Hercules dropped anchor in the small bay. He anchored so that their bow was facing the shore. If they had any trouble then the bolt thrower would be positioned to fire.

The small boat was lowered and they could see the welcoming party on the jetty. Unlike their first landfall, there was little sign of arms or weapons. As Rufius descended into the boat with Hercules and Gnaeus he wondered if that was a good thing. The men he could see were obviously warriors unlike the fishermen of Cnut's stead. He looked up at the pouting face of Furax. Hercules had insisted that he stay aboard and for once Rufius did not disagree. They both knew the danger they were in; they were going into the lairs and dens of the sea wolves and they did not know how they would be received.

Rufius had managed to pick up some words of the language these people spoke and, as they greeted the welcoming party he was able to introduce them.

The chief was a round warrior who had a pair of beady eyes which gave him the appearance of a pig but Rufius noticed the bracelets which marked him as a warrior. It would not do to underestimate him. "I am Gurt, the headman of this place. Why are you here?"

Rufius recognised the suspicion. They had arrived in the depths of winter, uninvited, in a foreign looking ship. Rufius smiled, spread his hands and began to explain. "I am Gaelwyn of the Brigante. We are traders from Britannia. The markets in Gaul are less welcoming than they were and we are seeking new markets for our wares and new sources for those things we cannot source ourselves."

Gurt seemed a little more relaxed at that news. "What can we possibly have that you do not have in Britannia for are the Romans not the richest people?" The sharp eyed chief was curious about these visitors for none of them was as rotund and soft as the ones he normally dealt with. Two of them looked to have the lean look of the wolf while the Captain had the gnarled look of an old pirate. They were not what they seemed.

"True, they are rich and they build in stone. Their homes are heated and they even have baths." Rufius smiled as the warriors shook their heads at such amazing and outlandish ideas. "But they require many slaves and they are not only scarce in Britannia but expensive."

Gurt grinned and his men laughed as he said, "Perhaps that is because many people from Britannia are now slaves here."

Rufius nodded as though that was understandable. "Then do you have slaves to trade? We have some fine goods to offer in return."

Gurt's face fell. "No we have none but there are other places, further south which have them." The wolfish smile which appeared on the warrior's face told Rufius that if they went further south then Gurt and his ships would be waiting when they returned north.

"We have jet, pottery and spices to trade. Is there anything you might have to trade in return?"

"Spices? It may be that we could use some spices for we have heard of a demand for them further south. And we have skins and fish to trade."

Rufius caught Hercules' eye and the old man shook his head. "I am sorry but we have sufficient of those. However as a mark of our good intentions please accept this gift." Rufius handed over a dolphin carved from jet.

The headman was impressed. "Thank you. Forgive me, I didn't catch your name?"

"Gaelwyn, Gaelwyn the Brigante."

Gurt and those close to him followed the Romans and watched as they went back to their ship. They took in every detail of the vessel and Rufius noticed one of them counting the crew.

As they rowed out to the ship, under the watchful eye of Gurt and his greedy companions Rufius asked Gnaeus. "Were those the ships and the men who took Marcus?"

"No, nothing like them. What did you make of that comment about the spices?"

"You noticed that too. I think that means that somewhere south of us are people who like spices and they may well be Roman. It may not be Marcus but at least it is a lead and gives us some hope."

As they climbed aboard Hercules said, "And I think that the sooner we get away from here the better. It strikes me that we are just a little too attractive for our new friends."

"And I agree but I wonder if we might try a little test." Hercules and Gnaeus looked at the decurion who had a strange smile on his lips. "If the people south of us, those with the slaves, are dangerous, then these villagers, or pirates, will probably attack us tonight for they would not wish to lose the chance to raid and take us when we return. If, on the other hand, they are not dangerous then they will let us leave to attack us on our return journey."

"That sounds very risky."

"I don't think so. If we anchor in the middle of the bay and we keep half of us on watch then we should be able to see them if they come out to us. Don't forget they will have to pull their boats off the beach and we would hear that."

Hercules looked up at the pennant flying from the mast. "The wind is in our favour. We will try it."

Furax tried to keep awake but as he fell asleep he was covered in the wolf skin. The cold clear night meant that they had a clear view of the boats but it was unbelievably cold. As the moon rose they could see that the whole of the village was silent and no-one was stirring.

"Do you think he lives still Rufius?"

Rufius looked up at the moon. "I do, Gnaeus, and yet, if you ask me how I know I could not answer you. It is, perhaps a feeling." He shifted a little and rubbed his feet which were becoming blocks of ice. "I would be happier if we had heard of a sword for I am sure that whoever took Marcus and his weapon would have recognised it for what it was."

"I still feel guilty."

"What for?"

"I didn't protect him."

Rufius burst out laughing and the sound seemed to carry across the bay. "You protect Marcus? There was only one other trooper who could best Marcus and that was his brother. "He ruffled Gnaeus' head. "All that you did was to obey your decurion's orders. That is all any of us can do."

"It is just that this land seems, well it seems nothing like our land. It is more primitive and, well more dangerous."

"True Gnaeus and this is a measure of the success of Rome for I daresay that before Claudius came to Britannia our land was like this and yet in eighty years it has changed beyond recognition."

"I do not think they are coming. Let us leave."

"You are right Hercules and with the clear skies we should be safer."

The crew hoisted the sail and the light breeze which was coming from the land edged them south and east, away from Gurt and his longships. The coastline was unlike Britannia and there were no cliffs just low dunes and rolling low hills. The ports were, largely, on the beach with no docking facilities at all. The next port they visited lacked longships but it looked far more business-like and more like the ports they had expected. It had long halls with a long wooden jetty and three ships the same size as The Swan tied up to solid-looking bollards. They pulled in at sunset having seen no sign of Gurt or his ships. They all knew that it was not good news for he would be waiting for them on their return but that was in the future.

As they stepped ashore they managed to find a friendly headman who spoke their language well and was effusively friendly.

"My name is Gudrun Gudrunsson and I am headman of this port. Welcome."

Hercules was immediately suspicious but after they were invited into the longhouse for some honeyed mead Hercules began to mellow. The villagers were pleased to have outsiders visit them and the headman told them of the dangers of the longships. "Many years ago, in my grandfather's time, they would raid us and take all that we had. We were grateful when they decided that there were richer pickings in Gaul, Germania and Britannia. It was in my father's time that we decided to become, like you traders." He pointed vaguely to the east. "We trade with the lands at the end of the dark sea. They have some good timber which make fine ships and the animal skins we trade there are softer and warmer than any we have. We do well." He leaned over to Hercules. "But had I been the captain of your ship, I would have travelled here with other ships. We find there is safety in numbers. There are many pirates out there and we arm our sailors. Those who took from us in the past will not do so again. Now, what is it that you wish to trade?"

They went through the same routine as before and showed the pots to the headman. He was impressed. "We have some fine timber? Skins? "

Hercules shook his head. "They may be fine but we need a more valuable prize. There is a shortage of slaves in Britannia." He shrugged his shoulders. "The Romans cannot get enough of them; they probably have one to wipe their arse."

The headman laughed. "We have some. There is a tribe further south, the Tencteri, who go to foreign lands and return richer but they do not bother us. They have slaves. We do not need many but the ones we buy from them are good quality. Many of them are from Britannia."

Gnaeus and Rufius masked their emotions as Hercules asked, "Have you any spare? We would take as many off your hands as you can let us have. The pots are fine and…" he nodded to Rufius who took out a carved piece of jet in the form of a bear, "and as a token of good intentions accept this from us, trader to trader."

The headman turned over the jet. "This is a precious object and I thank you."

Hercules waved his arm expansively at the long house, "You have shown us hospitality. It is the least we could do."

"We do have two spare slaves, women. They are good workers but the man who bought them no longer needs them." He lowered his voice, "His wife and children died and he lives alone. He is ready to join them. He lives up in the hills. I will visit him in the morning. Now as to the pots..."

Hercules and the headman wandered over to the fire to haggle. "I thought that this might be the place where Marcus had been taken but ..."

"Gnaeus do you not see? These may have been sent our way by the Allfather for if they were captured in Britannia then they will know where Marcus is. For the first time since we began this quest I have a strong hope that we may find him."

The two slaves were young women of about eighteen summers. When they heard the Brigante language their faces lit up and they boarded The Swan eagerly although it was not a sign of freedom, it was at least a little closer to their home. The headman was a shrewd businessman. Hercules did not know how much he had paid the slaves' owner but he knew, from the rapturous look on his face, that the pots the headman had received far outweighed the pittance he had paid.

"You are more than welcome here again Hercules."

"And you too Harald Snorrisson, come to Britannia for there they have need for fine wood and you could trade for the pots yourself."

As they sailed away Hercules wondered about a trade route to this part of the world but the thought of the longships put him off. He concentrated on sailing south having been given good directions and a chart from the headman who had been eager to build on the relationship.

The two girls were pleased to be away from the strange land but Rufius could tell from their faces that they worried why the boatload of men had bought them. "I am Morag and this is Agner. We were taken two summers since from the land close to the place of the jet. The family who bought us were kind but since the woman died..."

Agner carried on. "He behaved strangely and we feared what he would do. When the headman came we knew that our prayers to the Mother had worked." She looked intently at Rufius. "And what will our work be?" The look in both their eyes told Rufius what they feared.

"We will return you to your homes and you will be free." The joy in their faces and the embraces they gave each other was a visible sign of their relief. "However you must aid us in our quest. For we bought you as a key."

The girls looked perplexed. Morag asked, "A key? I don't understand."

"We are looking for a friend who was captured by raiders to the Dunum. You are the first Brigante we have found and we think you may have been captured by the same band. If you have then you can tell us of the place and make it easy for us to rescue our friend."

"We will tell you all we know. The man who took us was a man called Trygg. He was not cruel but he has many warriors. They had five ships."

Gnaeus asked, "Is he a big man with blond braided hair and a full beard."

"Yes, that is him."

"Five boats with a dragon head?" Again they nodded. "Sounds like him Rufius."

"Let us not get carried away. Even if it is the same man we don't know that Marcus is still there." He turned to the girls. "Describe his land."

"There are two islands, close to each other and the land and he has a fort on the mainland. "

"Were the slaves kept in the fort?"

"No there is a slave hall on one of the islands. Some slaves worked on the mainland and the other smaller island but they were all kept in the slave hall."

"Do they have slave sales?"

Morag nodded. "Yes, they hold them at the new moon."

"Every new moon?"

"In summer, yes but when we were there some of the slaves who had been there longer told us that they only have one in winter."

Rufius looked up at the sky, seeking the hawk. "Then let us hope they have not held it yet."

Chapter 9

The execution of the former headman of the citadel was witnessed by the whole of the community. His craven cowardice meant that he did not warrant a warrior's death and he was chained to a rock at low tide. Had he sent someone else in his stead then he might have been seen as a hero but the fact that he allowed two slaves to lead the defence of their citadel sealed his fate. As the sea came in his cries became more pathetic and strident. Marcus almost felt sympathy for him as he tried to stand on his toes in the bone-chilling, icy waters, to gain a few more moments of life. It was, in the end, futile but Marcus wondered if, in the same position, he would behave any differently. Life was something to cling on to and Frann and his unborn child had made his existence and survival even more important and precious; it was not something to be squandered idly.

As the waves finally crashed over him Trygg finally averted his eyes and came over to Marcus. "Now, before they have fled too far I will take my men and we will make sure that these Suebi have returned to their homes." He looked at the horses. It would impress the people if we rode."

It almost sounded like a plea to Marcus who was not sure if Trygg, who had had barely six lessons would manage to stay on his horse. His sons would manage it easily. "If your sons come they will manage it easily as for yourself," Marcus paused, knowing that his next comment could determine his future. "The mare, Magpie, is a quiet beast and we could try her." Magpie was black and white and the name seemed to suit.

Trygg looked disappointed. "The stallion. He is the horse for a chief."

"Let us try him but I warn you Trygg Tryggvasson, he is not an easy horse to master, even for me."

The chief's face lit up. "I am sure that you have taught me well. Saddle him."

Marcus did not like to say that Cato was not totally saddle broken but the chief would take that as an insult and so the decurion saddled the black stallion. Cato was not happy with the saddle and snorted at Marcus. "It is not my doing Cato. You are master of your own fate." The horse snorted and Marcus held on to the reins as Trygg emerged. "I would not wear the sword chief for you will need to balance on the horse." He looked dubious but unstrapped the blade and handed it to the waiting Snorri. He looked less confident as he neared the horse. Marcus had taught his pupils how to grasp the mane and the reins and throw the right leg over. He handed the reins to Trygg whilst holding on to the halter. As the chief's leg came over the back of the horse there was a cheer from his bodyguard and he sat astride the stallion looking like the cat who has stolen the cream. Cato just snorted.

"Let him go Roman and I will ride."

Reluctantly, and knowing what would happen, Marcus let go of the halter and, released from his grip Cato took off. He ran straight at Snorri and the guards who were standing by the open gate. The chief had no control over the horse and the guards threw themselves to the ground. As soon as it had escaped the enclosure it reared up, depositing Trygg, unceremoniously on his back and the black stallion galloped off. As Snorri and the others went to help up Trygg, Marcus went to retrieve the Sword of Cartimandua. The moment he held it in his hands he felt power surge through his body. He seemed more alive than any other moment in the last four months. Overhead the hawk screamed as it plucked a dove out of the air and Marcus felt like taking the sword and killing all around him, was this his chance of freedom? Then he remembered Frann... As he glanced over to Trygg and his guards he knew that he would be able to despatch all of them in a couple of blows but, out of the corner of his eye he saw the crestfallen face of Drugi who knew what Marcus intended. Marcus followed Drugi's gaze to Frann who stood watching him. Realising the futility of his action he slowly slid the blade back into its scabbard.

Trygg came over with a rueful look on his face. "Thank you for my sword Roman and you were right about the black one." He looked over to the horse which stood defiantly a hundred paces away. "Will you and Drugi recapture him?"

Marcus grinned. "No, he will come." Taking an apple from his bag he held it aloft and shouted, "Cato! Cato here!" It looked for a moment as though it would ignore the command but then it galloped towards the group. Snorri and the bodyguards scattered but Trygg stood his ground as the stallion came up to take the proffered apple.

"I can see that I have much to learn Roman."

"Look on it like this. If I tried to sail your ship what would the result be after five lessons?"

Enlightenment lit up the chief's face and he nodded as he rubbed his back. "You are also wise. I will ride the mare and we will see if there are any Suebi left to hunt."

Marcus would have enjoyed the hunt for the Suebi had it not been for the brooding presence of Lars. Lars, whose scarred face seemed to bore into Marcus' back as the warband trotted through the forest, Lars whose mutterings seemed somehow threatening and Lars, whose hand never strayed far from his dagger. Marcus resisted the temptation to turn around and say something. He was acutely aware that he was just a slave. He saw that Drugi had noticed Lars' attention and the look on his face told Marcus that his friend was not happy about it either. The rest of the warband were in good spirits. It was the first time that Trygg had led them from the back of a horse and they all thought he looked almost kingly. The chief, for his part was not confident and, despite his smiles, was clinging to the mane of the mare. Marcus rode next to him and said, quietly, "Relax. She is a gentle horse and she will not throw you. Use one hand on the reins, as I do, and sit lower in the saddle." The chief looked dubious but he did as instructed and he smiled as he found the motion easier and that he did not fall off.

"I think it will be a long time before my warriors ride." Trygg's dream of a mounted warband had faded with his crash to earth from the back of the black stallion.

"Were I you I would not use my older warriors as riders." Marcus pointed at the king's sons whose ponies were darting through the trees, their riders fearless. "I would use the boys. Train them on ponies and when they are big enough you will have a fine herd of horses for them to ride."

Trygg nodded as he digested that information. There was a roar from their right and, turning Marcus saw yet another wounded Suebi being butchered by the jubilant Tencteri. The unfortunate corpse was stripped of anything valuable and the warband moved on, already enriched by the plunder from the dead. "Drugi go ahead, take the Roman with you and see where they are."

Drugi grinned and loped off. As they were moving through trees there was no disparity in the speed of the hunter and the speed of the horse. Marcus resisted the temptation to speak, he knew that Drugi would be listening for clues to the Suebi whilst smelling the air and looking on the ground. Being higher up gave Marcus a better view and a movement up ahead caught his attention. He gave a short whistle and Drugi looked around. Marcus pointed to their right. Tying Cato to a tree Marcus and Drugi slipped through the woods. Hearing a noise they dropped down on all fours and began to crawl through the tangles and snow-covered undergrowth. The bushes above their heads were covered in snow still but to their right, they were bare having had the Suebi survivors trampling through them. They were a sorry sight. There were but fifty of them left and they were resting in the clearing. It was obvious that they did not know they were being pursued for it was two days since their attack. The disadvantage of fighting in winter was the shortness of the days. The Tencteri had eaten well and rested whereas the Suebi had expected to feast on Tencteri provisions.

Drugi tapped Marcus on the shoulder and they backed out. When they reached Cato, Marcus mounted, leaving Drugi to keep watch on the raiders. As he rode back to Trygg Marcus reflected that he had the same understanding with Drugi that he had had with Macro and he had with Rufius, that ability to know without speaking and act with the confidence that your partner would be there for you.

"The Suebi are up ahead. They are tired and there are but fifty of them."

His eyes eager with anticipation Trygg asked, "How far?"

"A thousand paces."

The chief turned to Snorri. "Split the men into two groups. You take one to the west and attack the enemy. They are a thousand paces ahead of us. I will take the rest." As Snorri led his band away Trygg slipped from the mare. "I think I will fight better on foot." Although Marcus felt happier on a horse he knew from the tone of Trygg's voice that he expected the slave to join him. Reluctantly sliding off Cato he tied them both to a tree, along with the ponies, and then, as an added precaution against theft, he hobbled them.

Marcus found himself on the left side of the chief as they moved purposefully through the woods. Suddenly materialising from a bush Drugi stood and held his finger to his lips. He pointed forwards and held both hands up twice. Trygg understood, the enemy were twenty paces on the other side of the bushes and trees. The chief waved his men to either side of him and then, drawing the Sword of Cartimandua led them forward.

To call it a battle was ridiculous and to Marcus, it was not even a skirmish. The fifty warriors they fought were tired, hungry and dispirited. They had been driven from their target by arrows and water. They were humiliated. The eighty Tencteri were rested, fed and fresh. They were undefeated and they were hungry for revenge. It was no contest and none was left alive. Trygg ordered his men to decapitate the Suebi and he had the heads placed on sharpened stakes in a semi-circle facing Suebi land; a warning to other Suebi that they crossed the grotesque barrier at their peril. As they rode back to the citadel Marcus couldn't help thinking that fighting in a warband was no different to fighting in a turma, as long as you won.

The reception afforded to the returning warband was all the sweeter for the chief as he rode in on Magpie for all could see their leader, the conquering hero. Behind him his sons were just as proud as they rode back on the ponies, the blood spatters on their tunics showing that they had been blooded in this, their first battle. As they rode close to the rocks on the beach Marcus stole a glance at the unfortunate warrior who had been executed there; his bleached body already showing the ravages of the unseen sea life. It was a reminder to Marcus that he was still in a precarious position and he too, could end up as food for the fishes.

The trouble began at the feast. Drugi and Marcus had tried to get out of it; Drugi did not enjoy that kind of thing and Marcus just wanted to be with Frann but the chief was insistent that the two slaves be honoured for their defence of the citadel. Marcus wondered if they would be given their freedom but Trygg was too clever for that. Whilst they were slaves they had to heed his orders. As freedmen they had choices. Neither Marcus nor Drugi drank much but the Tencteri did. A trader from the east had arrived and brought with him a consignment of the clear spirit they brewed across the dark sea. It was a potent drink and already many warriors were passed out having failed to drink in moderation. Marcus had been aware that Lars was consuming great quantities of the spirit and the Roman hoped that he too would pass out because he was becoming tired of the aggressive stares from Lars and his brothers. Marcus was wondering when he could slip away when Drugi grabbed his arm and pointed. Lars had left. His brothers were lying in a pool of their own vomit but Lars had disappeared. Fearing the worst and dreading what he might find Marcus leapt to his feet and raced out of the hall. Drugi was close behind.

There were no sentries at the gate which was wide open. Cursing the lack of discipline in the warband Marcus ran even faster to his hut. Before he got there he could hear the screams from Frann and the drunken voice of Lars.

"You little bitch! I'll show you pain like you have never felt before. That whore of a sister of yours took hours to die; you will last but a moment."

Marcus kicked the door open and there, with her legs spread wide lay a terrified Frann and between her legs was Lars. The only weapon Marcus could see was the branch of a tree waiting to be chopped into logs. He picked it up and struck Lars so hard that he fell off Frann and over the fire. Marcus helped Frann to her feet and put her behind him. Lars roared to his feet, his head bleeding heavily from the blow. "You fucking slave! Now you will die and then I will fuck your whore to death!" He pulled out a wickedly long sharp dagger and advanced towards Marcus.

Marcus edged to his right saying, "Frann, get out and find Drugi."

"I am not leaving you."

"I can fight him if I am not worrying about you, now go!" He did not see her go but the quick blast of cold air behind him told him that she had left. Marcus knew that the blade would rip him open if he allowed the barbarian to close with him and he needed a weapon. He kept edging right until he reached the fire. Without taking his eyes off Lars he reached down until his hand found the end of a log from the fire. He held the smouldering brand before him. It was little enough but he could use it to keep the drunken man at bay until he had worked out a strategy to defeat him.

Lars feinted with the knife and Marcus swung the brand, an ember flew off and struck Lars in the face, enraging him even more. He moved surprisingly quickly for a large drunken man and he leapt at Marcus with his dagger aiming for Marcus' eye and his other hand, aiming for Marcus' throat. The Roman managed to halt the dagger with the brand but the hand found his throat and the rapist began to squeeze the life from the Roman. Lars was a powerful man and Marcus felt himself blacking out. In desperation, he reached up with his left hand and, finding Lars' one good eye poked as hard as he could. He felt the eyeball and tried to tear it out. Lars reared up screaming and Marcus could at last breathe. Unfortunately, he had lost his grip on the log and, weaponless, he dived at Lars' legs, knocking him to the ground. The blade of the knife came around in an arc and Marcus held on to it for all he was worth. He felt the point inexorably turning into him and he grabbed it with both hands. He looked into the scarred face of Lars and saw his own hand had severely scarred Lars' cheek. The red-rimmed eye told Marcus how close he had come to blinding him and he was suddenly filled with anger. "You are a sad rapist and you are going to die."

In answer, Lars spat a gob of blood and phlegm into Marcus' face. He remembered something Gaelwyn had told him about fighting. And with all the force he could muster he rammed his knee into the groin of the half-blind savage. The shock and the pain momentarily relaxed his grip on the knife as he half-rolled away and the momentum carried Marcus' hands upwards to slice through the stomach and into the heart of Lars who died with an expression of shock on his scarred and bloody face. Marcus rolled over on to his back, eyes closed, gasping for breath. When he opened them he saw Drugi and Fran peering down. The two of them looked sad. Drugi said, "I am glad he is dead for he deserved to die but I wish it was not you who killed him." Marcus looked up, not understanding the meaning of the words. "You are a slave and you have killed a freeman, and Lars has brothers. This is not ended, Roman."

Marcus and Frann discussed fleeing but they had nowhere to go. It was the middle of winter and, although Frann was barely pregnant, she was pregnant and Marcus could not risk his unborn child in a foolhardy dash across the peninsula to the coast. As Drugi pointed out they would catch them anyway. Even if they did evade their pursuers what would they do when they reached the coast? How would they get a ship? They were slaves and had no money. Their only chance was for a ship to come to Hjarno-By and for them to stow away. Even that seemed ridiculous as they had only seen one trading ship since they had been at the citadel. By the end of the night, they had decided that Marcus would have to stay and face whatever consequences resulted from the killing. He knew that it was a matter of honour and blood honour at that. There would need to be bloodshed at the very least.

"Whatever happens we need to get some money, coins, gold, whatever it takes to buy a passage on a ship. If nothing else the death of that piece of offal has clarified my thinking. From now on we work out how Frann and I can escape."

Drugi shook his head. "No Roman for if you and Frann escape then I would have to be with for my life would be forfeit. Our destinies are bound together." He looked at the ceiling, "The hawk saw to that. Your brother was a clever man Roman, and he still plans and weaves."

Marcus remembered then that Macro's mother had been Morwenna, one of the cleverest and most devious planners he had ever encountered. Although they had bested her there had never been anything wrong with her planning, it had always been the mistakes of others.

They decided that the best course of action was to see Trygg early in the morning and explain what had happened. It would not mitigate the crime but their honesty would put them in the right, initially at least. Of course when Lars' brothers found out then everything would change.

The hall looked as though a whirlwind had whipped through it. Bodies were scattered everywhere with spilt ale and discarded food. Someone had gone out in the night and the doors left open so that a chill wind made it a cold and sparse space. As they entered the hall Trygg and Snorri were just coming too. "Ah

Roman, I see that you truly are wise and know when to stop drinking. I think Thor has his hammer inside my head this day." He suddenly saw that there were three of them and that they looked serious. "What is amiss? Have the Suebi returned?"

"No chief, although if they had, then they could have walked in and slit your throats for the gates of the citadel were left open all night but that is not why we are here. There has been a death." By now others were waking up. Trygg climbed the dais to his seat and, wrapping his wolf pelt around his shoulders he gestured for them to continue. "Last night Lars tried to rape my pregnant woman." It had been on the tip of his tongue to say wife until he remembered that he was a slave and could not marry. "When I stopped him he pulled a knife. We fought and he is dead."

Snorri snorted, "I knew we should have thrown you overboard Roman. You bring bad luck to this land."

"Snorri! Did he bring us bad luck when he saved our lives with the boar? Did he bring us bad luck when he saved the citadel? You are a brave and loyal warrior Snorri but you have the brains of a fish! Now be silent and get that fire lit. It is colder than Hell in here." Snorri reddened but went off to organise the fire. "The brothers of Lars will want blood for this. Yours, Roman, and I am helpless to aid you."

"I know Chief Trygg. I am a stranger to your ways. How are these things settled in your land?"

"The family who are aggrieved fight with the taker of blood. They would fight you blade to blade but as a slave they would wish to fight you without you bearing arms." Frann gave a small cry and grasped Marcus' arm. The chief gave a sympathetic smile. "If it was up to me I would allow this Roman a weapon but it is up to the council and they will decide. Where is the body?"

Drugi spoke. "Outside my hut."

"You six, take the body to Lars brothers. You three had better stay here. Snorri, summon the council." Trygg shook his head. The Norns are cruel Roman, they give you hope and then they snatch it away. Even with a weapon you would struggle against Lars' brothers for they are fierce and worthy warriors."

Lars two brothers were both younger than the scarred savage but they had the same evil look on their face. They stormed into the hall with daggers drawn. Snorri's voice roared out. "How dare you dishonour the chief with drawn blades! Sheathe them or suffer the consequences."

The two men reluctantly did as ordered, but then rushed towards Marcus. "The younger of the two, Carl, pointed an accusing finger at Marcus. "This slave murdered our brother and we demand his life."

Trygg nodded and turned to Marcus. "What have you to say to this Roman?"

It was a subtle difference but Trygg had called Marcus a Roman rather than a slave. It was wasted on the two brothers. The older, Stig, laughed. "It matters not what he says for he is a slave."

Marcus spoke quietly. "Your brother tried to rape the slave Frann and then he attacked me but the gods were with me and he died by his own blade."

The reference to the gods and the suggestion that they had sided with Marcus infuriated the brothers who both shouted at the same time. "We demand his death!"

Marcus' and Trygg's words had not been intended for the brothers but for the council who waited to one side. Trygg addressed them. "What does the council rule?"

The ten men spoke quietly for a while; Frann nervously gripping Marcus' arm in fear. The oldest shaman stepped forwards. "The slave did kill the freeman Lars and the brothers have the right to his life but Lars violated the hut of Drugi the hunter and this gives the slave the right to defend himself."

Marcus breathed a sigh of relief. The council could have decided that he could be killed whilst bound. Stig and Carl grinned at each other. "The slave can not have a blade." They were anticipating a slow death for Marcus as he tried to defend himself with his bare hands and they would hack him to pieces, slowly.

Marcus had been expecting this. "But I can have a rope."

The two brothers looked at each other, suspecting a trap. Stig spat out scornfully, "To hang yourself or to hold up your breeks when you fill them?"

Marcus ignored the jibe. "A rope?"

Stig shrugged, a rope would not withstand their blades. "You may have the rope and when you are dead we will use it to hang your body for the crows to feast upon."

As they were led by the council out to the area designated as the arena, Drugi said quietly to Marcus, "I hope you know what you are doing Marcus, a rope?"

Marcus shrugged, "I could not have a blade and a staff or a club would merely slow them down. I need something to help me win." They both looked up into the empty sky but there was no sign which would help them.

Snorri handed a length of rope to Marcus. He gave him a sympathetic look but a look which also said that the gesture was futile. Marcus made a large knot at one end and coiled part of it around his left arm, while he held the knotted end in his right. He whirled it gently as he waited for Stig and Carl. Trygg could see how the rope could be used defensively but he could not see how it would be an effective weapon. Still, the Roman had proved resourceful before, perhaps he would surprise them again.

Stig and Carl had both chosen axes and Marcus breathed a sigh of relief. Had one chosen a spear then he would have only lasted a few moments. The warriors of the tribes surrounded them with their shields making a large circle and Marcus felt like a gladiator in an amphitheatre. Marcus stepped forwards and the two men began to circle him. They intended to eliminate any chance he had to defend himself and attack from two sides at once. They would feint and prod and make him become defensive. Marcus had no intention of staying on the defensive and he whirled his rope around his head and advanced on Stig, who was the closest. He flicked the knotted end and it smacked into Stig's eye which erupted in blood and white viscous liquid as it was torn out. "Just like your brother!"

Marcus knew that the disabled Stig would soon attack him again and he had to attack Carl quickly; he turned to face the advancing Tencteri warrior who had seen the fate of his brother and he held his axe up to protect himself from the knotted rope. Marcus had anticipated such a move and he reacted accordingly. This time he whirled the rope to strike and wrap itself around the haft of the axe. As Marcus pulled back it was torn from Carl's grip to land safely out of reach behind Marcus. Carl grabbed his dagger and lunged at Marcus. The decurion could not avoid the charge but he fended off the wickedly sharp blade with the rope coiled around his left arm. As Carl slid by Marcus wrapped the rope around Carl's neck. He began to pull on the rope and saw Carl's eyes bulge.

Suddenly Marcus heard the screech of the hawk and turned just in time to see a bloody and enraged Stig swinging his axe at Marcus. Using Carl as a shield to protect himself from Stig's attack Marcus waited. Stig had begun his swing and had no chance to slow down the blade, the axe sliced into his brother's stomach and his lifeless body slid to the ground. His death took with it Marcus' only defence as the rope was still around Carl's neck. He dropped it and, before Stig could swing again he jumped feet first at Stig's knee. He heard a reassuring crack as something broke and Stig fell to the floor in agony. Before Stig could react Marcus went behind the warrior and, holding his neck in his right arm pushed his knee into Stig's back. He pushed with his knee and his arms exerted as much pressure as he could. Stig's remaining eye bulged. The crack of his neck breaking seemed to echo around the stunned arena. Drugi, Trygg and Frann had surprised but happy expressions while the others were just stunned that a man with merely a rope had killed two of the deadliest warriors ever to wield an axe. The fact that one brother had been responsible for another's death seemed to confirm that Marcus was the innocent party and that the gods had decided in his favour.

Marcus looked up at the circling hawk, "Thank you, brother."

Chapter 10

The snow had begun to melt on the ground around Rocky Point and the days were lengthening. Rather than making life easier it made it harder for, as the legionaries began to build the wall higher and start the construction of mile castles and fortlets so the Votadini and Selgovae began to make their presence felt even more. Ten legionaries of the Sixth had been slaughtered in a surprise attack before they could reach their weapons and Centurion Brocchus was not a happy man. He and the Legate rode into the fort one cold and damp morning. Additionally, the melting snow had churned the paths into a muddy morass giving the whole fort a depressing feel.

"Livius we need a strategy to keep the barbarians at bay."

Quintus looked angrily at the map on the wall. "The Gauls are doing their best Livius but they are losing men at an alarming rate. If we have to keep half of our men armed as sentries then the wall will never be completed."

Livius looked at the map and then shouted, "Julius bring in the rotas." He turned to the two visitors. "If we pull the turmae from the west then we can strike at their homes in the north. It will make them pull back but we will be leaving the west overexposed."

Julius nodded, "The strategy might work and it will keep them looking to their homes. They do not need to worry about attack at the moment as were are too busy building to be aggressive. The Emperor is there and he has extra men. I will take the responsibility." He paused, "No news from Rufius?"

"No, I had expected him back after the winter solstice but you yourself know how unpredictable a sea voyage can be." The clerk returned with the lists. "If I leave the Gallic turmae to defend the road I can take the ten turmae of my ala and we should be able to leave in the next three days." He looked at the Centurion of the Sixth. "Will that do?"

"Aye, we will keep a better watch until then."

The captives had given Hercules a good idea of what the settlement at Hjarno-By looked like. Hercules looked at the crude drawing and shook his head. "If these girls are right then we cannot enter the bay for we would be trapped which means we would be on the seaward side. If a storm blew up..."

"We will cross that bridge when we come to it."

The girls had described the walls around the settlement and the large slave hall. "That is where Marcus should be if he is still alive."

One of the girls shook her head fearfully. "There were no men there sir. We only saw women, girls and boys. The men were always killed. If your friend was taken, he will have been put to death."

Gnaeus looked crestfallen. Rufius put his arm around his shoulders. "You saw him taken alive. Neither of us knows why this Trygg chose to capture him but there will be a reason and I can see no reason why Marcus should have been killed once they reached here. The Parcae are fickle creatures Gnaeus, besides, we have a duty to try to bring back some of the captives if we can."

Gnaeus and Rufius had been drilling the ex-soldiers they had recruited in Eboracum. It was not that they had to give them new skills but help them to remember old ones. The few who had never used a bow were taught how to fire them and they practised repelling boarders with two teams, one commanded by Rufius and one by Gnaeus. They were learning to be marines. Furax had been delighted when he was put in charge of operating the bolt thrower. He happily drilled with the men, never actually loosing a bolt but setting it up to be released. His enthusiasm made up for his age and Rufius was pleased; when they did have to use it they would be able to keep up a healthy rate.

Cassius and Metellus were both delighted to be reunited with the rest of the ala. Although they both enjoyed their independent commands, the cold lonely winter had been devoid of the banter of the ala. Both of them, too, had their thoughts with their comrades Rufius and Marcus. As they rode north, skirting the main Votadini settlements, they talked of what their friends would be experiencing. "It will be hard for them Cassius. I remember when we were in Gallia Aquitania. Every man is a potential enemy and you do not know the language well. You have to live on your wits."

"And do not forget that Marcus is a captive. All of the efforts of Rufius and Hercules may come to nought. They may discover the corpse of a Roman if they find him at all."

Cassius looked eastwards, even though there was a forest there to hinder his view. "I for one would not enjoy the sea voyage of Rufius and Gnaeus. Those pirates who took Marcus are more skilled than the peaceful Hercules."

"I think that Hercules is something of a pirate and he can handle himself." Livius turned in his saddle to look down the column of cavalry. "The men seem in better mood."

"Yes Prefect. The fact that we did something to try to rescue Marcus helped their mood and this chance to hit back will also do them good. Where are we heading?"

"I want to take us close to Bremenium," Bremenium was the deserted fort on Dere Street. "They may have fortified it, in which case we would avoid it, if not then we would use it as a base and attack their settlement at Horseshoe Rock." Horseshoe Rock was halfway to the coast and a prosperous community. By attacking it Livius hoped to draw off the warbands from the wall.

"Risky. We will be thirty miles from our own lines with every barbarian in the land looking for us."

"That is why I am hoping that Bremenium is still deserted for it would enable us to hold them off and then return swiftly down our road." He looked at his two subordinates. "This is not a suicide mission. We just need to buy the wall builders time to finish some of the wall. Once it is complete from the Tinea to Rocky Point then we will have breathing space. The sooner we have a barrier, the sooner the tribes can be controlled. It may not be solid yet but the noose is tightening."

Metellus took his five scouts forward on foot. They had left their mounts with a guard at the edge of the forest. They could see the ruined wooden walls of the Roman fort but they could not tell if it was occupied. Metellus signalled the four men who would circle the walls while he led the remaining trooper towards the main gate, now hanging forlornly on its one remaining hinge.

The trooper said nervously, "Looks deserted sir."

"Precisely but don't forget son these barbarians are lazy bastards. They could be living there and just not be bothered to fix the gates. That is why we will win in the end, we are better builders."

The ground around the gate was muddied and Metellus could not tell if it was recent or not. He drew his sword and stepped gingerly into the fort. The debris on the ground showed that someone had been in to steal as much as they could but there was an empty air about the place. Suddenly the trooper next to him gasped. In front of the burnt out building which would have been the Principia were ten spears each topped by a rotting skull. The last defenders of the auxiliary fort were still at their post.

The four other troopers arrived. "Nothing to see sir. There were muddied prints but they could have been from before the snow."

"Right one of you, fetch the horses and send Marius back to the Prefect. The rest of you let us remove these skulls before our comrades see them. We will lay them honourably in the ground." By the time the ala arrived the skulls had been buried beneath crossed spears just outside the fort.

Livius nodded at the grave as he dismounted. "The last of the defenders?"

"So it would seem. Everything which could be taken has been but it is defensible sir. They haven't filled in any of the ditches."

"Right, Cassius get your turma to reseed the ditches with lillia. Metellus, you take your turma east for ten miles, see if there are any Votadini nearby and we will put this fort into some sort of shape."

A day later and with half a turma guarding the fort the ala set off for the hill fort at Horseshoe Rock. Built in ages past it had been a place of refuge for the people of the Votadini but since the invaders had been sent packing south of the Stanegate it had become a settlement of markets and iron workers. Livius did not enjoy the task he had been given but he knew it would hurt the Votadini. By destroying their metal workings he would damage their ability to arm their warriors and, in addition, they would need to use warriors to defend every settlement.

The ala rode through the night to arrive at the edge of the forest just two hundred paces from the entrance to the hill fort. Metellus had reported that they had but ten guards on the walls and the gates were opened at dawn. The ala would be approaching from the dark of the west into the sliver of light that was the winter dawn. He hoped that they would not be seen until the last minute. Cassius led the column as they trotted forwards; the gates were opened by two sleepy guards who were eager for their beds. To their horror they saw the column of cavalry galloping towards them. They were caught between two stools; close the gates or sound the alarm? Their procrastination cost them their lives and the settlement its prosperity. The two luckless guards fell to javelins as the turmae thundered in. One turma dealt with the guards on the ramparts as the other decurions led their men to the barracks and the iron workings. Livius had counted on a blacksmith's hut with a forge and he found it. "Use the coals to start fires. I want every building set alight and every warrior killed. Try to spare the women."

An hour later as dawn fully broke, the sky was filled with thick black smoke as Horseshoe Rock began to burn. They had no time to rest on their laurels and they rode swiftly back into the forest. Livius hoped that the Votadini would think they had fled south and ignore the possibility that they had headed west. It was a gamble but if they succeeded then he would have achieved his objectives; disrupt the Votadini and save his ala.

As The Swan edged its way towards the islands Gnaeus peered anxiously from the prow. Rufius was behind him. "Well?"

Gnaeus took one more look to be sure and then turned with a grin of relief on his face, "I am not certain, they could be, they look to be the ones." He pointed at the six ships drawn up on the beach, the men, like ants busy cleaning the weed and growth from their hulls.

"And it looks as though we have made it just in time for they are preparing for sea."

Having gone ashore a number of times before, they had the routine well practised. The First Mate would remain on board and take charge of the crew. Furax, to keep him under control would be given charge of the bolt thrower. As Rufius had said, if he has to fire it then it means that we are in trouble ashore and any help will be welcome. Hercules, Gnaeus and two of the bigger ex-soldiers would row ashore and haggle. This time they varied their routine by anchoring after dark and keeping a good watch on the islands. No-one visited them which gave them some comfort for they had feared that the islanders would be belligerent.

As they waited on watch, Furax reluctantly asleep Hercules put into words the thoughts that they had all had but dared not voice. "This is the last throw of the dice, you know that don't you? If we find no news of Marcus here then we will have to return home. The Senator wanted you back after the winter solstice, we are already overdue and they will be worrying."

"I know Hercules and the Prefect will need me back at Rocky Point sooner rather than later. Tomorrow is an important day for us and I hope that the Allfather and Macro are here and watching over us."

King Lugubelenus was incandescent with rage when he heard of the destruction of his iron workings. His weapon production would drop dramatically just when he needed to increase his numbers. "Send a mounted warband south and find these Roman horsemen. They will head for Coriosopitum. "

As his lieutenant raced off to fulfil his king's orders Queen Radha took her husband to one side. "Do not forget, husband, that these Romans are cunning. It may be that have chosen to use their road in the west. They could make swifter progress and it is unguarded."

"You have the mind of a man my love. Angus, take another warband to the Roman road and seek them there."

The ala left Bremenium with a sense of relief; they had reached it in safety and had not been attacked. There was something of an anti-climax to the journey south for they had expected the barbarians to follow their trail and try to take them.

The day was a stormy blustery day which made riding both uncomfortable and slow. The troopers wrapped up as best they could in their cloaks but the relentless rain and hail hurled at their backs insinuating itself into every nook and cranny of their bodies. The icy droplets fell between armour and tunic making them sodden and cold. The road had not been used for some years but was, at least, firm under foot. The encounter when it did come was a surprise to both the Votadini and the troopers. The troopers suddenly saw figures filtering from the trees just as the barbarians saw and heard the horses. Both groups reacted instantly; the barbarians fired their sling shots and the troopers threw their javelins. Soon the two groups were locked in individual combats. Livius sought out Cassius. "Take your turma and ride half a mile down the road. Make a defence there. Metellus, take Calgus and Drusus, ride back up the road and take them in their flank. Antoninus gather the wounded and follow Cassius. The rest of you follow me!" As the decurions all split up, causing the barbarians confusion as they wondered which enemy to follow, Livius led this remaining turmae into the woods where the slings of the Votadini were less effective. The javelins of the troopers and their extra height gave them the advantage over the nimbler but less well-armed enemy. Increasing numbers of Votadini swelled the ranks of those fighting and Livius suddenly found that they were making less progress. This was not a band of a few warriors, this was a sizeable warband. He turned to the signifier, "Sound fall back!"

As the strident notes sounded the well-trained troopers began to withdraw. The exultant Votadini sensed victory and began to surge forwards, a huge wedge of men aimed at the Prefect and the standard. They had nearly captured the eagle of the Ninth years before; they would not lose this prize. Livius and those around the standard found themselves in a desperate battle as warriors raced forwards to claim the honour of capturing a Roman standard. Just when they thought they had it in their grasp, at the moment when the signifier clutched at his leg, pierced by a spear, Metellus and his three turmae hacked into the unsuspecting flank of the exultant warriors who thought that victory was within their grasp. Their apparent success turned into a slaughter as the ninety men of Metellus' vexillation found unprotected backs before them. Soon the only Votadini in the woods and trees were the dead and the soon to be dead as Livius' troopers finished off those who had not fled.

As the ala reached Cassius and his defences Livius knew that they had succeeded; they had bought the Sixth time for the bodies which littered the forest were those of a large warband. King Lugubelenus had suffered a severe blow in his campaign to stop the wall being built; his men would have to watch their homes and the king would need to rebuild an army.

Chief Trygg wondered what to do about the Roman. He had never seen anyone killed by a rope before and many of his warriors, whilst respecting Marcus' skill, felt that he had somehow tricked Stig and Carl. There would be much bad feeling. He now wondered about his decision to bring the Roman to his home. He had benefited from the horseman's presence, there was no denying that, but at what cost? Three of his best warriors lay dead, all killed by one man. He would visit Britannia with more caution next time. If one horseman could do that he would be well advised to avoid their forces until his men were better armed and better trained. The horse side of the Roman's influence was less problematic. He had seen how to train the horses and he was sure that Drugi could continue the Roman's work. The horses and horsemen were important against the Suebi but they would never be taken on raids so, for the moment, they were not a priority. The problem still remained what to do about the Roman?

Marcus was having the same discussion with Drugi and Frann. He knew that he had outstayed his welcome. Whilst Lars and his brothers had never been popular they had some allies amongst the brethren and many others had felt their honour betrayed that a man with a rope could kill two warriors wielding axes. Marcus had a number of problems; how to escape quietly and with Frann; that required a boat and a sail to aid them. Secondly, he needed the Sword of Cartimandua which resided either about Trygg's waist or on the dais on the great hall. Once he had taken the sword then there would be a hue and cry and he would be pursued for Trygg would know who had taken it as clearly as if Marcus left a written confession.

"Drugi, when we escape, will you come with us?"

Drugi did not answer at first. He was comfortable where he was and no-one bothered him but he liked the Roman and Frann the slave. He knew he would miss them. More importantly, however, was the hawk, for it had spoken to Drugi and Drugi was entrapped in its spell. He would have to aid Marcus and once he did that the Norns had decreed that Drugi would be hunted down and punished for his disloyalty. It was not his decision; the fates had made it for him. "I will help you two to escape and that means I will come with you." He looked up from the deer he was skinning. "Where would we go?"

"Why, back to Britannia of course."

"Would I be welcome there?" Drugi was not afraid, he could live alone if he had to but he knew nothing of Britannia save that it was a Roman province.

"Of course and you could still hunt. The difference would be that you would be a free man."

That thought had not occurred to Drugi. He had been a slave for most of his life and he was used to it. The state did not upset him unduly but the way Marcus had been treated worried him. He had no woman and, as yet, no thought of one but if he did that slave would be subject to the same repression as Frann; she could be taken and used by another. Drugi knew that he would react in the same way as Marcus but he was not sure he would have been as resourceful in the arena.

Snorri arrived at their hut just before sunset. Although there was still snow, the days had become longer and a little warmer. "Chief Trygg will send a boat for you in the morning. " He looked pointedly at Frann. "All of you. He and the council will decide your future."

Frann looked worried but Marcus knew that his Fate was being decided elsewhere; all he could do was survive and keep his wits about him. Somewhere above was a hawk which seemed to know more than he did what was going on. Drugi, however, had become less compliant since his meeting with Marcus and Fran. He had lived amongst these people for a long time and knew their ways. "But the Roman did no wrong. He did not use a blade and he defeated the brothers. Odin was with him."

Snorri looked a little embarrassed. "He did well and I admire his courage, Drugi, but Chief Trygg has the welfare of the tribe at heart and he sometimes has to make decisions which go against his feelings."

With that enigmatic statement, Snorri left and the three of then continued to plan. "This helps us a little anyway."

Drugi looked at him in amazement. "How?"

"We will be close to the water and the ships. We could steal a boat and sail away."

Frann shook her head and cuddled into his arm. "Drugi is right for they would soon catch us. Unless the Roman fleet sailed into the harbour we will have to await our fate at the council meeting."

Marcus kissed her on the head but said, defiantly, "I will not go quietly anywhere. We make plans. When they come for us we must take all that will aid us. Weapons, clothes and food."

Drugi had preserved venison in great quantities and Marcus knew that, if they escaped, they would, at least, have the luxury of food.

"I will pack some dried deer meat and some water skins." He began to place wrapped little parcels into a leather bag. "Will they not think it strange that we take them?"

"I do not think it will be Snorri who comes for us, it will just be some of the warriors. We take them on the boat as though Trygg has sanctioned them. We will need to keep them where we can get at them."

The next morning Marcus went to the enclosure where he fed and groomed the horses. He held out an apple for Cato. "This may be the last time I see you old friend. If I do not return then take your herd and grasp freedom." The black stallion gave a whinny and nuzzled the decurion. He believed that the horse had understood him but he would do all in his power to free the horse if he could not return to Drugi's domain.

The boat was a small skiff and the two warriors made no comment as the three of them placed their precious items in the bottom. The harbour was remarkably empty and Marcus felt his heart sink. He had hoped that there would be a foreign ship and, somehow, against the odds, they would escape. The two warriors made no attempt to help them unload. One of them turned to

Marcus, "We have been told to look after your horses until you return."

Marcus felt a wave of relief wash over him. He might yet return to Drugi's hut. "I have fed them this morning but they will need water this evening and, if it is cold then put their blankets on them." The snort from the warrior told Marcus that the horses would not be given a blanket but at least someone would be there for them.

There was no one waiting for them at the jetty and for the briefest of moments Marcus thought about flight but one look at the empty bay, without even a fishing boat, convinced him that they would have to await a better opportunity. The only boat he could see was a small longboat, obviously intended for warriors; although small it was still too big for the three of them to manage. The trio headed up towards the settlement and the slave hall. They attracted little attention at such an early hour and they trudged towards the hall where the guards stood impassively. Marcus' notoriety evoked an appraisal by both warriors and Marcus afforded himself the ghost of a smile. The two warriors were thinking how they would have defeated the Roman with the rope, each convinced that they would not have fallen for his tricks. The fire in the hall had gone out but the room still felt warm from the heat of the bodies. As their eyes became accustomed to the gloom Frann spotted an empty place and they arranged their belongings. Drugi had not been in the hall since he was a child and it was a salutary reminder of what slavery really meant. The slavery he had experienced was not the same as that of these wretches. As the slaves rose, Drugi could see that they were pale and emaciated whereas he, Marcus and Frann looked healthy by comparison. It hardened his resolve to join Marcus and Frann if they should manage to escape. He still could not see it but then many things had happened around Marcus which were inexplicable.

Without instructions and without a task to perform the three companions bound by an invisible bond lay down on their bearskins. For Marcus this was just the same as being on patrol. When you could, you rested for you knew not when you would have to go without sleep. He glanced over at Frann who gave him a weak smile. Once again he worried about her ability to survive an escape attempt and then he remembered another two Brigante captives, his mother Ailis, and Metellus' wife, Nanna. Both had emerged stronger from their ordeal. Frann would as well.

It was almost mid morning when Snorri came for them. He looked at them sympathetically, Marcus could see that the bodyguard's initial view of him had changed but it would not affect his duty. There were more people about and they looked at the three slaves who had been the talk of Hjarno-By. The normally dull winter had been enlivened by their adventures and everyone had a view on Marcus' disposal of the three brothers. Some held the view that it was somehow dishonourable, that was the general view of the warriors, but the others, the fishermen, the old and the women applauded the ingenuity of the Roman. As they passed the crowds there was a buzz of conversation and speculation for everyone knew that the council and Chief Trygg had decreed that they would pass a judgement on them.

The council meeting was in full flow when they arrived and Trygg gestured for Snorri to keep them to one side. The other business of the day was being concluded and there were visitors from beyond the Tencteri addressing the council.

"We see great opportunities for trade with these peoples. They bring things we cannot get elsewhere." The grey-haired man displayed the clay pot. "Look at the quality of this and," he proffered a piece of carved jet, "the quality of their gifts. We, as you know Chief Trygg, are a peaceful people, unlike Chief Gurt. We would hope that the Tencteri would welcome these traders as we can only benefit from trade with those from inside the Roman Empire." Marcus' ears suddenly picked up that vital piece of information- traders from the Roman Empire!

The council nodded as they passed the pot from hand to hand, admiring the quality of the fired and glazed vessel. Chief Trygg turned the intricately carved jet over in his hand. "This is a precious gift. We have acquired much of this precious black stone but I have never seen such workmanship. Who are these people?"

"As I said, it is but one ship and they are heading here but the trader is called Gaelwyn of the Brigante."

Marcus felt a shiver race down his spine as though someone had poured icy water down his back. Gaelwyn of the Brigante! That could not be a coincidence. There was a ship from his home and it was coming for him. He struggled to keep his face impassive but he was desperate to tell Frann and Drugi his news.

"They also wish to buy slaves. It appears the Roman appetite for them in Britannia has outstripped the supply."

Chief Trygg and his warriors laughed. "Perhaps that is our fault, for Britannia provides us with a fine source of slaves." When the laughter had subsided the council spoke for a few moments and then Chief Trygg addressed the visitors. "Like you we do not wish to wage war in these waters. There are much better pickings abroad. If Gurt and his pirates do disrupt our trade then perhaps we may have to teach them a lesson." At this there was much banging of hands on tables as the warriors saw another opportunity, as with the Suebi, to show their neighbours their newly acquired power and confidence. Trygg held up his hands for silence. "As for the trader, this Gaelwyn will be welcome here and you should know that we will have a sale of slaves in seven days' time." The quick, unconscious glance he sent at the three slaves was a warning to Marcus of the council's decision. "And you and your people will be welcome to attend."

"Thank you, Chief Trygg of the Tencteri. And now we will return home."

When the visitors had left the doors were shut and Snorri brought the three slaves forward for the council's decision. The serious look on Trygg's face told Marcus that none of them would like the decision.

Chapter 11

"The council has deliberated long and hard about Marcus the Roman and his actions. While none of us doubt his courage and his bravery nor the service he has done us his continued presence brings with it discord and disunity amongst the people. This cannot be good. He and the woman Frann will be sold at the slave sale in seven days." Some of the people in the hall shook their heads; Marcus had appeared as a sign of good fortune. Many said that the loss of the three brothers was a good thing for they were always fighting and causing trouble. The warriors approved of the decision and generally nodded, for they wanted this warrior of Rome away from their land. They preferred their slaves subservient and they had seen that this Roman never bowed his head.

"As for Drugi the slave, some of the council wished him to be sold as well for he has been closely associated with the Roman." It was obvious which of the council had voiced that view for they reddened. "However Drugi is invaluable to us and it would be a waste to lose such a useful slave. With the departure of this Roman, we will need someone else to train the horses and that will be Drugi's task. Take the slaves to the slave hall and return Drugi to his hut on the mainland."

As they left Drugi's head was bowed in distress. Marcus said to him, as quietly as he could, "Fear not Drugi for a ship comes for me." Drugi looked up in surprise and delight. " Can you get a rowing boat?"

Drugi nodded, "For what purpose?"

"When you see the trader arrive here then we will be making our escape. Return to the jetty after dark when that happens and we three will escape together."

"How?"

Marcus shrugged but he was grinning. "I don't know yet."

Drugi's face showed that he was not convinced but suddenly there was a shriek as their hawk plunged down from the sky to take an unsuspecting gull. Drugi's expression changed instantly and he grinned. "I will be here."

"And Drugi, release the horses before you leave. I would not want them mistreated and Cato and his family can have their freedom."

"It will be done as you wish."

When Hercules awoke the next morning there was a film of fog lying across the bay. He could make out the shape of the land but it was indistinct and grey. The pinpricks of light they had seen the night before had shown them that the islands had inhabitants but, in the dark, they could not make it out clearly. They were largely going on what the two Brigante girls and the headman had told them. Full daylight would reveal all. Rufius and Gnaeus joined the captain as they watched the thin sun begin to burn off the grey cloak of fog. "Well, Rufius today is the last day of the search. If he is not here then we return to the Senator and Britannia."

Gnaeus face fell but Rufius nodded. "The captain is right Gnaeus, The Legate and the Prefect will be expecting us home and Marcus, if he is still alive, would not wish us to risk our lives on a futile quest. If he lives and he is not here then I do not doubt for a moment that our resourceful friend will find a way to return home, eventually."

It was obvious to Gnaeus that the two of them had given up hope. Gnaeus too had had his doubts but he had thought each time they had landed that this would be the place where the decurion would be discovered and each time they had had their hopes shattered. If only he could be certain that these six ships were the ones he had seen on the Dunum. He thought that they were but that could be wishful thinking and he was no longer certain.

Furax stepped up to the rail. Gnaeus felt himself smile; the boy was always cheerful and always happy. He knew that Furax still believed they would find Marcus even though wiser heads knew differently. Rufius ruffled his hair, "Still like your bed eh Furax?"

In answer Furax laughed and stood on the thwarts, precariously clinging to one of the stays for the mast. "Have we seen the town yet?"

"No it is hidden by the fog."

"Well the mist is clearing, look!"

It was almost as though someone had drawn a curtain back. The light from behind the boat suddenly pierced the gloom and dispersed the last of the grey revealing Hjarno-By. The longships which Gnaeus had seen the night before were still drawn up on the beach but they could now see boats leaving the harbour for the fishing grounds and tendrils of smoke rising from the halls. Hercules shouted down to the crew. "Prepare the boat."

Just at that moment, Furax pointed to the sky above the town. "Look! The hawk! I can see the hawk!" Circling high above the town, like a beacon, was the hawk and suddenly they all knew that they had reached their destination.

In the settlement, Marcus was praying that the Roman trader would appear soon. This day would determine if Marcus was rescued or not. Marcus was now hobbled, just as he had hobbled his mounts. It was a mark in the change in status. The warriors had thought it highly amusing to see him shuffling through the village. He and Frann escorted Drugi to the jetty. "Remember Drugi keep watching for the trader, on that day you return here."

Drugi shook his head. "I admire your confidence but I do not know how you can know."

Marcus pointed above their heads, "The hawk is one clue but the name Gaelwyn of the Brigante that was the name of my uncle. It would be a huge coincidence if another Gaelwyn had that name and was seeking me."

Drugi was dubious. He embraced Marcus and as he did so whispered. "I have slipped a blade into your belt. It is small but sharp." Then, as Chief Trygg was approaching said, "Farewell Roman it has been an experience meeting you…" suddenly his voice faltered as the mist cleared and he saw over Marcus' shoulder, The Swan. Quietly he added, "Do not turn around. Either my eyes deceive me or your friends are here. I see the trader. I will return on the morrow before dawn breaks." He bowed to Trygg and, lowering himself into the small boat began to row to the mainland.

"Having said goodbye to your friend Roman you and your woman should return to the slave hall. Your days of relative freedom, are over. For the next seven days, you do not leave the hall." The friendly tones of the previous week were gone and it was a slave master who ordered Marcus back to the hall.

The handful of guards pushed the two of them towards the road which led to the gates. Halfway along, where the track curved Marcus risked a glance to his left. Keeping his face as impassive as possible he saw, to his delight, Hercules, Rufius and Gnaeus sitting in the small boat which was rowing ashore. They had come for him; the problem was that the freedom he had had the previous day had melted like the fog and he was a guarded prisoner once more. As he entered the fort he put his arm around Frann who was despondent at their state. He whispered in her ear. "Fear not my love, for tonight, with the aid of the Parcae, we shall escape."

Her face turned to him with surprise written all over it, "How?"

"That I do not yet know. We will have to work it out over the next few hours." As the door slammed behind them it sounded and felt, final. Marcus hoped that his friends were thinking the same as he.

As the skiff pulled towards the jetty Rufius turned to Gnaeus. "Did you see Marcus?"

Gnaeus had seen someone who looked like Marcus but he could not be sure. "It looked like him but…"

"Keep your eye on him and the woman he is with. Let us see where they go."

Hercules murmured, "Well no-one is asking me but I think it was Marcus as well but did you see? He was hobbled."

"I know but let us take it one step at a time. Hopefully, this deception will be our last one."

The welcoming party were all armed but the three men all saw, immediately, the Sword of Cartimandua hanging from the belt of the warrior they took to be chief. It was confirmation that they had found the place to which the decurion had been brought. When they stepped off they all gave a small bow. "Thank you for receiving us. I am Gaelwyn of the Brigante and I come here to set up trading links."

"My friends from further north told us of your coming. Please come to my hall where we can speak in a warmer environment." As they walked, he pointed to their ship, The Swan. "A tidy looking ship but you have no oars. Why is that?"

Rufius looked at Hercules and nodded, subtly. "We can carry more cargo if we are not encumbered by oars and we have a smaller crew." He grinned, "More profits for us."

"But it does make you vulnerable to attack does it not? Especially if you are becalmed."

Rufius wondered if there was a hidden message in the words. Was he threatening to take their ship? He seemed to be the man they had been told of, a reasonable leader who was no Gurt but perhaps he was a wolf thinking that the sheep had inadvertently come into his lair. "So far we have only met with peace and hospitality. Are there pirates around here?" Rufius acted the innocent in his words and his facial expression.

"Not here but further north there are some dangerous waters. You may find your journey north more dangerous for, as you can see, the seafarers of the dark sea are preparing for their summer work."

"Ah. Thank you for the advice, we will be careful when we return."

"You intend to travel back soon then?"

"We heard that there was to be a sale of slaves and we would like to buy as many as possible for there is a great demand for them in Britannia."

"Really?" Trygg showed that he too was also an actor. He, of course, knew all of this and he knew that they could get an even greater price because of that. They sat around a huge table and the chief ordered a slave to bring some honeyed mead. "Now we have slaves but I am interested in the goods that you bring, that you think we might need."

Gnaeus brought out the sample pot which was passed around the other members of the council who were at the table. Their admiring glances were not an act for the quality was far superior to anything local. Rufius brought out a small amphora which he opened; the smell immediately filled the room. "And we have spices from the east. These are rare and justly expensive." The appreciative sniffs told Rufius that if he had been a trader he would have made a sale already. "And we have more of this, but this a gift for our hosts." Rufius took out a beautifully carved jet hawk.

Trygg nodded his admiration. "This is interesting. We have had a hawk which has enjoyed our hospitality for some weeks now." He smiled ruefully, "Many of the doves we would have eaten in winter have been devoured by our greedy visitor. Perhaps this token will help to ward him off and send him away."

"Perhaps, and now Chief Trygg having seen our goods do you think that we can trade?"

Hercules smiled in admiration. Rufius had perfected the act of being a trader well and all of his behaviour seemed both natural and appropriate. He did not know that when Rufius had been an Explorate he had had to play a variety of parts and adopt many disguises.

The Chief scanned the faces of his peers and they all nodded. "I think that we can trade. Certainly, your goods are ones we cannot buy locally." He smiled and Rufius shivered, for it was the smile of a wolf. "The only other way would be to take them."

Rufius laughed, "Then we have come to the right place. Would it be possible to see the quality of the slaves so that we can agree on a price?"

"Oh we can go to see them but I am afraid that the auction will be in seven days for there will be others who wish to buy them. We have had a good crop this year." Gnaeus felt sick at the way that Trygg was speaking about human beings. He had never owned a slave although he understood why they were needed but after this visit, he began to question the justification. "The slave hall is next door. We will be making this hall ready today for a feast we hold tonight. We defeated some Suebi raiders and we are holding a feast to celebrate."

As they stepped from the fuggy warmth of the hall to the chill air of the fresh morning Hercules shivered. The Mare Nostrum, even on its coldest day was much warmer than the air through which they walked. When he returned to the Senator if he returned to the Senator he would suggest that he return to more familiar seas to make a profit from all that they had traded so far.

Rufius immediately became wary when he saw the two guards at the door of the slave hall. They were both armed and alert. When they were swung open the smell of the unwashed slaves hit the three men like a slap in the face. Gnaeus was worried that he would actually vomit and he had to put his hand to his mouth to hold back some of the stink. This was less well lit than the main hall and the fire barely glowed. Those slaves not working outside were huddled together looking fearfully at the visitors.

The shaman who had shown such keen interest in the pots led them into the hall. Trygg hung back to see the men's reaction. "As you can see we have a surplus. They are mainly women and children, although we have one man. Some of the women are with child which, of course, proves their fertility and of course would demand a higher price. Some of the boys are approaching manhood but most of them are young enough to be trained to whatever purposes their new owners choose."

Rufius found something distasteful about the way the old man went on and kept licking his lips as he looked at the boys and young women. He had seen Marcus when the old man had pointed him out but he avoided any eye contact. Instead, he led the other two towards a group of women and children who looked to be a family. Their faces showed terror as they were displayed and paraded like animals. Rufius hated the role he had to play but he knew there was no other way. He had to convince them that he was a slaver. "The buyer does not need to keep family groups together does he?"

"No of course not, split them up any way you wish; provided, of course, your bid is successful."

Rufius had seen enough and, looking at the young trooper's face, he was not sure if Gnaeus would be able to hold on to the contents of his stomach. "Well, we have seen enough." He looked at Chief Trygg. "Seven days you say until the sale?"

"Seven days."

"Good. That will give us time to prepare our hold for our new cargo. We will then have to agree on an appropriate and suitable price for our goods." Rufius affected a rapacious look, "Those prices will, of course, not be dependent upon a bid as you will be the only buyers. I assume that tomorrow will be too soon." He smiled sympathetically. "I assume that you will be recovering from the celebratory feast. So shall we say the day after tomorrow?"

"That will be acceptable." Trygg looked curiously at Hercules, "Captain, do you not wish to tie up at the jetty for storms do blow up quickly in these waters."

"Thank you for the offer but we do not wish to give the crew the temptation of your drink and the slave women. We have few enough crewmen as it is."

"As you wish then. If you need to buy any provisions I am sure it can be arranged."

As they watched them row back to The Swan, Trygg turned to Snorri. "I do not trust them. Have some warriors keep an eye on them."

Snorri looked at the departing boat. "They seemed genuine to me."

"Perhaps but two of them, the younger ones looked to have the lean and hungry look of predators. If that had been a dragon ship I would not have been surprised. See if you can find out how many they have in their crew."

"We could easily take the ship if you are concerned. Our ships are almost ready for sea and that old tub could not outrun us."

"No, for I genuinely do want to begin trading with others and this may be the perfect opportunity. Just keep an eye on them for a couple of days and report to me."

Furax couldn't wait to find out what they had seen. He pestered them from the moment the boat pulled up at the stern. "Furax, wait until we are aboard and then you will find out all."

As they waited, hidden below decks Rufius peered out of the small ventilation hole to look at the distant harbour. "Only keep one or two men on deck captain. I want them to think we are undermanned. And you had better have one of them keep a watch on movements to and from their ships. If they suddenly decided to put to sea then I want to know."

"Well we have seen Marcus but I have no idea how we are going to rescue him. He was hobbled, there are guards on the hall, guards on the gate and guards on the jetty."

"True Gnaeus but the Parcae have helped us for they have arranged for them to be drunk tonight and we know how the Germani like to drink don't we?"

There was a silence as they all contemplated their plan of attack. Rufius wished that Metellus was with them for he had the best mind for strategy and plans. Rufius had no doubt that he could get into the fort unseen but getting Marcus out was another matter and the other nagging doubt was the woman he had seen with Marcus. If they had to get her out as well then it would be difficult.

Furax broke the silence with the impishness of youth. "Well! Have you a plan or not? How are we going to rescue Marcus?"

Hercules cuffed the boy around the neck but then said, "The cheeky monkey is right Rufius. How do we do it?"

"The chief said that we could buy whatever we need, so at dusk, we go in to buy some fresh meat or milk. That would be understandable. That gets us through the guards on the jetty. After dusk, we go back to the jetty and dispose of the guards there, substitute our own men. Then we wait until the feast is in full swing. If it is anything like a Brigante feast there will be a lot of movement in and out of the gates, we dress in the clothes of the two guards and get to the slave hall. Gnaeus and I should be able to take the guards and then we rescue Marcus."

Hercules looked doubtfully at the slight Gnaeus, "I don't know, the guards on the slave hall looked big to me."

"We may not even have to deal with the guards. They may just bar the doors and join the fun. It is what others would do. It may be that the guards are not there at night. "He sighed. "Look, I know that the plan is flimsy and as Explorates we were always taught to scout out thoroughly but we have to strike tonight. The feast is too good an opportunity to let slip by. We could watch to see if the guards do stay there all night and try tomorrow but either way, we have the same problem."

"It will work Rufius, it has to."

"Thank you Gnaeus but your kind words will not make it happen, we need a lot of luck and a lot of drunken guards for it to succeed."

Marcus and Frann had very similar emotions and feelings as they huddled together in the slave hall. "They were your friends?"

"Yes, they are my friends. I told you they would come."

"But there are guards at the doors."

"Do not worry they will find a way but we need to be ready to leave quickly and quietly. The first thing we need to do is to move closer to the doors."

The places near to the doors were the least desirable as the wind whistled beneath the ill-fitting opening and it was further away from the feeble fire. Marcus knew that they had to sneak out and, much as he would hate to leave the captives, helplessly trapped, he knew that their only chance of success lay in secrecy. What he did not confide in Frann was his plan to go into the main hall and steal back the Sword of Cartimandua. He suspected that Rufius might try to prevent him too but he would have to take that chance. He had been given an opportunity to redeem himself and he knew that Macro's presence, in the form of the iconic hawk, was a message to him and one he could not ignore.

"Reach behind me into my belt and find the knife Drugi gave to me. Hide it where you can get at it and be careful, for it is sharp. When all are asleep we will cut my bonds and prepare to escape."

Frann prepared them some food; it was not that they were hungry, they were not and were both too nervous to enjoy the food anyway but it passed the time and fitted in with the behaviour of the other slaves, huddled together trying to cook a meal from their meagre rations over a fire far too small for the task. The other slaves seemed to resent both Frann and Marcus, probably because Marcus was the embodiment of what they had all lost, a man. Both of them were either ignored or just the object of stares and mumbled curses. The effect was to force Frann and Marcus closer together.

As they played at eating their food Frann broached a question which she did not wish to ask but knew that their future depended upon that answer. "If… when we reach Britannia, what of us? I know that, for both of us, it was convenient and necessary to be together and for me to be with child. In Britannia, you will not need a woman. What of me?"

Marcus pulled her closer to him and kissed her gently on the top of her head. He had not planned on meeting her and falling in love but that was the way the bones had fallen. "You are my woman and when we reach my home I will make you my wife and you will live with my mother and my brother and you will be safe." As they lay in silence Marcus did not see the tears of gratitude streaming down her face.

They had both dozed off when the door burst open and Snorri stood, framed in the fading light of the sunset. He had with him two guards and they dragged the decurion roughly to his feet. While his hands and arms were secured Snorri quickly examined Marcus' clothes; he ran his arms down his breeks and patted them. He felt all over Marcus' body for anything which was hard. Finally, he checked that the hobbles were still secure and had not been loosened. Without a word, Marcus was dropped to the floor and the three of them left. Marcus thanked the fates which had warned him to give the knife to Frann. The killing of the brothers had changed the way that Chief Trygg viewed the Roman. He had gone from being an amusing asset to a threat and Rufius' rescue could not come too soon.

Chapter 12

The skiff was well loaded as it glided, silently into the jetty. Apart from Marcus and Gnaeus, there were four ex-soldiers. Their weapons were secreted in the bottom of the boat and all six of them carried concealed knives. The two sentries looked bored and unhappy that they were not at the party and walked, belligerently, up to Rufius. "What do you want?"

Feigning an innocent expression and with just a hint of outrage in his voice Rufius spread his arms. "Your counsel and the chief said that we could buy provisions for we have travelled a long way. Is this not the case? Should we sail for another port?"

Not wishing to be on the wrong end of Snorri's boot the surly guard backtracked. "No, but there is a feast in the hall and most people are there. You will be lucky to find anyone who is sober."

Smiling Rufius said, "Don't worry about that," he jangled a bag of coins. "We have brought plenty of silver with us." He turned to the two men in the skiff. "You two keep an eye on the boat and no sloping off for a quick drink." Rufius reflected that they could all go on the stage with such acting skills. The two men looked suitably annoyed. Their real task, as outlined on the ship had been to find a second boat; partly to make it easier to get the whole party to safety and to eliminate any pursuit.

The four of them made their way through the huts and halls which filled the space between the port and the walls of the palisaded settlement. The guards had been correct. There were not many homes which showed a glimmer of light. The first two they tried contained women but they had nothing to sell. The last one they tried sold them a skin of milk and some cheese. Rufius took the risk of wandering up to the gates to see the state of the guards. Both looked alert but relaxed. As the four men walked up to the gate they did not react aggressively and Rufius gestured at the hall which was filled with a cacophony of noise and shrieks. "Good feast eh?"

"Aye." One the two guards nodded in a good-natured manner, "I am sure that you would be made welcome."

"Thank you but the captain wants these provisions quickly but thank you for the offer. We will see what he says when we return."

As they walked slowly back to the jetty, Marcus turned to Gnaeus and said. "That is a little bit of good fortune. We don't need to sneak in we can just walk in. You and Decimus wait here, keep an eye out for any relief guards. If they send any more warriors down then dispose of them. We will take care of these two guards at the jetty."

The two guards were talking with Rufius' two men as they descended to the jetty. They both turned as they heard them approach. The two ex-soldiers slid their knives out of their scabbards and into the men's throats faster than a blink.

"Take off their clothes and then get rid of the bodies. Any other boats?"

The two men began the grisly task of stripping the bodies. Lucius nodded towards the end of the wooden walkway. "There is one up there. It is about the same size as this. Nothing else though."

"Right when you are dressed fetch it down here and keep watch." The two bodies were dropped almost silently into the black waters of the bay. Rufius felt a shiver across his spine. The creatures of the dark waters would soon feast on the corpses of the two unfortunate men who had managed to draw the deadly duty.

Returning to Gnaeus and Decimus, Rufius looked at the moon which had just disappeared behind a cloud. "This is the hard part. We have to wait until the warriors are drunk before we risk the rescue."

Gnaeus looked up the slope to the two guards. "We could go into the fort, though. Have a look in the hall, that way we will get a better idea of when they are drunk and we will be closer to Marcus." Rufius knew that Gnaeus was keen to affect the rescue but he could not see a problem with the idea.

"We will go into the fort but keep to the shadows. I will decide if we go in the hall or not. It is one thing to evade the guards but I don't want to arouse the Chief's suspicions. He asked too many strange questions this morning."

The two sentries had obviously been brought some ale by a sympathetic friend and they were both far more relaxed and less alert. "Ha, so your captain let you ashore eh? Good lads. If you go to the hall tell them Orm and his brother would like some more of that ale."

Slapping him on the back, Rufius grinned and winked at Orm. "We will and see if there aren't a few women eh?"

Orm shook his head sadly. "No women tonight. Nor until after the slave sales." He laughed lecherously, "It'll have to be a sheep or your hand tonight. Still you sailors are used to that eh?" The two brothers laughed until they cried at their own joke allowing the four Romans to move into the shadows towards the Great Hall. This would be the hardest part of their rescue attempt. Rufius wanted to wait until the small hours when everyone would either be drunkenly asleep or too befuddled to know what was going on. Spying out the hall had not been part of his plan but he recognised that it would give them a better idea of how soon they could start their attempt. Gesturing for the three of them to stay in the shadows, Rufius moved to the steps leading to the hall. Two men were lying ungainly across the steps leading to the doors and the decurion avoided them, staying to the shadows. Although the noise from inside was like a battle he heard someone belch and then lurch towards the steps. He ducked behind the wall and saw Snorri emerge from the hall, unsteadily reaching for support; he steadied himself and dropping his breeks began to urinate on the two recumbent bodies that were totally oblivious to the steaming torrent. He laughed a giggly, silly little laugh which did not seem to go with the body. When he had finished he pulled up his breeks and rolled back into the hall shouting something to an unseen companion.

Rufius risked a move to the door. He peered around the jamb; the light from the hall meant that he was still in darkness, and he saw that many of the warriors were passed out on the floor while others were having drinking contests or arm wrestling bouts. Chief Trygg was seated at the head of the table beneath the dais with his throne behind. He looked befuddled and drunk but he was still conscious. Above his head, resting majestically across the throne, glistened the shining, magnificent

Sword of Cartimandua. Having seen enough Rufius slipped back outside, gesturing for the others to join him.

The four of them crouched in the dark behind the slave hall. "It will not be long now. Most of them are out of it." He glanced up but the moon was hidden. "We will give it a little longer. Are the two guards still alert?"

Gnaeus shook his head and grinned, his white teeth standing out in the dark. "No sir, drunk, worse than Orm and his brother."

"Good. Gnaeus, take Decimus around the other side. When you are there signal to me and we will take them. Then we will be ready for the rescue when it quietens down."

It seemed to take forever for the two men to get in position but Rufius knew that it was better to be slow and silent than rush and risk a commotion. As soon as he saw the signal, he and the others slipped along the wall like shadows from the moon. The two guards were soon slumped on the floor having been struck silently and efficiently; there had been no noise. Rufius did not know if they were awake or not but they could take no chances. The two ex-soldiers took out their cudgels and ensured that the sentries would not wake before morning. The door had a simple bar as a lock and they slowly lifted it so that the door would be free to swing open when they were ready. It was tempting to open it and bring out Marcus but Rufius wanted as many of the slaves as possible to be asleep.

Suddenly there was a commotion from the Great Hall and eight men tumbled to the ground. Rufius gestured for Gnaeus to stand back and he slipped on the sleeping guard's helmet. The eight men began a brawl which gradually took them to the gate where Orm and his brother just stood laughing. Some of those fighting took exception to this and soon Orm and his brother were embroiled in the fray. After a few moments, there were six still bodies lying close to the gate and the four survivors cheered each other, slapped backs and then staggered back triumphantly to the hall. Rufius had no idea if the six were dead or alive but it seemed likely that they would remain inert for a while. It had cleared one problem for them; there was no longer a guard at the gate.

They waited for someone else to come out. Gnaeus was finding the tension unbearable but Rufius was patient. There would be a perfect time to escape and he was trying to get as close to that time as possible. When it had been silent for a long time he nodded and they slowly opened the door. Once again a wall of foetid air hit them but Marcus and the woman leapt silently to their feet and quickly joined Rufius. There was not the time for welcomes and Rufius led them, along the shadows to the gate. When they reached the gate leading them to safety Marcus halted. "Take the woman to the jetty."

Rufius looked in amazement at Marcus. "Why? Where are you going?"

"I'm going to get the sword."

Before Rufius could stop him he had taken off for the Great Hall. Rufius cursed. "Gnaeus come with me. You two take her to the boat and then back to the ship. Warn Hercules that we may be leaving in a hurry." Frann looked terrified as the two men half carried her away but she remained silent.

Rufius caught Marcus' arm just as he was about to leap up the steps. "Wait! This is stupid but if you are going to get the sword then let us do it properly. It is hanging on the throne. Get a helmet and a sword. If we walk in there like this we will stand out. Let's play drunks."

The three of them soon looked the part and they staggered, with trepidation in their hearts, into the Great Hall. There was barely any movement and Rufius could see that the drink and violence had taken their toll. He pointed to the throne which shone in the firelight above the unconscious form of the Chief of the Tencteri. They moved cautiously through the bodies, careful not to step on any. While Gnaeus and Rufius kept watch, Marcus slipped to the throne and grabbed the sword. Hardly daring to breathe they made their way back to the main door. Suddenly a figure lurched drunkenly towards them, it was Snorri. He did not recognise them but he recognised the helmet. "Harald? You still fucking sober? I thought you passed out hours ago. Here let's go and shag some slaves eh?"

As soon as his face drew next to Rufius he realised it was not his friend and he stood there with a stupid expression on his face. Marcus swung the scabbard of the sword to crash into the bodyguard's head. His mouth and nose exploded in a mess of blood, teeth and gristle and Gnaeus caught him before he hit the ground. He was alive but out for the count. The three men quickly fled. No-one else was stirring and it was only as they left the gate that Rufius realised that he should have locked the slaves' hall for the slaves were not drunk and if they saw the door open they would leave and that might alert the warriors. He realised it was too late to do anything about it and they ran down the slope to the jetty towards the boats and safety. The two guards they had left breathed a sigh of relief as the three of them appeared.

Marcus grasped Rufius' arm. "Thank you, old friend. Where is Frann?"

"Your woman?" Marcus nodded, "On the boat."

They were just climbing into the boat when a silent figure suddenly rose menacingly from the shadows. Rufius and Gnaeus' hands went to their weapons but Marcus restrained them. "Don't worry. He is with us. This is Drugi."

The huge hunter grinned as he joined them in the heavily overloaded boat. "Your friends are not as silent as you are Roman."

As they rowed away Rufius looked up at the giant seated in the rear of the boat. His weight made it precariously close to the water. "Where did you find this Titan?"

"This Titan, is the finest hunter since Gaelwyn, probably including Gaelwyn, and we owe our escape to him. Without him, this would not have been possible." As they rode to The Swan which Rufius could see was preparing for sea, Marcus looked at the beached dragon boats. "We'll have to do something about those."

Rufius threw his hands into the air. "Marcus, have you lost all your senses. First, you want the sword and we nearly get caught. Now you want to do something to their ships. What in the name of the Allfather can we do?"

"Sink them because if we don't they will follow us and believe me they are faster than this ship and then Chief Trygg will have even more slaves; including Furax and Hercules. Now you do not want that to happen do you Rufius?"

Rufius knew that, infuriatingly, Marcus was right. As they clambered aboard Frann hurled herself at Marcus to hug him tearfully while Hercules and Furax looked up at the giant who appeared on their ship. "Get us under way. Furax, get the bolt thrower ready."

"Bolt thrower? We have no time for that."

"Yes, we do Hercules. Sail slowly towards the dragon ships, we are going to try to sink them, or at least damage them to prevent them following us. Marcus has pointed out that they will follow us otherwise."

Saying a silent prayer to Neptune Hercules wondered if he would ever get back to his beloved Italy.

"We need to aim below the waterline, two bolts to each boat, at the closest possible range; we need the maximum damage. Gnaeus keep your eye on the fort and let us know if there is any movement."

Furax and the crew aimed their weapon at the acutest angle possible. When they were fifty paces away they fired and quickly began reloading. They were closing too quickly and Marcus shouted, "Shorten sail, slow down!"

Cursing the trooper Hercules did as he was told. They managed to hit the other five with two bolts each but their first target had only been holed by one. Rufius was not convinced that they had struck them all in the right place and he was also doubtful that it would hold them up for long. Had they been in deeper water then they would have sunk and been harder to repair. As it was he suspected they had only delayed pursuit by a day at the most. It was now important to put as much distance between the barbarians and themselves as possible. Having taken not only their Roman prize but also the famous sword they would be angrier than a hive of wasps which has been poked by a child- they were that child! "That's all that we can do Marcus. Hercules, you can sail as fast as you like now."

"About time too!"

Back at the village there was a strange silence punctuated by the snores, belches and farts of the inebriated warriors. The foxes and rats ventured out to feast on the pieces of discarded food and detritus which had been left after the feast. The dead bodies had not attracted attention as there were piles of much easier pickings lying both in and out of the hall. As a sharp frost hardened on the warrior's bodies there was a stirring in the slave hall. One of the boys had felt the cold draft from the half-open door. Urination was normally carried out in a container in the corner but the boy saw the glint of moonlight through the door and went outside to relieve himself. To the young boy's eyes the sentries looked asleep rather than dead but he could see the gates to the fort wide open. He ran back to his mother and shook her awake.

"What is it child? Get back to sleep." The mother knew that they needed every moment's rest that they could get for they were worked long and hard.

"The gates, they are open."

Suddenly awake the mother looked and saw that there was, indeed, light coming from the door. She went and peered nervously out and saw that her son was correct. She slipped back inside and quickly woke her sister and her two children. "Come! Quietly and follow me."

The younger sister did not question the elder sibling's command for they trusted each other implicitly. On reaching the door, they saw that freedom lay ahead and they raced out with the three children. As they left the fort one of the foxes barked in shock when they silently passed. Inside the slave hall, another mother woke at the sudden noise.

The fugitives fled down to the jetty. There was only one way off the island, by boat, and they just hoped that they could find one. The passage to the southern stretch of the mainland was but a hundred paces and they knew that inept as they were if they could find a boat then they could achieve freedom. On reaching the jetty they saw, to their disappointment that there were no boats. Beneath the black waters, they could see the remains of sunken and damaged boats but none which were usable could be seen.

Picking up the discarded bearskins of the dead sentries, the resourceful elder sister wrapped them around the children. "Wait here and I will look for another." The younger sister held the three children fearfully as she stared up at the village, just waiting for the alarm which would signal the end to their brief foray into freedom. She caught a glimpse of movement at the gate as other slaves realised that they were free and she felt her heart sink. They had come so close and yet failed.

Suddenly she heard a, "Hssst!" Looking along the jetty she saw her sister waving. Running as quickly as they dared along the icy wooden jetty they ran to where Drugi had left his boat. It was small but it was a means of escape and the five of them boarded and pushed off just as the first of the escaped slaves arrived at the end of the jetty. The other shore was closer than they could have hoped and they were soon halfway across; their fellow captives staring helplessly at the only means of escape. Two of the younger women jumped into the icy waters and half waded, half swam towards the departing boat. One of the girls barely made it ten paces to the slowly moving boat before she succumbed to the cold and sank slowly beneath the waters. The other had more resilience and, despite her freezing joints kicked on. The elder sister took pity on this brave soul and they stopped rowing. As the girl reached the boat the sister said, "Hang on to the back and we will take you with us." The six refugees stood on the shore, the swimmer shivering, draped in a bearskin as they looked at the jetty which was filling up with freed slaves who had nowhere to go.

As the elder sister led the party south the younger one took an oar and pushed the small rowing boat back to the island. If the Norns so willed it, then others would have the same chance of freedom as they were grasping for such hope with both hands.

The sound of the fox and the movement through the open gate had woken Orm. The blow he had suffered in the brawl had been slight but the ale he had consumed had taken him to the depths of sleep. He stood, wondering what had occurred when he saw the stream of women and children running towards the jetty. It took him a few moments to discover that he was not dreaming and they were fleeing. He grabbed his spear and yelled, at the top of his voice, "To arms! To arms!"

On the jetty, there was a collective wail as the refugees realised that their bid for freedom was over. Some sat, silently sobbing on the jetty, oblivious to the cold. Others fled along the shoreline to try to find a hiding place on the island. One or two jumped into the water to try to grab the rowing boat which had floated tantalisingly close. One or two of the women slipped back to the nearby houses to wait and hide.

Chief Trygg jerked awake, his head pounding with the sudden movement. Orm appeared at the door of the Great Hall. "The slaves! They are free! They are escaping!"

The angry chief shook awake the bleary-eyed men around the table. "To your feet! The slaves!" He turned around to grab his sword and saw to his horror that it was gone. Although his mind had been befuddled a few moments earlier, he had a sudden clarity of thought, the Roman had, somehow organised the escape and taken the sword. He took his dagger out and banged hard on the discarded helmet lying at his feet. "Get to your feet you lazy whoresons! The Roman has taken the sword! On your feet!" He had a cold hard fury about him. He had been deceived and, what made it worse, was that he had known there was something wrong. He cursed the Roman but he also cursed Lars and his brothers; but for Lars' lust, Marcus would have been safely on the mainland, well away from his friends.

Marcus stood staring over the stern. To his left, the first lightening of the sky could be seen. Nestled in his arm was Frann who could not quite believe that they had escaped. He turned to Drugi, "The horses?"

"Cato and his family are free, running wild in the forests of Uiteland but the ponies did not wish to go," he shrugged. "The Norns."

Marcus nodded. He was, in some way pleased, for he had liked the sons of Trygg and enjoyed watching them ride. He had seen in them a love of horses and riding which mirrored his own. They would grow to become the first horsemen in their tribe. They would be happy, as would Cato and the small herd they had created. He regretted leaving Cato for he was the finest horse he had ever ridden. When they returned to Britannia he would ask Nanna to find one as good. He laughed aloud as he wondered what made him think they could escape.

"Well, I am pleased that you have something to laugh about decurion."

Marcus could hear the censure in Rufius' voice; he was still unhappy about their diversion to rescue the sword. "Nothing ill came of it Rufius and we could not leave the blade in a foreign land."

Rufius' face was angry. "You young fool! Have you become your reckless brother? Do you think this is a game? We have travelled halfway around these northern waters to find you and you want to go back for a piece of metal." He gestured at Furax and Hercules. "These men risked their lives for you."

Marcus faced up to Rufius, truculently. "I did not ask you to. I am grateful but I would have found a way to escape."

"You are your brother again. Within seven days you would have been sold. How would you have escaped then… with the sword, your woman and your unborn child?"

Drugi spoke suddenly in the embarrassing silence which came between the two Explorates and his deep slow voice made them all start. "I think that Odin or your Allfather determined all of our actions and the Norns wove a web so complex that all of our decisions were not ours." They all looked at this giant of a man as though he had suddenly materialised on the deck. He shrugged, "I was content living in the land of the Eudose but I am here. Why? I did not intend to leave my hut ever and then this Roman came into my life." He shrugged again and then grinned, his smile lighting up the stern. "My Roman friend has not told you who I am but I am Drugi the hunter and the woman with my Roman friend is Frann the mother of his unborn child."

Marcus looked with increasing respect at Drugi. He was wiser than any. His brief interjection calmed the atmosphere and made smiles appear on the faces of all of his friends. "Are you one of the Titans? Are you a giant?"

The wonder in Furax's voice made Drugi smile. "No I am but a slave or I was a slave and now I breathe free air. It feels good."

Hercules sniffed, "Aye well we are not out of the fire yet. "

Marcus said, "It will take them some time to repair their boats."

Rufius shook his head. "There is another dragon fleet awaiting us in the north. We are between pirates. I would put your woman below decks for when the dawn breaks we may well be fighting new foes."

Chapter 13

As soon as he saw that the trader had disappeared then Chief Trygg knew how the Roman and his woman had escaped. The floating bodies of the drowned slaves was a stark and visual measure of the cost of the feast which had seen five warriors killed and others injured. As the slaves were rounded up, Chief Trygg contemplated his next action. Snorri's sudden arrival brought even more unpleasant news. "They have damaged the ships. There are holes in all of them."

Snorri expected a raging torrent of anger and abuse from the chief who had lost his sword and so many slaves. Instead, there was an air of resigned calmness about him as he nodded. "Get them repaired. Have the slaves rounded up and prepare the crews for sea."

Snorri looked around at the devastation. "But the ships will not be ready before nightfall and, even then, I am not sure how many of them will be ready. The Roman ship will be long gone by then."

Trygg's voice was quiet but firm and cold as he turned to his lieutenant. "Even if it takes a month to repair the boats we will follow. We know where he will go and we know where to find him. This will not be over until I have the sword and the Roman lies dead at my feet. Now go!"

The chief now finally understood that the hawk had not been an omen of good fortune as he had thought but was a warning, a sign from the gods of impending doom. The symbol of Rome was the eagle and this was its lesser cousin. He was being punished for his arrogance. He would not make that mistake again. Once he had visited Britannia again, killed the Roman and retrieved the sword he would begin his conquest of the whole of Uiteland. The easy defeat of the Suebi, for which he thanked the Roman, had shown him the way forwards. He had lost some of the slaves but he would still make a hefty profit. He strode over to the bay where the dragon boats lay to view the damage. All but one of them was sunk to the oars. The remaining boat still floated half in and half out of the water. He could see Snorri and his men hauling the ship to the beach. He had hope;

he could follow with one boat filled with his best warriors and then the others could follow in a few days. Perhaps the gods were giving him back some of the fortune for, with a keen crew rowing hard, he might catch them before they turned west.

Hercules looked nervously up at the masthead pennant. The wind had shifted from the south-west to the north-west; they were being driven further east than was good for them. All of them feared Gurt whose settlement lay close to the north of the peninsula. He could wait there knowing that the trader would have to pass his waters. Without oar power, The Swan would be helpless, even with their bolt thrower. Their only hope was a favourable wind and inclement weather which might swamp the dragon boats. He looked again northwards wondering if he could head further north and then turn west. That too brought its own problems for it increased the chance that their pursuers might catch them and also put them closer to potential enemies who were, as yet, unknown. Despite his misgivings, he felt that they now had a chance; he had thought it a forlorn hope for them to go after the young decurion but the Parcae had been with them and perhaps the god of the sea, Neptune. He smiled as he saw Furax showing the giant the bolt thrower. They had both made an impression on each other.

"And with this, we can send a bolt more than five hundred paces."

Drugi looked dubious. "Are you mocking me young Roman?"

Furax's face became very serious. "No, honestly, ask Rufius. He will tell you."

The sincerity in the boy's voice convinced the former slave and he looked at the intricate workings. This was a well-made machine. The Romans had to be highly skilled if they were able to produce these in any quantity. "Are there many of these wondrous machines?"

"Every Roman ship and legion has many."

Drugi looked aft to the land he had left. Trygg might get a shock when he caught up with them. He had been impressed when he had seen the bolts crash through the hulls of Trygg's ships but if they could fire further than that then the Roman ship might escape. The hunter was philosophical about their flight. He knew that, if they were caught, he would die; Trygg would show no mercy despite all of Drugi's services to him. But he had the feeling that his death would not be aboard this ship; he could have died many times during the escape but the Norms had not wanted him dead. When they did he would die, until then he would take each day as it came.

"Now then young Furax, I believe you were going to show me the rest of this ship?" Furax eagerly took Drugi by the hand and led him below decks.

"Furax has found a friend then Marcus. Where did you find him?"

"He is the reason we are here for he aided us many times. He has been a slave since childhood but the hawk spoke to him and he threw in with us and I thank the Allfather for that." Marcus turned to Gnaeus. "The two troopers who were with me on the Dunum?"

"They were killed. We gave chase but had to halt at the mouth of the Dunum. It was hard to see you leave."

Marcus clasped Gnaeus' hand. "I thank you for your loyalty. You are a good friend."

Gnaeus shook his head. "It is more than that, I am an oath brother remember."

Hercules' voice was a reminder that they were not safe yet. "Winds shifting again. We'll have to tack and head nor-east." He looked meaningfully at Rufius. "It means we are heading further from home and we have still to pass the pirates."

"Pass the pirates?"

"Yes, Marcus. Trygg is not the only raider around here. We visited another village and I know that Gurt will be waiting for us. We are not out of the woods yet and we may have to fight." He gestured at the broad back of Drugi disappearing below deck. "Can he fight?"

"He is a superb archer and strong as an ox. He can fight. I have stood with him and fought off a Suebi warband. It is a good thing you brought the bolt thrower. It may be the difference between death and survival."

Gurt and his crews had calculated that The Swan would be returning to their waters within a few days and so the wily captain had spread his line of five ships out in a broad line so that they covered a wide area. He had them provisioned and manned well for he knew not how soon the ship would arrive. The delay did not worry him, it was early in the season for shipping but other boats could pass and the wolf would have them. He knew that the trader would avoid the coastline and so the left-hand ship of the line was just out of sight of the horizon. The ship which was the furthest east could see another two miles to the west; if the trader travelled any further west then they would be in the seas controlled by barbarians far more fearsome than Gurt and his men and that would bring the Brigante called Gaelwyn more trouble than Gurt's five ships. His ships were all facing northeast as he assumed the sailing ship would try to outrun him. Gurt was a master at the board game called ducks and drakes played with four white stones and a black one. This time he had five stones to play with, whilst not a duck, The Swan would soon be his.

While Hercules fretted and worried about the wind Rufius organised the weapons on deck. They had the bows, swords and spears in long wooden boxes below deck and they brought them up to secure them to the sides of the ship. When they were called to action they would not have any time to go below decks. The small quantity of shields they had brought were already secured to the masts, ready to be untied and used at a moment's notice.

Gnaeus whistled in admiration as Drugi brought a huge box of swords up. The rest of the crew had struggled, in pairs, to do the same. He turned to Marcus. "He is a strong one. Are the other barbarians as strong?"

"He comes from the east in the land of the Wends. He was enslaved as a child." Marcus shook his head. "Having been a slave, for no matter how brief a time, I now have a different view on slavery."

Gnaeus shrugged. "My people are like your family Decurion, they own no slaves."

"No, but we frequently come upon them." He looked darkly across the empty sea towards Hjarno-By, unseen in the distance. "We have been in taverns where men use the women."

Gnaeus looked dumfounded. "The men pay the women."

Marcus shook his head. "They pay their owners, they pay the men who own the women. I am just glad that neither Macro nor myself abused women like that."

Rufius overheard the conversation as he wiped the oil off a sword. His friend had changed. He had grown up and learned about life. It was a good change. He had been worried, when they had gone back for the sword that he was becoming like his brother. Now he knew different; the sword was a symbol of the Brigante people. Becoming a father was giving Marcus Gaius Aurelius a different perspective on life.

"The wind is changing." Hercules cursed the precocious wind. He had never known a wind change direction so many times. The thick scudding clouds above told him that the gods were angry but why could they not ensure that the wind blew in the same direction?

Drugi came next to the old sea captain. "Why do the crew have to keep changing the sail? They make it smaller, larger, they turn it? Why?"

"It is the wind. Unless the wind is blowing directly at us we can sail forwards but we have to keep changing direction to do so." He made a zig-zagging motion with his hand. "If the wind is behind us it is easier to sail and we travel much more quickly."

"Ah like the bird. The eagle holds itself against the wind." He peered forwards. "Well, captain, you will need your crew to climb again."

Hercules looked up at the pennant which still blew in the same direction. "The wind hasn't changed."

"No but unless my eyes deceive me there are dragon boats ahead and we are heading directly for one."

With a sinking heart, Hercules knew that the sharp-eyed slave was right. There, on the reciprocal course to them, was a dragon boat. The question which he needed the answer to was, was it alone or part of a pack? He turned to Rufius. "They have found us." He pointed to the north-west.

Rufius had expected this but it did not make it any easier to countenance. He yelled, "All warriors on deck." The ex-soldiers were only used for sea duties in times of dire need and they all raced to the deck. With Drugi and the Roman troopers, they had fifteen men and Furax who had given himself the job of directing the bolt thrower.

A fearful Frann and the two Brigante slave girls appeared at the hatch, their faces filled with terror at the thought of being returned to the life of a slave again. Marcus saw the fear on his woman's face. "It is not Trygg go below decks and hold on tightly. We may have to move quickly and suddenly." Her pleading eyes filled with tears. "Trust me. I was not saved from slavery to die in this lonely, cold and dark sea." As the three women went below reluctantly, Marcus wondered at the lie he had just told. The dragon boats were smaller, more nimble and would be filled with warriors. The Swan would be both outnumbered and outmanoeuvred. Marcus knew that they were dependent on the wind whilst the dragon boats had oars and the wind. It was an uneven contest. Perhaps a couple of triremes might have made a difference but The Swan was an old trader, not a warship.

"Hercules. Hold this course until we discover if this is just one ship or many." Hercules nodded but the glum look told Rufius that the captain thought he had sailed his last voyage. "The rest of you get a bow and a quiver. We have plenty of arrows. Gnaeus bring the amphorae of Greek Fire."

As Gnaeus went below deck, Marcus paled. Greek fire was like magic, two substances which when mixed and lit, would continue to burn, even on water but the danger was always fire. The ship firing the weapon was in just as much danger as their target. Rufius saw the look on his friend's face and understood. "We will only use it when we have to but we have sacks of sand which will put out any stray sparks." He shrugged. "We have to do all that we can, even if it frightens every single person on this ship." He turned to look ahead. "Any other ships yet?" When he received no reply he shouted, "Furax, up to the top of the mast. You have the best eyes."

Drugi watched in amazement as the young boy scampered to the top of the swaying mast. "He is like the squirrel. I know not how he does not fall."

Gnaeus smiled. "It is the bravery of youth."

"Two other ships." The voice seemed to be disembodied as they could not see the boy.

"Where away?"

"West."

Rufius looked at Hercules. "There will be a line of them. The one we saw first is the last in the line."

Marcus and Gnaeus joined Rufius who, as senior decurion, took all the decisions. "I am thinking this, if we head for the second in the line the other two will converge on us. They do not know about the bolt thrower and, I am certain that they have no long range weapons. We fire at two hundred paces. We should be able to fire three in the time it takes to cover fifty paces. Then Hercules turns," he looked at his hands, he had not worked out yet the nautical terms, "to the right then our archers can send two volleys at the last ship in the line. They will not expect us to attack them. Once we have crossed through their line we sail with the wind, in whatever direction that takes us. They will have to turn and we will gain time. I know that they are faster and can catch us but if we can avoid them until dark then we might escape."

Hercules' voice drifted over. "You are not expecting the old girl to turn like a foal are you?"

Rufius grinned. "You know you can do it. If you had any doubts you would have told me."

Hercules mumbled something about eggs and sucking and then shouted to the crew. "When I give the command I want you to give me full sail and we will be turning to starboard. The wind will be across our quarter and The Swan should fly."

Marcus murmured to Rufius, "I think the old bugger is actually enjoying this."

Furax had descended. Rufius grabbed him by the shoulder. "Right Furax, you wanted to be part of this adventure well as of now everything will depend on you. I want your first bolt aimed at their mainmast. It doesn't matter if you don't hit it but you will scare the living daylights out of the rowers and might disrupt their rhythm. More importantly, you might get lucky and hit the steersman. The next two bolts you fire below their waterline, we need their ships filling with water to slow them down and when you reload you keep firing at the other ship, the one at the end of their line. Is that clear?"

The grinning boy said, "Absolutely and the Greek Fire?"

Rufius shook his head. "That is the last resort. Let us hope that they have never seen a bolt thrower before and it terrifies them into running away."

The pirates were confident and Rufius could see why. Already two more sails could be seen to the west. Gurt had brought his whole fleet and no doubt every warrior he could. An early season gift like The Swan was not to be ignored. The pirates were heading quickly for The Swan, the five ships converging to close the distance between them and their prey. They would swarm around it mobbing like birds do when a predator threatened, but the dragon ships were the predators. Hercules was holding the trader back, the sails had a couple of reefs in them, and this made the pirates' speed seem even greater.

Furax's voice sounded shrill in the cold winter air as he peered over the bows. "Three hundred paces."

"Stand by. Archers, be ready on my command. Furax, you judge the distance." Furax did not turn but nodded his concentration on the target total.

They could make out the faces of the enemy now and, at the prow, were helmeted figures, the assault party no doubt, who would leap aboard once they had closed. Perhaps they thought that The Swan's captain was panicking by heading straight for them but they were supremely confident that, once they made contact, they could clear the decks of the tubby trader in moments with their superior numbers. They could not see the ex-soldiers crouching in the thwarts of The Swan. The story of the Trojan Horse had not made it as far as Uiteland and they would learn that not all traders were harmless; this one had teeth.

When Furax released the catch the bolt flew straight and true; the crack resounding like thunder. Already reloading he did not have time to watch but Rufius did and he laughed out loud as the assault party dropped like stones to avoid the deadly and unexpected missile. Some of the rowers took evasive action which resulted in the boat changing direction slightly. The bolt missed the mainmast but, as it sped past the mighty timber, it sliced through a rope and thudded into the chest of the spare steersman, hurling him overboard. The steersman was already compensating for the loss of power down one side and the bolt next to him made him overcompensate and the longship lurched towards the next boat in the line. The cut rope made the sail ruffle and lose power. Rufius and the crew cheered when the next bolt thudded into the hull below the waterline. The next boat was Gurt's and he watched in horror as the second ship in the line lurched towards him. His converging course meant he was heading over towards the stricken boat anyway and he too had to turn to starboard. Before the third bolt had struck home Hercules and the First Mate were pushing the tiller for all they were worth to make the turn. Even as he pushed, his crew unfurled the sails and the old tub leapt forward as though it was a greyhound released from a trap.

The last boat in the line, whose captain had been expecting to board the starboard side of The Swan, saw to his horror, the trader heading for his bows. The Swan was a bigger heavier boat than the nimble dragon boat, although he knew the trader would be damaged, his own boat would be sunk and he yelled, "Back oars!" in an attempt to avoid a collision.

Before the captain could give another command fifteen arrows flew high into the air to be followed a heartbeat later by another fifteen and, before the first had struck, a third flight was launched. There was carnage amongst the unprotected rowers; their shields lay protecting the side of their ship and they wore neither helmets nor armour. At point-blank range Furax fired a bolt which went through the steersman and shattered the tiller. The dragon boat lurched, out of control, towards the other stricken and sinking ship. The Swan was suddenly in clear water and rapidly heading north towards safety.

Gurt looked at his fleet which was in complete disarray. There was only the last ship in the line which had any control and Gurt yelled to the captain. "Follow him. We will join you."

The captain of the last ship, The Crow, was not convinced that the pirate leader was correct. He could see one boat, the first attacked, slowly sinking and the other boat which had been attacked was dead in the water. This Roman ship was not a sheep; it had sharp teeth and could use them. He obeyed his orders and slowly the ship turned to starboard to follow the white-sailed ship which was disappearing to the north-west. Gurt and the other undamaged boat rowed slowly around to pick up the survivors of the wreck. When he saw the dead on the last boat he knew that he could only pursue with three ships, there would be barely enough men to row the damaged ship back to port. His lieutenant must have been reading his mind. "Is it worth it? It is one boat."

Part of the pirate leader's mind knew that he was right but his pride demanded that he continue. His men respected a strong leader and one who let a fat little merchantman get away would not last long. "No, we go on. We will catch him fear not and his little surprise is at the front of his ship. Not the stern."

They had just transferred some rowers to help the stricken ship return to port when they heard the cry from the lookout. "Dragon ship."

"Where away?" Gurt looked north wondering if his ship had returned and why.

The lookout shouted. "South!"

They turned and looked at Stormbringer, Trygg Tryggvassons' boat which was powering towards them. Gurt knew of Trygg's reputation as a sailor, a pirate and a raider. They did not come into contact with each other as Gurt had not yet had the courage to sail across to Britannia. He would have been wary had it not been the single ship. He looked at his men. He had more than enough men left to defeat the Tencteri if this was a warlike act and if not it would do no harm to talk with the chief.

Trygg hove to close to the stern of Gurt's ship so that the two captains were barely ten paces apart. "Have you seen a trader, filled with Brigante or Romans?"

Gurt waved a remorseful hand at the wreckage bobbing up and down on the icy black waters. "One of my ships is following her. She is heading north-west."

Trygg nodded. "She is heading for Britannia. What do you intend chief?"

Gurt was still in two minds but having sent one of his men after her he would have to follow eventually. "I am going to follow her."

"Good." Trygg always saw the bigger picture. He did not like Gurt and he knew that one day if he was going to rule Uiteland he would have to fight and destroy him but the most important matter was to recover what had been stolen. "I propose we join forces and follow this Roman to Britannia. My ships will soon catch us up."

Gurt looked suspicious. "And how do we share the proceeds?"

"All I want is the Roman slave who escaped, Drugi the hunter and the sword. You can have all the rest."

"In that case, we have a partnership." Gurt paused for he did not totally trust this Trygg. "But this is temporary?"

"Of course."

The three ships headed north-west. The men were largely rested and the three longships were soon ploughing purposefully through the water, hot on the trail of The Swan.

"Captain. There is a dragon ship two miles astern of us."

"I had hoped that a bloody nose would discourage him but obviously not." Rufius looked at the sun slipping down in the west. "Two hours until sunset."

Hercules shook his head. "By then she will have closed up and this time she will be wary. The others will be close behind."

Rufius slapped his hand on the guardrail; he turned to Gnaeus and Marcus. "Move the bolt thrower to the stern and bring up the Greek Fire from below. Captain, slow us down. I want her to catch us before dark."

"Before dark! Are you mad?"

"No, I want to sink her and sink her quickly. You are right. She knows about our weapon in the bow so she will keep astern of us. We won't be lucky enough to hit the tiller a second time and she can keep us at bay until her consorts come. No, we must knock her out, with fire. The others will head for the burning wreck and that will give us the chance to head due west and escape." Rufius was not a gambler but he knew that the night and the dark was their ally. They needed a head start and a fire aboard the dragon ship could be all that they needed.

Hercules wasn't certain but the troopers were. Buoyed by their success against the other ships the ex-soldiers felt that they had a good chance of hitting the dragon ship. The captain shrugged. It was as good a plan as any.

Chapter 14

The Captain of The Crow could not believe his luck. The trader had slowed dramatically; he still could not see Gurt and the others but he knew they would be just over the horizon. He had had a lantern hung from the stern to guide them. He would just follow this wallowing tub and then, when the others arrived they could pick at her from the rear; he would have no difficulty in maintaining contact with her and his rowers were not even using their full power. Then they would get their revenge for their lost comrades. "Get us under their stern and get some archers here. Let's see if we can get the old man on the tiller."

The men grinned as the boat powered through the water; the low dragon boat seemed to fly through the water. When they were about one hundred paces from the stern of the slow-moving trader, the captain ordered his archers to aim at the stern. Their bows were only short ones and he needed for them to be closer than eighty paces to stand a chance of hitting the target. The lookout at the front shouted, "Captain that is a strange-looking tiller." Suddenly everyone on the ship saw a light at the stern. Was their captain giving them a light to follow too?

They had seen neither a bolt thrower nor Greek Fire before but that night they saw and heard them both. With a terrifying crack, the fiery bolt flew, straight and true for The Crow. At such close range, there was no time between the sighting of the bolt and the striking of the fire. The Captain had no time for any command as the bolt struck first the sail and then embedded itself in the mast. One of the sailors threw a bucket of water on to the flames but, to their horror, the flames spread. A second fiery bolt struck the ship towards the bow and that too began to burn with a fierce white heat. When a third set fire to the prow the Captain knew that his Crow would never fly again and every man threw himself overboard as the flames quickly ripped through the wooden ship devouring every part of her like a hungry beast gorges on a helpless prey.

On board The Swan none of them could quite believe the devastation created by this magical substance. None of them, Rufius included, had ever seen the weapon used before. It seemed such a terrible weapon and yet it had saved their lives and bought them valuable time. Already the wind, which had fanned the flames and helped the conflagration to spread quickly, was pushing them northwards into the increasing darkness. Rufius turned to Hercules, "I think we can head west now captain and you can say a prayer to your god Neptune that we can evade observation until we reach Britannia.

Gurt's ship was in the lead and the lookout shouted, "I can see a light to the north."

Gurt nodded. "Good. He has lit a lantern."

As they closed the steersman said, "I don't think that is a lantern captain. Look it is spread across the waters.

Suddenly a body bumped into the bow of the ship and Gurt shouted, "Stop rowing." The wind drifted them up to the wreckage which was strewn across the sea. There were burnt and damaged bodies amongst the still burning timbers of the ship. The other ships came up to join them and they trawled for survivors. There were but three.

One of the warriors was so badly burned that Gurt nodded to the warrior cradling his head to slit his throat. The other two would survive but the shocked expressions on their faces told the others that they would never forget the experience they had endured. "It spat fire captain. And they must have used witchcraft for when we poured water on the fire it burned brighter and harder. The ship caught fire in a heartbeat and then the ship just disappeared."

Gurt glanced around at the white, frightened faces of his crew. He too was shaken. What could have destroyed one of their ships so quickly? Was the apparently harmless trader a dragon in disguise, sent to punish them for their piracy? The ship rolled a little as Trygg's ship nudged alongside. Gurt looked over at the Tencteri warrior. "The Roman ship spat fire and The Crow sank. There are but two survivors. It is witchcraft."

Chief Trygg laughed but it was a cold hard laugh which echoed and rolled across the silent sea of death. "No, it is the Roman war machine. My ships and your ships were struck with giant arrows from a Roman war machine. This fire is also a

Roman trick. I do not know how they made it spit fire but they did."

One of the survivors shook his head. "But the water would not put out the fire! It was magic."

"No, it is just another Roman trick we do not understand." Chief Trygg looked impatiently at Gurt. "Well Captain, do we pursue or do I continue alone with my boats?"

Gurt looked astern of the Tencteri ship and saw another three of Trygg's ships. He had lost three of his own ships already and many warriors. If he continued he could lose it all and, for what? It was but one ship. "It is but one ship…"

"No, it is not just one ship which we seek, for I intend to punish the Romans. They have dared to come into our waters and they will pay a heavy price for that. Join with me Chief Gurt and we will raid the coast of Britannia and your ships will have so much booty that you will be throwing valuable items over the side just to sail home safely."

Gurt knew of the success of his neighbour. It was well known that his visits to Britannia brought him much plunder. If he did not join him then he would have a poor season and one of his warriors might seize control of the band. "You know the waters and the land, we will follow you." Gurt was ensuring that, if they ran into the fiery trader again it would be one of the Tencteri ships which was lost. He intended to lose no more ships.

Once Chief Trygg took control they changed course. The wily pirate knew that he could search the seas and not find his prey but he knew where it was heading; the land along the valley of the Dunum. Marcus had told the Chief of his home and described, in great detail, what it looked like. The Tencteri had a good idea where it was. He led, instead, the fleet around the coast of Uiteland. They hugged the coast for a night and a day and, as dawn broke on the second day found themselves off the settlement known as Cnutstead. Trygg had left Hjarno-By hurriedly and while he had enough men and arms he was short of food. He hove to and signalled to Gurt. "The men will need some rest before we sail across the waters to Britannia. I am going ashore to re-provision."

"My boats are well provisioned. We will rest. When do we sail?"

"We have plenty of time to get across the waters to Britannia When I return to my ship join me and we will talk more of how I intend to punish the Romans and their allies. I will tell you of their waters and the currents and eddies which catch an unwary sailor."

Cnut did not like the look of the warriors who waded ashore from the dragon boat. He wondered why the others were moored offshore. They had been lucky of late and, since the Romans had left their jet gift, they had prospered. This visit did not bode well and Cnut sent the women and children into the dunes and woods to hide.

When Chief Trygg stepped ashore he could see that Cnutstead was a poor place but the racks of drying fish told him that he would be able to stock up. "Hail headman I am Chief Trygg of the Tencteri."

"I am Cnut headman of Cnutstead and I have heard of you. You are a long way from home Chief Trygg. What can my humble village do for you?"

"We have run out of provisions and need your fish."

"We have little enough for our own people and we can spare you little."

The normally patient Trygg was tired and still smarting from his humiliation at the hands of the Romans. He suddenly saw the jet carving hanging from Cnut's neck and knew that the Romans had visited here too. In his mind that made them allies of the Romans and fair game for his warriors. "You misunderstand me old man. We intend to take it. You can get more." He turned to Snorri. "Search the huts and bring all the food!"

There were only ten men in the village, including old Cnut but they knew they had to defend their village and its paltry supply of food or the women and children would die. It was futile but Cnut roared, "No!" and drew out his short seax.

Trygg had been itching to kill someone since the Roman had fled and he took out his sword, which seemed now, after having handled the Sword of Cartimandua, to be a lesser weapon, and ran the old man through. The others fell quickly to these experienced warriors who had fought Suebi and defeated them. The fishermen stood no chance. As his men took their ill-gotten gains back to their ship Chief Trygg looked down at the despoiled bodies of the stead and regretted his action. He had killed because his heart had been filled with hate and, as Snorri took the brand to burn the settlement, the Chief relented. "No, leave the houses. We will return to the ships."

Whilst the warriors slept as best they could aboard their ships Trygg took Gurt through his plan. "The river we will use to take us onto their land is wide but it twists and turns. When I have been there before I have not had enough ships and men to truly take the plunder that we could." Gurt looked at him with an intense look of concentration. He would learn much from this war chief and use it to his own advantage later. "The villages which line the river see our ship's masts and they lock themselves in their forts. We could take them but we would lose many men. With this number of boats, we could send two of the boats along the river while the rest of the ships disembarked at the mouth of the estuary. Once they had seen our ships pass by and leave them unmolested they would relax and they could be taken when they open their gates."

"A good plan but I do not know the land and the settlements."

"That is why I propose that Snorri goes with you and I take one of your boats with me. That way we have the best of both worlds."

"You are choosing the most dangerous task for yourself. Why?"

"I captured a mystical sword which brought us great victory over the Suebi. It was taken by a Roman who lives along the Dunum. I intend to find the Roman's home and retake it."

Gurt chewed on some of the salty dried fish and washed it down with some weak beer they had liberated from Cnutstead. He wrinkled his nose in disgust. "You defeated the Suebi? Were there many of them?"

There was an implied criticism in Gurt's voice which Trygg chose to ignore. He understood the scepticism; no-one in Uiteland had ever defeated the mighty Suebi before. The Suebi were fierce and uncompromising fighters and their numbers were always superior to the warbands they encountered. "I will be honest with you Gurt. Had it not been for the Roman we would not have defeated them but it was he who organised the defence of my burgh and the Suebi were slaughtered as they broke against his defence. He helped to lead the pursuit and we massacred every Suebi who came north. The trail south is still littered with their bones."

"I can see why you want this Roman back."

Trygg snarled, "I do not want him back. I want him dead. I learned enough in his time with my people to become a better and a wiser leader and I have been shown how to defeat the Suebi. The next time they attack will be their last."

The next few days were torture for the crew of The Swan. The fickle winds scurried and flurried this way and that and all the time they were looking over their shoulder for the barbarian boats which they expected to see loom over the horizon each morning as dawn broke. The only three immune from the fear were Frann, Drugi and Furax. For Frann this was simple, every sea mile took her further from slavery and closer to her home and she had her man with her. The two Brigante girls fussed over the pregnant Frann; Hercules shook his head at the giggling, shrill female voices which seemed strange on his boat. The only female Hercules cared for was his ship. Frann was oblivious to any criticism. Since they had lost sight of the Tencteri she had seemed freed from worry. The Mother was truly watching over her and as her belly swelled she felt the new life kicking inside her. She spent every moment she could on the deck, normally with Marcus but, if he was in a debate with the others, she would just stare at him; grateful that she had met him and thankful that he appeared to love her almost as much as she loved him.

For Furax and Drugi it was a mutual appreciation society. Furax told Drugi of life in Rome and the sea whilst Drugi's tales of hunting filled the boy with wonder. "I still do not understand what you say about the people who live in Rome. Do you not know them all?"

Furax laughed until the tears rolled down the street. When he saw the offended look on Drugi's face he relented. "I am sorry Drugi. How best to explain? You know the place we rescued Marcus from?"

"Hjarno-By?"

Furax could not get his tongue around the words and so he just said, "Yes, that place. Well, how many people would you say lived there?"

"Oh too many to count. Many years ago it was small with but two or three hundred but now there are many more."

"Rome has hundreds of such villages inside its walls and all of them are much bigger than your village. If you stood in the middle, in the Forum, and you counted every person who passed in one day, you would run out of numbers."

Drugi found the concept incredible but he believed the boy. "And how are these people fed?"

"Ships like this one, arrive every day and bring food from all over the world."

"Where do people hunt?"

"Hunt? There is nowhere close by."

"Then I do not want to live in Rome. Too many people and not enough animals." He began to become nervous about Britannia. "Tell me Furax, for I know you will not lie to me, is Britannia like Rome?"

"Like Rome? I have not visited all of Britannia but the Senator," Drugi looked confused, "the man who owns this boat and an important Roman, a chief amongst Romans. He told me that you could take every person who lived in Britannia and there would still be more people living in Rome. No, Britannia is like your land but with more forests. I like it."

"Thank you, my young friend, you have put my mind at rest."

Rufius and Marcus smiled at the two new friends who were totally engrossed in each other's worlds. Frann nodded to them and said, "I will fetch some food for you two."

Marcus shook his head. "You are not a slave anymore."

Indignantly she said, "I know which is why I asked you. I want to do this!"

As she stormed off Rufius laughed. "This is why I do not envy you and Metellus. Women are different from us men. They are hard to fathom." Marcus looked embarrassed and watched as

Frann and the two Brigante girls descended into the bowels of the ship. "You are much taken with her."

"I did not intend to be; she grew upon me and the next thing I knew I could not be without her."

"I think the poets call that love but I am not sure. You and she will be a family but where will you live? Or were will she live for you are still a soldier?"

"I had thought to take her to mother and Decius. She would be safe there."

"I am not so sure. The Legate told me that he had read many reports about the increasing raids from the east. We did not know of them because they were at the coast but it may be that something needs to be done to defend the Dunum from the raiders."

"I cannot keep her at Rocky Point; the frontier is even more dangerous."

"I know but that is where we will be heading first."

"Not Morbium?"

"No the Legate will need the three of us. We have been away too long. He will need to know that Hercules is safe and then give him his orders. He can drop Frann off after."

Marcus shook his head. "No, I will ask the Prefect if I can take Drugi and Frann with Hercules. It is not right that they arrive unannounced."

"I am not sure that your wish will be granted." Rufius wondered if it was something in the blood of Marcus and Macro which made them believe they had a destiny outside of the ala. For Rufius the ala came first. Perhaps that was the effect of the sword or the Brigante blood. "This fellow Drugi, he will live at the farm as well?"

"I don't know. I feel obligated to him but he is a free spirit and I would not want to tie him down."

"He reminds me of Gaelwyn and Gaelwyn was free in the valley of the Dunum. Perhaps Drugi will be too."

The two former inhabitants of Hjarno-By peered anxiously over the bow to be the first to see Britannia. The strangely shaped rocks to the south of the Tinea looked to them both as though the gods had carved them. To those returning they seemed commonplace, having viewed them often. Drugi shook his head in wonder. This place must be special to the gods that they have carved such objects from the land. All of them were surprised by the progress on the fort which now stood at the south side of the Tinea Estuary. There were many ships moving between the stone jetty and the northern shore where the eastern end of the wall was clearly visible. There were three triremes of the Classis Britannica moored there as well as other merchantmen busily offloading their wares.

"This has come on since the last time I was here."

"The Emperor was keen to secure and defend this end of the wall." Rufius pointed to the huge vicus which had sprung up. "That was but two huts when we set sail. It is growing at a prodigious rate."

Drugi turned to Furax. "This is the biggest town in Britannia?"

"No Drugi. When we left it was but a small fort. All these people have come since the waters and the land warmed. They will be traders such as us."

Drugi looked across the river at the line of what looked like ants labouring up the path to the fort which stood at the top of the low ridge. "Are they people?"

"Yes Drugi, they are offloading the ships and then they will be taken by road to the forts."

"What is a road?"

To the Roman boy, Drugi's question made no sense but then he realised that what was familiar to him would be foreign to the former slave. "Imagine a trail but ten paces wide, covered with stones and straight, with no turns, that is a road."

"I should like to see one of those."

"Don't worry you will."

Just then a small sailing boat belonging to the Classis Britannica left the trireme in the estuary. When it drew close the officer in charge shouted, "Welcome Captain. The Legate asked that we tell you, when you arrived, that you should land your charges at Coriosopitum."

"Thank you. Tell your captain that we were pursued by some dragon boats for part of the voyage. There may be raiders and pirates about."

"A little early in the year for pirates isn't it?"

"Not these. They are annoyed that we sank two of their boats."

"This sank two dragon boats?" The incredulity in his voice made Hercules redden.

"The Swan may be graceful but when she bites you had better watch out!"

As the captain ordered half sail Furax turned to Drugi. "You will have to wait to see your road. We have a few more miles to sail."

Drugi did not mind for he had never seen as much activity nor so big a river. Little boats scurried from one bank to the other, each one seemingly laden with goods of one description or another. For the first couple of miles, there was much evidence of building until the river took a turn north-west and the gentle banks became quieter. Drugi was fascinated by the wealth of wildlife which proliferated in the water and on the shores. As the river slowly turned to give him a new vista he asked more and more questions of Furax about the wildlife they saw. Furax struggled to come up with the answers and Old Hercules found himself smiling. "It makes a change for the lad to have to answer questions. Usually, he is pestering the life out of folk with his constant interrogation.

When the boat began to slow and the sails were lowered, Drugi looked at Furax. "We are here. You see that bridge there…"

Drugi's mouth dropped open. He had never seen a bridge before, especially not a stone bridge. "The Romans are a mighty people that they can tame the river and span it like that."

They moored at the small wooden jetty. Marcus took Frann's hands. "I want you to stay on board while I go and visit with my Legate. We will be sailing with Hercules down to the Dunum."

Drugi looked like a child who has had his toys taken. "Do I have to stay too, Roman?"

"No Drugi you can come but," he said turning to Frann, "this is a dangerous frontier and a difficult walk. I would be happier if you stayed here."

She looked worried until Hercules put his arm around her shoulders, a strangely paternal act, "Don't worry love. I'll not leave without him and we can have a bit of something to eat eh?"

The bridge and the fort all looked so familiar to the troopers and Furax but to Drugi it was a constantly unique experience. The guards at the bridge recognised them but stared in awe at the giant with them. "Have you the password sir?"

Rufius laughed. "We have been away for some time and I assume that the passwords will have changed."

The optio was young and uncertain what to do. Three of the four sentries smirked at his discomfort but the fourth, an older soldier, tutted and said, "Why don't I escort them to the Prefect eh sir? That way they can't steal the fort's silver."

"Good idea."

As they walked up to the fort Drugi looked at the metalled surface beneath his feet. Furax suddenly understood and said, "Yes Drugi that is a road."

The Prefect was relieved to see them. "Your Prefect and the Legate have been worried about you. They thought you had perished in the lands beyond Rome. "He looked up at Drugi, "Now I see that you were just collecting some of the wildlife."

As they sat and drank watered wine, another new experience for Drugi, Rufius asked, "How goes the wall building sir?"

"Over the winter we made more progress than the Emperor thought we would but, since the snows began to melt we have had increasing attacks. Your lads have been kept a little busy." He took an appreciative swallow of the wine, his bulbous red nose attesting to his fondness for the fruit of the vine. "Half of my men now do duty in the wall. I can see us being moved up there as soon as they have finished the fort."

Rufius took an immediate interest. "Finished a fort? That is quick."

The Prefect looked ruefully around his well-apportioned quarters. "Yes, a little too quick for me. I have become used to the bathhouse and my comforts, still the Emperor wants experienced troops stationed there and those troops are us."

"Do you mind if we show our friend here around the fort? He has never seen one."

"Of course. Just tell him to mind his head. The buildings were made for Romans, not giants like him."

Drugi was impressed by everything, from the granary to the aqueduct and the bathhouse. No matter what happened in the future Drugi would not regret coming to Britannia with Marcus. It was a world apart from his hut and his animals and the harsh cold winters of Uiteland. Furax almost fell over laughing when Drugi stepped on to the floor warmed by the hypocaust and jumped. "Where is the fire?"

When Marcus showed him he scratched his head and asked, "How does the heat get from there to the room we were just in?"

"It travels under the ground." The look on his face told Marcus that he thought it was some magic trick.

Drugi had finished his exploration of the fort by the time Julius Demetrius arrived. The cooks had been warned by the Prefect that they would need to cook for their guests and, as Marcus and Rufius filled the Legate in with the details of their adventure, they ate. Drugi listened to not a word for he was too interested in all the foods they were eating and once again Furax had to do the explaining.

"I am pleased that you are returned safely Marcus but, I am also disappointed. Rufius has done his best to protect you but, as I can see the Sword of Cartimandua hanging from your baldric I know that you took risks to get that damned sword back."

"Legate, if it had not been for the sword then Trygg Tryggvasson would not have spared my life and this would be a moot point. Besides, as you know this is the heart of the Brigante and after the recent rebellions we need all the Brigante support we can get."

Julius Demetrius was not convinced but he had more pressing matters on his mind. "Now that you are returned we need to use your skills here. Rufius you and Gnaeus will return to Rocky Point. Gnaeus you are to be made up to acting Decurion until Decurion Marcus returns."

"From where sir?" Marcus was ready to argue with the Legate if he was sent to the other side of the country.

"We have four turma of replacements at Morbium." He looked at Marcus wryly, "you were, I believe, the training officer and horse master for the ala were you not?"

Reddening but with a sheepish grin, "Yes sir. It just seems a lifetime ago."

They all looked sadly at each other remembering that the lifetimes were Gaius' and Macro's. "I think that you need to knock them into shape. The Gallic cohort is seriously under strength and your ala needs more men. You have ten days to achieve that."

"Ten days from when sir?"

"Ten days from now. I suggest that you accompany me to my ship so that I can give my captain his orders."

With their rapid goodbyes to Rufius and Gnaeus spoken, they hurried back to the jetty. "Hercules I want you to drop Marcus and his," Julius' eyes were drawn to the pregnant Brigante woman, the two Brigante girls and Drugi, "retinue at Morbium and then I need you to sail…"

"Senator, the ship needs work. We have had a hard winter."

"I know and if I could spare you I would but with these pirates around the shores, I need you to act as a messenger. You are to return to Ostia and send this package to the Emperor's secretary. Use the Praetorian messenger at Ostia. Then you can refit and refurbish your ship."

Mollified, Hercules smiled, "Well in that case…"

"I suppose we didn't make a profit while you were gallivanting in the wild north did we?"

Sniffing his indignation Hercules said, "Well there you are wrong. We have some fine animal skins and some excellent wood which will fetch a fine price in Ostia."

"Good." As he stepped off the ship he shouted to Marcus. "Ten days mind, and that means ten days until you are here with the one hundred and twenty-eight men."

Chapter 15

The dragon ship fleet headed gingerly westwards, always nervously on the lookout for the masts of the Classis Britannica. Trygg had made it quite clear that they needed somewhere close to the mouth of the estuary where they could hide Gurt and his two ships. That meant approaching the estuary in the early hours of the morning. Trygg's ship took the lead as he and his crew were familiar with the waters of the Dunum. They were just using oar power to minimise their profile and he had a young warrior at the top of the mast. He knew from the smell that they were within two miles of the mouth of the Dunum; the land had an earthier greener smell than the tang of the sea. Suddenly the masthead lookout shouted down, "Three Roman ships lying off the entrance."

Cursing his luck he ordered the steersman to head south and run parallel with the coast. He knew of another bay some twenty miles further south. It was large enough to hide the ships but it would delay them by a day. Three Roman ships, fully armed, were just too much for his small fleet. Using a shielded candle, he signalled to the next ship to follow him. If they all repeated the instruction then they would be safe. It was an agonising wait for the ships to tack in turn and all the while he could see the thin sliver of lightening sky which heralded the dawn. He had to move faster and he ordered his rowers to increase their speed. The next ship was Snorri's and he would follow. He just hoped that the next two ships would also realise what he was doing.

By the time there was enough light to see the land they were almost at the hidden bay. There was a spit of sand which had been deposited by the river over years and by following the spit and the river, ships could be hidden from the sea. Unlike the Dunum and the Tinea, ships could travel barely half a mile before it became too shallow for any kind of ship. The other ships pulled up alongside Trygg's and he commanded them to drop anchor. Gurt was more curious than angry when he came aboard.

"There were Roman ships at the Dunum, three of them. They will have moved on by the morning."

"And if not?"

"Do not worry. I will send four of my men back up the coast. They will light a signal fire on the hill above the estuary if it is clear tomorrow, and if not then we return and wait." Gurt raised his eyebrows as an unspoken criticism. Exasperated Trygg said, "We have done the hardest part. We have reached Britannia undetected. We have plenty of provisions; a day or two longer waiting will not hurt us. Learn patience."

Not only did The Swan reach the Dunum quickly, there were still the three ships of the Classis Britannica there waiting for them. The captain grinned at Hercules as they bobbed next to each other in the choppy waters. "It seems your Legate wants you protected down to Dubris old man. You will have an Imperial escort."

"I have survived long enough without your help but I thank the Legate for his concern."

"We will wait here for your return. There is little need to hurry, by the time you have returned the tide will be against us anyway. We will leave this time tomorrow morning. Make sure you are here."

Even though the triremes did not need to worry about the tide for they had rowers; the captain had seen enough sailing ships to know that they would not be able to fight an incoming tide as fierce as the one on the Dunum. The channel was only narrow despite the fact that the estuary was wide and Hercules needed all the sea room he could get to tack his way out.

Furax was delighted. "That means I get Ailis' cooking and I don't say goodbye to Drugi until tomorrow." Hercules was also happy for he had had no time to provision his ship and the journey to Ostia was a long one.

The bridge at Morbium was as far as they could go. The ship suddenly seemed much emptier as the ex-soldiers waved their goodbyes along the road to Eboracum and the two Brigante girls said their farewells. They tearfully hugged Frann and wished her and her baby well. Frann looked seriously at the two girls. "I know your homes are nearby but should you ever need my help then come to me at the home of Marcus' brother, Decius." She looked carefully at the two of them. The girls had not thought of that aspect of their life and they headed south of the river more nervously and warily. "In the two years since you both left things may have changed."

The First Mate was left with the ship as Hercules and Furax headed down to the farm. Marcus had to go into the fort at Morbium to pick up his recruits. He knew that they would have had some training but it was important for him to find out how much. He left Frann and Drugi at the bridge as he went in to speak to the Prefect and First Spear. "I will not be long."

Drugi was happy. "I can watch the fish in the river Roman and see the animals I will soon be hunting."

"And I will look at the land I left as a child for I was born but ten miles from here." Frann was content now that her feet touched Brigante land once more. Her baby would be born in the land of his ancestors; the Mother was, indeed, all-powerful and all-seeing.

Leaving his two companions Marcus entered the fort. He was well known by all of the auxiliaries who wondered at his tale for they had all heard that he had been taken by slavers and yet here he was as large as life. First Spear was with the Prefect. "We were expecting you Decurion." The Prefect sat back in his chair, "To be honest we are relieved. First Spear has drilled your recruits with sword and spear but, as we all know, as cavalry they need to ride horses and to fight upon their backs."

"And I fucking hate horses!"

"Yes First Spear you have made that abundantly clear to everyone."

"I just didn't want the Decurion to think I hadn't done my job."

Marcus knew the Centurion well and there were close ties with his family, for his father had sacrificed his life to save First Spear and his vexillation during the Hibernian invasion. He had a sudden, terrifying thought. "There are horses aren't there?"

"Oh yes," said the Centurion indignantly, "Crapping and pissing all over my parade ground. The sooner they are out of here the better."

The Prefect shook his head. The Centurion was a good officer but his language left much to be desired. "Do you intend to take them from here Decurion?"

"Yes sir. There is an old gyrus from my fathers' time close to the farm. It will keep them out of your hair and give me the chance to get to know them." He looked at the sun through the Principia door, it was past noon already. "If you don't mind sir. I'd like to make a start."

"Right First Spear, take the Decurion to his men."

The recruits were being put through sword and shield training with the auxilia optios. First Spear barked and all movement stopped. "Right ladies. Your time here is over." Marcus smiled at the looks of relief on their faces. "The decurion here," he glared at them all, "is a particularly good friend of mine and has come to take you and show you how to ride your horses. May the Allfather help him. Go and get your gear and then fetch your horses. I want to see you all in a column of twos, now go!"

As the two officers walked towards the horse lines Marcus asked, "What are they like?"

"Oh they'll do. Quite good with spears, not quite as good with sword and shield but they know the basic commands and orders."

"Thank you for that. I appreciate it."

The old Centurion looked sadly at Marcus. "After what your father did for us it was the least we could do."

"And have you a wagon or a cart I could borrow?"

"A cart?"

Marcus suddenly became embarrassed. "I have a woman and she is, well she is with child."

First Spear slapped him on the back. "Well done, you little bugger! Yes, of course, we have a cart." He saw a soldier slouching near the stables. "Oy shit for brains, go and bring the cart from the Quartermaster and a couple of horses and be quick about it."

The cart arrived at the same time as Marcus' horse and the two officers led them to the bridge. When First Spear saw Drugi his jaw dropped. "That's not your baby is it?"

Marcus laughed. "No that is Drugi the hunter, he was a slave who helped me to escape."

"If he gets bored with hunting tell him I will have him in my cohort any time!"

Drugi helped Frann into the cart and then looked helplessly at Marcus who, mounting his own horse, shrugged, "A new skill for you Drugi, driving a cart."

Climbing aboard he grabbed the reins and gave a tentative flick; the horses did not move. Drugi looked around in panic. Marcus rode up to the rear of one and slapped it hard on the rump. The cart lurched off down the road. "Recruits! Ho!"

The column moved off, their speed dictated by the cart which moved somewhat erratically down the road, moving more like a snake than anything. Marcus shook his head, it was a good job that there was a road, otherwise, the cart could have ended up in the land of the lakes.

Ailis and her family had been warned by the voluble Furax of the imminent arrival of her son. The stoic, grey-haired lady did shed a small tear as she silently thanked The Allfather and The Mother for returning him and Macro for watching over his brother. She had never doubted that her brave son would return but, as the months had passed, she worried about how he was suffering. She had been a captive and a slave for many years and, like Marcus, her captors, the Caledonii were a cruel and uncompromising people.

Her tears shed she began to organise the sleeping arrangements and the food. Decius' wife, an excellent cook herself was sent to organise the food while Ailis fussed over the beds. She noticed Hercules standing self-consciously at one side while Furax played with the dogs. "You will be staying old friend?"

"We wouldn't want to put you out. We could always sleep at the fort."

In answer Ailis put her arm around him and cuddled him. "We wouldn't hear of it. Besides you put yourself in great danger to go and find him." Pecking him on the cheek she led him by the arm. "Come you can help we organise the beds and we can talk at the same time."

Although Hercules was uncomfortable around women, Ailis had this ability to make any man feel welcome. He eagerly followed her, the gnarled sea dog a temporary domestic servant.

"How is our boy?"

"He is well." He knew the question behind the words. "He was not treated over cruelly. He is healthy."

As they turned over the hay filled mattresses she squeezed his arm. "Thank you for that."

"There is one thing." Hercules did not like gossips but he thought that Ailis should have a warning about Frann.

A cloud passed briefly across Ailis' face. "He has a wound?"

Hercules laughed, "No, at least not a painful wound." Ailis' puzzled look made him shake his head," I am sorry domina, I am used to speaking plainly with rough sailors. Your son has taken a woman and she is with child."

The relief on Ailis' face took Hercules aback as did the tears which flowed down her face. The gruff old man did not know how to deal with tears no matter that the cause was a good one. Throwing her arms around him she said, "They are happy? Was she a captive too? How long until the birth?"

Hercules backed off, panicked by all the questions. "She is with child," he mimed a bump. "They look happy and she was a captive I believe." She threw her head back and laughed. Relieved, Hercules added, "She is Brigante I think for she spoke with the other slaves we rescued in their tongue."

"The Allfather does know all things. Thank you, Hercules. You are a true friend and we are lucky to know you."

Blushing at the compliment Hercules followed Ailis from the sleeping wing of the villa back to the kitchen. She paused at the door. "Thank you for telling me but I will not tell Decius and I will let Marcus think he tells me for the first time. It will be better that way."

Hercules was glad that he was a sailor for he could never fathom out the minds of women.

The clattering of hooves on the metalled track brought the whole household out to greet the returning hero. While Ailis and Decius threw their arms around Marcus and Decius' wife nursed their second child, the rest of the workers started in astonishment at Drugi who climbed down from the cart and yet still seemed bigger. He helped Frann down just as Ailis turned. Marcus held his mother's hand and Frann's. "This is my mother, Ailis. Mother, this is the mother of my child and the woman I wish to take as a wife, Frann."

The women all embraced and Decius came over to clasp Marcus' arm. "I was worried, brother, that I might never become an uncle." He stepped away and said wryly, "I wondered if all that riding had worn away your manhood."

Marcus punched him playfully on the shoulder. "There is nothing wrong with my manhood. I was just waiting for the right woman."

Decius glanced over at Frann. "Then you did well brother." Catching sight of Drugi he asked, "And who, in the name of the Allfather is this?"

To Drugi, Marcus said, "I apologise friend, my brother has a habit of speaking a little too plainly sometimes and forgets his manners.." To the others he said, "This is Drugi who was also a slave of the Tencteri and who helped us to escape. He is a mighty hunter; the equal of our uncle Gaelwyn."

Decius was the first to greet him. "Then you are truly a mighty hunter. Welcome to my home. And I apologise for my rudeness but your size took me by surprise. Will you stay?"

Drugi looked embarrassed. Marcus interjected, "If it is still empty I thought he could live in Gaelwyn's old hut until he knows what he wants to do and where he wishes to go. It seems... right."

Decius roared, "A splendid idea and I will enjoy speaking more with you Drugi the hunter." He began to lead them into the house but Marcus shook his head.

"I am afraid that I will have to delay my arrival for a short time. I am here because I am training recruits. When I have had them build their camp and prepared their meal, I will return to eat with you but then I must rejoin my men." He looked apologetically at Ailis and Frann who were still linked, arm in arm. "At least I will see you over the next ten days. The alternative had me on the frontier."

Ailis shook her head. "I am the wife of a soldier, son. It is your lot. And it will give us chance to get to know your bride to be. We have a wedding to plan."

The recruits were still where he had left them and they were still mounted. As he rode up they all sat upright on their mounts. Whilst at Morbium they had been told of the exploits of the Second Sallustian Ala and, more especially, the exploits of the brothers Macro and Marcus; the warrior who wielded the Sword of Cartimandua. They were in awe of him already. The fact that he had been a prisoner in barbarian lands and then escaped merely added to the legend.

Marcus halted his horse. "Thank you for being so patient but here is your first lesson; when you stop, unless there is danger nearby, dismount, for your horses are valuable and need their energy." One or two started to dismount, "Not now!" Shaking his head he realised the size of the task he would have to undertake. "Nearby is a gyrus where we will begin training but first we will have to build a camp. I will be watching you while this takes place because some of you are going to be given some responsibilities to help me. By the time we rejoin the ala some of you will be chosen men for your turma." The carrot dutifully dangled Marcus led the column off to the gyrus.

The men were exhausted by the time that they had built their camp and fed their horses. "I am returning to my farm for a meal but I will return before nightfall. Turma one, it is your duty first." He pointed to a recruit who looked attentive. "You will be in charge of the sentries until I return." The young man beamed with pleasure. "The rest of you eat and rest for tomorrow the real work of becoming a trooper begins."

Drugi had thought he would be uncomfortable sitting at the fine table eating with this fine and noble family but he was made inordinately welcome. Decius, in particular, kept plying him with questions whilst Decius' wife, Mara kept filling his plate whenever he wasn't looking. Furax just enjoyed something he had never experienced whilst growing up, a family and, for once, he was content to sit silently and let the atmosphere wash over him. Hercules the eldest man in the room also felt the same. Married to The Swan and the sea this was as close as he would ever get to children and grandchildren and he too relished the moment.

The main topic, of course, was Marcus' rescue but all conversation around the table stopped when Marcus and Drugi spoke of the hawk. "As soon as it appeared then I knew I would be rescued or I would escape. I knew not how but I knew that it would happen."

Ailis nodded. "We too saw the hawk and knew that your brother was watching." She paused. "Have you seen it since you left this island?"

"No. Not once."

"Perhaps our brother has fulfilled his oath?"

Marcus shook his head. "I don't know. I feel, and that is all, a feeling; I feel that he is still watching." He shrugged. "As he only appears to arrive when there is danger, perhaps that is a good thing."

Frann spoke and as she did, Drugi nodded, "I do not think that Trygg has forgotten us. Taking back the sword will have hurt his pride, and his standing with the tribe. He has grand ideas for the tribe and the sword was part of it. I am just glad to be away from the slave hall." Ailis touched her arm, remembering as she did so her time as a slave.

Drugi's deep sonorous voice was remarkably soothing but his words were heavily laden with frightening thoughts. "As slaves Frann and I were unimportant but we had ears and we listened as they spoke of their plans. The council and Chief Trygg were going to use the sword as a means of uniting all the smaller tribes against the Suebi. There would be only one person to lead them, one king…"

Marcus nodded, "Trygg." Frann and Drugi nodded. "Then we had better take precautions. I will warn Nanna and Hercules can tell the Prefect at Morbium of our fears. And now," Marcus stood, "I at least have work to do and I must leave my family," he spread his arms to include all of them, "to continue to enjoy this happy event."

After he and Frann had said their farewells she returned to the house she now called home. "What did he mean take precautions?"

Decius waved an airy arm around the room. "You may have noticed that we are more than a home, we are a small fort. We will dig the ditches even deeper, spread lillia and keep a closer watch." He looked sadly at Frann. "This has happened before and the last time my father died defending this house. You need have no fear, sister. This Chief Trygg has bitten off more than he can chew if he thinks he can take on the Aurelius brothers."

Marcus found it hard the next day to concentrate on the training of his recruits. They were all keen and enthusiastic and none had so far run. Marcus knew that desertion after initial training was an issue for some thought being a trooper meant just riding around all day killing barbarians- the reality was somewhat different. The main reason for his distraction was Frann. He knew that his family would make her feel welcome but he felt guilty that he was not there. As they all stood there next to their horses, he knew that he would have to start.

"Gentlemen, I am going to divide you into two halves. It will make the simulation of a real skirmish more realistic." He strode along the front rank trying to identify faces; he would need some help from those amongst his recruits who showed the most aptitude. "The Centurion who trained you is an infantry man. They like to fight shoulder to shoulder with a line of interlocked shields. In the cavalry we can't do it that way. The horse's arse gets in the way." They all laughed at his joke. "That is before the horse's arse sat on the horse gets to work." His second attempt at humour visibly relaxed them." He held up a branch he had cut from the wood. "I want you all to go and cut yourself a branch about the height of a man. We are going to hold it like a spear. I don't want to lose too many of you too early."

When they returned he divided them up and then had them mount. He instructed them to hold the shield in their left hand and the branch in their right. This was the first time they had had to hold two such unwieldy objects and they found it hard. One of them raised his branch, "Sir, how do we hold the reins?"

"In your shield hand but eventually you will have to ride without using your reins such as when you are in close combat and when you use a bow."

Another recruit shouted, "use a bow!"

Grinning Marcus shouted, "That comes later. You will need to learn to ride with your knees and your body weight but before we start that you need to know the most important lesson of all," They all looked at him intently, "how to fall off the horse." Some of them thought he was joking. "I am deadly serious. In my last battle in Britannia, a Hibernian struck at my horse and I was thrown over his head. Had I not known how to fall I would have been dead."

He dismounted. "I will show you the technique." He put down his branch and took up his spear. There was a small raised mound of earth and he used that for his demonstration. He ran up one side and, when he reached the top he discarded his spear, tucked his head under and rolled with the shield taking the blow of landing. They applauded but Marcus silenced them with a raised hand. "It is easy from that height but when you fall from the back of a horse the blow is harder. Use the shield to take the blow and relax, you need to roll. This is something you will need to practise on your own after we have finished training but remember, if you are in the front rank you will need to protect yourselves from the hooves of the second rank and, if you are the second rank, you need to be able to move your horse to avoid unhorsed troopers." The looks on their faces showed Marcus that they had understood the complications of charging into battle on a horse. "Right, we are going to simulate a charge at each other at the trot. When you are within ten paces of an opponent throw your branch. It will not fly far and it will not hit unless you are very lucky, but it will show you the problems you face. You need to throw and then protect yourself with your shield as your opponent will be doing the same."

Their first charge, even at a trot, was, as he expected, an unmitigated disaster. He had counted on that fact. Almost a third of them fell off while another group couldn't control their mounts and ended up charging an empty section of the field. When they finally sorted themselves out they looked totally dejected. "Don't worry about that disaster. No-one is hurt but you need to concentrate more. Your horses are good horses but they need control. Keep a tight grip with your left hand. Grip the flanks of the horse with your knees and ankles. Make the horse do what you want not what he does. When you throw your branch, throw from the shoulder, don't lean back as you did when you were on foot. Now let's try it again."

Over the course of the morning they gradually improved but by the noon break they were exhausted and a number of them had the bruises to show they had either fallen or been struck by a lucky branch. Marcus wondered how they would react to having to prepare their own food when he heard the wheels of a cart and saw Drugi and Frann appear. The former slave did not look anything sat on the cart but when he descended the recruits' jaws dropped to a man. Drugi was used to this reaction, "Your mother thought they might be hungry Roman and she has sent bread, cheese and some ham." He winked at Marcus, "And to stop me becoming lost she sent your woman to help me. You see to your woman, I will feed these boys." As Marcus helped Frann down, he heard Drugi roar, in a voice which would have made First Spear proud. "Get in one line. One man comes for the food for four of you." They looked at him. "You Romans can count?"

While Marcus and Frann watched, Drugi fed the whole contingent and then he came over to them. "You were right Roman this is a good place to live. I thank you for my new home it is a fine hut and I will honour your uncle."

"You are welcome Drugi."

"He looked sheepish and then pulled, from under the seat of the cart an enormous ram's horn. "I found this in Gaelwyn's hut, hidden beneath some animal skins. What is it?"

"I haven't seen that in years. It is the Brigante war horn. It was used to summon help or sound the charge in the time before the Romans came. It hasn't been used since I was a boy." Drugi looked at it in anticipation. "Go on, my friend, try it." Drugi put his mouth to the horn and blew. It sounded like a small dog breaking wind. "No, you need to make this sound." Marcus put his lips to the back of his hand and blew, much as a child would.

"Ah, now I see." The next time Drugi blew, the sound echoed across the hills and flocks of birds lifted in the air. The recruits looked up in shock.

Drugi looked expectantly at Marcus who nodded, "Of course, keep it. It seems fitting somehow to pass from one hunter to another. He looked nervously at Frann. He hoped that she too had been made welcome but… "And you Frann, what of you?"

"Your family are so kind and I am very happy." She patted her bump, "And, more importantly, our son is content." She looked at him seriously, "You are a warrior and you lead men. Do not worry about me for I am safe and happy. There will be no men coming in the night to take me." She pointed at the recruits. "This is what you do and I am proud of you."

The recruits did not know Marcus but they did notice a change in him during the training session following the meal; he was happier and full of energy. By the time they made their weary way back to their camp they were exhausted, bruised and mentally drained but they had made huge progress. They could charge with their javelins and throw them without falling off. They could halt their horses rather than chasing over the countryside and they had a confidence about them that had not been there in the morning. In short, while they were not troopers, they looked, at least, as though they might become them in time.

Nanna had reached the farm just about the time that Marcus was doing his last rounds around his camp. Although not lonely, Nanna missed the company of others; she got on well with her servants but that is what they were, servants. Her husband was many miles away and so she took the opportunity of visiting Ailis to discuss the problems of these pirates. She was a little sceptical for she had not seen any evidence of raiders although she did know that Marcus had been taken. She enjoyed riding through this country. Her childhood had been filled with horses and now, after her marriage to Metellus, she had the chance to work with and to ride fine horses. It was a pleasure to be riding through the crisp late winter evening, the hooves crunching through the early frost, anticipating the warm welcome at the farm. She had told her servants not to expect her back for she knew that Ailis would expect her to stay. When she had first arrived she had felt guilty about imposing on her neighbours but she quickly discovered that Ailis enjoyed her company, especially at night for she missed her husband. As she had said to Nanna on one of her earlier visits, "It wasn't as though we spent each evening chattering to each other, more often than not we sat in silence but it was a companionable silence, and that I miss."

The extra security at the farm was obvious as soon as Nanna approached the entrance for there were alert guards watching. The gate swung opened silently and Ailis was there to greet her. Ailis was always happy and cheerful but she appeared to have a twinkle in her eye. She could not wait to tell her friend the news. "I am to be a grandmother again!"

Nanna was delighted. "That Decius, he cannot keep his hands off that Mara."

"Oh no Nanna, it is Marcus. He has a wife and she is Brigante."

Realising that there was a tale here Nanna could not wait to meet the woman who had won the heart of Marcus. Nanna had more than a soft spot for Marcus; he had saved her from the barbarians and she knew she owed her life and freedom to him. As soon as she saw Frann she embraced the girl. "What a bonny girl! Marcus is, truly, a lucky man!"

Frann could not believe her good fortune. Not only was her new family welcoming but all those associated with the family appeared to be the same. Having spent years in captivity it was something she appreciated. On their first night together Ailis had told Frann the true story of her captivity. It was a tale she had not told her sons but she could tell a fellow slave and the two women bonded immediately. It was the reason Ailis had behaved the way she had for she understood, above all others, the pain and the horror, not to mention the degradation, of slavery.

Chapter 16

Gurt watched the stern of Snorri's ship as it edged northwards up the east coast of Britannia. The stern light was his only guide as it was still not yet dawn. This was the second time they had made the trip for the previous night there had been no fire and Trygg had retraced his steps back to their hidden estuary. Gurt had not been convinced that there were any ships.

"Your men might not have reached there. It could be that there are no Roman ships and we are wasting our time going backwards and forwards."

Trygg knew his men and had chosen well. "They will have reached the hill and there will be Roman ships."

The discussion, if one could call a couple of words a discussion, had ended swiftly with Gurt dismissed like a kitchen slave. He did not enjoy the experience. Now, a whole day later, he glanced up at the cliffs which towered above them. They were relatively close in for Trygg said that the water was deep enough for them up to fifty paces from the rocks; Gurt did not like having to rely on another captain's judgement but he had little choice. The six ships they had were a large group of vessels and Gurt knew it made observation easier but he would have preferred to be further away from the sharp teeth like rocks which seemed to snarl and roar from the white capped water at the foot of the towers of stone.

The whole of the crew were nervous; to venture this close to Roman ships had been bad enough once but to risk it a second time seemed to be tempting the Norns. It was hard not to order the steersman to head for home but then Gurt thought of the face he would lose. This way he could follow the infamous Trygg and any blame for any disaster would be laid at his door. Suddenly a light flared from the top of the cliff. The ships were gone! Excitement and fear gripped the pirate captain in equal measure. They would gain some plunder but they would be taking eggs from the eagle's nest and hoping that the eagle stayed away; it was a gamble with great rewards but should the Roman eagle return then many hearths at Gurtstead would be cold.

Dawn's first fingers began to spread out across the black sea as the six ships closed slowly towards the estuary. Glimmers of light showed Gurt that it was indeed a wide estuary. He became aware that he could make out the ships ahead of Snorri's and they seemed to be pulling away from the final two in the line. His first panic subsided as he remembered that they had to get upriver and moored before dawn truly broke. The place where they had captured the Roman was deemed to be the best place as it was overhung with huge trees and ships could only be seen from the riverbank. Snorri's boat began to turn to the northern bank and Gurt prayed that Snorri knew the passage as well as his chief. He had been impressed with the Tencteri lieutenant for he was quiet and modest with the ability to listen. Gurt found that he could talk with him whereas when he spoke with Trygg he felt he was being talked down to. There was a slight levee on the north bank and as they approached it Gurt saw Snorri order his oars up as the ship was steered close to the bank.

"Up oars. Follow the Tencteri."

When they finally reached the bank Gurt saw that the levee was deceptively high and effectively hid the ship from view on the northern side. The southern bank was covered in heavy foliage and mooring was difficult. Here there were two tall stumps each about a hundred paces apart, perfect mooring posts. As Gurt met Snorri on the bank he mentioned this and how fortunate it was.

Snorri had laughed, "Not fortunate, we cut those trees down many years ago when we first came." He pointed to the other side of the river. "The river is wide here and we can easily turn around. Chief Trygg will have a harder task for where he moors the river will be narrow. He will need to turn his boats around. We will be the first to the plunder."

Most of the men were now on the bank. The six men detailed to watch the boats were already building a shelter and putting out fishing lines. As the oldest members of the crews, they had had their fill of running through enemy lands; they were quite happy to wait, watch and fish.

As the men adjusted helmets and shields Gurt could not help but notice how much better equipped Snorri's men were compared with his. Many had leather or mail armour; some was

Roman and some Suebi. Their weapons were also of higher quality with short Roman swords and javelins and the longer Suebi blades showing that they had taken the weapons from their previous owners. When they returned from this raid he hoped his men would be as well armed as his present allies. Snorri detailed two of his warriors to bring up the rear. When Gurt gave him a questioning look the Tencteri shrugged. "They know this land. If we get separated then you will have someone to guide you."

Gurt nodded, that made sense. With his shield and axe strapped to his back and his arms free he was able to move easily down the well-worn river trail. Snorri came down the line checking that all their equipment was secured. When he reached Gurt he pointed to his helmet. Gurt was proud of the helmet which had a nasal and the wings of a hawk protruding from each side.

"I would carry that until we near the village if I were you."

"Why? " The annoyance was tempered by curiosity.

"We have to move quickly and we are unlikely to be surprised. I have scouts out. This way will be more comfortable." He grinned, "But it is your choice." It was only then that Gurt noticed that the Tencteri were all bareheaded. The practical chief complied.

The trail along the bank was well worn but the recent rain and snow had made it somewhat slippery. After one of the warriors had slipped in and been helped to the shore, while his companions laughed and jeered, the remainder watched their footing and kept a safer distance from their fellows. They ran for about a mile and a half, by which time dawn had truly broken and Gurt could see the hills rising on the southern side of this flat valley. Trygg had done well to find this land of plenty. It was difficult to see them from the north and any observers to the south would have to have a boat. He was beginning to feel tired after the unexpected run when Snorri, at the front held up his hand and they all stopped. When those at the front began to don helmets and unsheathe weapons, Gurt's band copied their actions. Gurt made his way forwards. He had not minded following before but if there was going to be fighting, then, as chief, he wanted to make the decisions and to show them his bravery.

Snorri's scouts were there and Snorri held up a hand to silence them until Gurt arrived. "They have just opened the gates and they are loading a small merchantman with what looks like iron."

Snorri nodded. "Odin is with us for she would have spotted our boats and raised the alarm had we sailed close; as it is we can take the town and the ship." He looked at Gurt. "Eabrycg is the large port on this river. They have a long jetty and a long wall around the settlement. There are four gates, one on the river, one opposite and one on each side. We will attack the eastern and the northern gates. Tell your men to keep low. It is just two hundred paces away."

The land through which they were travelling was marshy and clung to their boots making their progress slow. The next time Snorri raised his hands they were but fifty paces from the eastern gate. Snorri waved Gurt and his men to head towards the northern gate. There was a shallow ditch which ran around the wooden wall but beyond it, closer to the raiders was a low line of bushes and Gurt led his men to the next gate.

There were no guards at the eastern gate; they looked to be helping load the ship and Snorri did not wait for Gurt to reach his objective. Raising his war axe he stood and they raced through the open gate. At that hour of the day there were few people about and the ones who were around were busily working at the quayside. They were not seeking slaves this time and Snorri's men had been given one instruction- no prisoners and no survivors. One of the sentries was lurching his way back through the settlement to his post on the eastern gate. He was armed with little more than a cudgel and looked to be half asleep. He glanced up to see the war axe scything down to take his head. His dead eyes watched as the raiders hurtled towards the ship. Out of the corner of his eye Snorri saw Gurt and his men enter and began to spread out towards the western gate. Trygg had told them both that he wanted no one to survive. His mistake on his last visit was to leave people alive who could raise the alarm. That would not happen on this visit.

The jetty had, perhaps twenty people busily loading lumps of raw iron ore on to the fat bellied trader ready to sail down to Eboracum and the enormous profits which awaited them there.

Even the sentries who were helping to load the ship were unarmed as they had laid down their weapons to help load before the morning tide. The captain saw the horde plunging down the small road to the jetty and shouted, "Cast off!"

It was a futile gesture for they had neither the time nor the opportunity to carry out the action. Snorri's men fell upon them like wolves in a sheep pen. Backhanding one unfortunate docker into the water with his shield Snorri leapt aboard and took off the captain's head in one blow of his war axe. The rest of the crew either fell to the deck to beg mercy or threw themselves overboard. Whilst despatching those who cowered on the deck Snorri shouted to the archer next to him, "Kill those in the water! No-one lives." The men in the water either drowned or were easily hit from almost point blank range by the Tencteri bowmen.

Gurt and his men had completed their mission and men stood guard on the three other gates. They then went from house to house, killing all who were cowering within. The men were lucky for they were slaughtered immediately but the women and the girls had to suffer the gang rape by men hungry for women after more than a week at sea and the dubious pleasures of a male only voyage.

When their appetites had been satiated Gurt and his lieutenants joined Snorri on the trader. "This is a welcome bonus."

"Aye Chief Gurt. Trygg will be pleased for there will be much profit here." Gurt's fertile imagination was working out how best to use this windfall and he greedily licked his lips in anticipation. "If you detail some of your men to crew we can sail her downstream to wait with the boats."

Gurt tried to find some weakness in Snorri's idea, some advantage to be had by his chief but he could see none. It was obvious that the trader would have to be escorted for there were too many pirates to allow it to sail alone. "Aye I will do. What next?"

"Have a short rest and some food and then down the river to the next settlement. Chief Trygg may have taken it already but that is where we meet." Gurt had obviously not been listening when Trygg had detailed their plan. "These are the largest two settlements on the river before Morbium. We can sail closer to Morbium which is where we think we will find the sword and there are many smaller villages just off the river."

Chief Trygg's band had tied their ships up as Snorri had done and they had also left six guards with the four ships. He led his men through the woods until they came to the open ground before the settlement. He had not been certain that it would have been settled again since his last visit but he had to find out. Ormsson and Sigurd were two young boys, not yet warriors but, if they claimed their first blood kill on this raid they would be. Trygg called them over and the hero worship and nervous energy was evident in both of them as they hopped from foot to foot whilst receiving their instructions. "This is your first raid as my scouts and all the warband brothers are watching you. I want the two of you to skirt along the woods and scout out the village. Do not let them see you. I need to know how many guards there are and how many people you see. The gates should be open but if they are not then do not worry, just count the people you see. Go all the way around making sure that you count them all. I am more concerned with how accurate you are rather than how swift you return." He put an arm on each of the boys. "If you do not count well then some of these men will die and that will be on your heads. The last time you did this you were watching others, you are now the eyes and ears of the band. Now go."
 Orm watched his son race off and prayed to Odin that he would do well. Orm still had the disgrace of the escaped captives to face once they returned to Hjarno-By; if his son did well then the Chief might consider that as mitigation when handing out his punishment. The other way would be for a brave or heroic deed from Orm but he did not think that this village would give him the chance.
 Snorri and his men had made good time from Eabrycg although Gurt and his men were out of breath with the unexpected exertion and struggled to keep up with the Tencteri. Snorri reported to Chief Trygg while their allies gathered their breath. "We had good fortune."
 "About time!"

Snorri shrugged, the Norns were the Norns, and you could not fight against them. "We found a ship laden with iron; we sent it to the other ships. All the other goods we took. There was little silver and no gold but we did find the black stone and much timber. We put it all on the ship."

"You have done well Snorri. The ship was indeed a gift from the gods."

Gurt had got his breath back. "The ship is mine you agreed, you just wanted the sword."

Trygg turned to the red faced pirate and his mouth opened in the grin of a wolf about to devour its dinner. "We will see, Gurt. In this land you have to earn what you get and fight to keep what you have. When we return to Uiteland we will discuss who owns what."

Gurt knew he was outnumbered but there were more of his crew with the boats. It would be likely that Trygg would suffer more casualties. He would bide his time. The chief was right, it did not matter and was not a problem until they came to Uiteland. Now their fortunes and their fate were bound together. He nodded his acquiescence.

The two boys came racing back. "The gates have just opened and there are but five sentries. We counted thirty people but there may be more inside."

"You have done well Sigurd and Ormsson. You may well become warriors this voyage. Now go around the village and wait a thousand paces up the river. Watch for any who come down and try to escape." The two boys scurried off delighted to be given another chance to prove themselves. "Gurt you take your men, follow the boys and you approach the village from the far side. Snorri take the north side. I will take this side. Attack when you hear me attack." He turned to Gurt, "You must make sure that no-one escapes along the river. Even if you are too late to attack the village you will stop and kill all the refugees." Gurt nodded. He did not mind if Snorri and Trygg's men suffered all the casualties.

The warriors who trotted up to the walled village were not worried. The last time they had come there they had easily taken it and this time would be no different. In contrast the people who had rebuilt and re-settled the hill top refuge had never imagined that it would be assaulted again. Refugees from other places had migrated to this place for its river, its hill and its walls. They were determined that they would not suffer again. The new headman had told them all that, once the land had dried out, they would deepen the ditches and raise the heights of the walls. It would become a second Morbium. As the silent barbarians crept up to the walls the ditches were still shallow and the walls not repaired. The headman's promises were as empty as the wind and the people were going to pay the price.

The one lesson they had learned was to keep the gates closed and a sentry upon the walls. The young man who had the dubious honour of watching the river could barely get his words out as he saw the mailed and armoured demons flooding up from the river. "We are under attack!"

Those few men who had weapons raced to get them. The women hid their children where they could and then picked up anything which could be used as a weapon. They had heard what had happened on the last raid and were determined that they would not end their days as slaves. There was one woman and her child who would not become slaves because she was going to leave. Deadra had hidden with her son Aed, the last time the raiders had come. All of her family had either been taken or killed. There were just the two of them left and she would survive. She saw that the western gate was ajar and she grabbed her young son and ran as fast as his eight year old legs could manage towards the west. They slipped out and she rolled them down the bank, beneath the elder trees and bramble bushes to land under a willow tree next to the river. Back in the village an eagle eyed villager closed the gate and they prepared for the attack. Deadra and Aed ran along the bank until they heard the noises in the bushes above- it was more of the enemy. They lay there shivering in fear as Gurt's band tramped towards the fight.

Trygg's band had the hardest task for the hill curved gently upwards, sapping legs unused to walking. Had the villagers had arrows then the attackers would have fallen like wheat to a scythe but as it was they were able to make the top easily. The gate was always the weakest point and, leading a wedge of warriors, Trygg hurled himself at the already weakened wooden gate. The weight of fifteen burly barbarians, with armour and shields was too much for the gate and it disintegrated before the force. Once inside it was a repetition of Eabrycg once more; this time with Trygg's men satiating their carnal desires. By the time Snorri and Gurt broke in there was no-one left alive and they searched for the few meagre possessions left by a village twice destroyed.

The path by the river curved in a long loop and the mother and son made good time for at least a mile and then they struck disaster. The heavy rains had flooded the flood plain and the path they were following was under water. They would have to cut across the open fields to the upper path half a mile away and there was no cover. All the while they did so they would be clearly visible. Deadra had no choice and they began to run as quickly as they could across the muddy, slippery fields. As they ran, her son constantly stopping to wait for his mother, she kept glancing over her shoulder for any sign that there were warriors in pursuit. She had to pause at the bank which led to the path as she could not catch her breath.

"Are you ill mother?"

"No son. Just tired." She grabbed her son by the shoulders, "If anything happens to me then you must leave me and tell the people lower down the valley that there are raiders."

The boy shook his head, "I could not leave you."

Deadra gave a sad half smile. "If I tell you so then you will have to leave me but fear not for if you live then I shall live in your heart. Now promise me." Unable to speak the boy nodded his unspoken promise. "Good. Now help your mother up this bank."

Trygg was impatient for his men to finish their examination of the village. He had known they would not be enriched by the raid; that was not the point. He wanted their presence on the river to be hidden from the Romans and those higher up the valley. He felt a thrill of excitement run down his spine. He was about to venture further up the Dunum than he had before. It was all new territory to him but it was also dangerous territory. He knew that there was a Roman fort somewhere up the valley but he knew not where it was. He was a cautious chief and he signalled for Snorri. He took him to one side. "Have

Harald take eight men and the goods we have acquired. Tell him to return to the ships and then bring one back to here."

Snorri threw him a curious look. "Just one?"

"We cannot afford more of our men away from the attack and I do not trust these women Gurt has brought. No, one boat will be enough should we reach here and find we need a speedy departure. Tell him to face the boat down river and moor in the middle."

When Snorri returned and nodded that his instructions had been given the chief roared. "We leave now! From this place onwards we are in danger from many enemies. Do not let your guard drop for an instant and remember- no prisoners. Snorri, scouts out."

Snorri ran up to Sigurd and Ormsson. "You two come with me. We are the scouts. "The two boys puffed up with pride, they were to be scouts and not just that but scouts with the chief's right hand man. Like two hunting dogs they sped off along the path. Unlike Deadra they did not plunge down the bank but kept to the escarpment. The sharp eyed Sigurd saw that the path disappeared into a new lake and pointed to the right where there was another, lesser path. When Snorri reached them he nodded. "Good lad. You will make a good scout. Now on."

The two boys were younger than Snorri who was heavily armed and they made good time. They could see, from their high vantage point, that the river took a large loop away from them but came back to them a mile along. They trotted on, both pleased that they had saved their warband a mile of worthless walking. Ormsson shielded his eyes against the thin, cold, winter sun. They would have just a couple of hours of daylight left. They knew that they would have to seek a camp soon for the nights were still cold.

It was Sigurd who saw the woman and the boy some way ahead. While Sigurd kept his eye on her Ormsson ran back the hundred paces to Snorri. "There is a woman and a child. They are heading west."

Not wishing to waste breath Snorri ran up to Sigurd who pointed them out. He was not sure if the two boys could take the woman and the child and so he led them. "We have to catch those two. Follow all my instructions. When I tell you go left and right of them and we will surround them."

Deadra had hoped that the Mother was with her and that she and her son would find sanctuary. She knew that the nearest farm was over a mile away but she began to believe that they would escape and then, glancing over her shoulder, she saw three men pursuing her. One was clearly a warrior from his axe and helmet. They would soon catch them and she took a momentous decision. She pretended to stumble. When Aed came back she said, "I have hurt my leg you must leave me."

"No!"

She pointed behind her. "See, they come!" Kissing him she pushed him down the trail and, as he tearfully ran away, she stood and plunged down the bank to the river. She would at least draw off some of the pursuers.

Snorri saw the women run down the levee. Two of them would follow her. The boy was small and Sigurd could follow him. "Sigurd, follow the boy, Ormsson with me."

The woman had her son's survival in her heart and she ran across the muddy fields as fast as she could. She stumbled once and, as she rose, picked up the small branch brought there by the floodwaters. She ran straight for the river. Behind her she could hear her pursuer's feet sloshing in the mud. She could not know it but Snorri was slowing, weighed down by his weapons and it was the boy Sigurd who was closing. The bank of the river rose, three paces before her and she turned and swung the branch like a club. Sigurd had almost been on the woman and was not expecting the blow which cracked into the side of the head. He fell like a stone. Deadra ran up to the bank and along the muddy riverbank. It was there that her good fortune deserted her. Just when freedom beckoned, she slipped on the bank and fell into the swiftly flowing waters. Her exhaustion, her heavy clothes and her inability to swim all conspired to quickly end her life and the brave Brigante mother slid beneath the black and icy waters praying that her son survive.

Aed was angry and that anger gave his feet and legs extra energy. He had watched, with his mother, when the raiders had come the last time and he knew what they did to women. He knew what they would be doing to his mother and he wanted to run back and stop them but he had promised his mother and he would live and he would warn everyone of their danger. The trail suddenly dropped ten paces down a steep bank. Already slippery with the mud he barely controlled his descent as he half ran and half slid down the slope. As he ran on he did not know that he had just made the path a deadly slide of shiny mud.

Ormsson was proud that he would be the one to capture the boy who he had seen was but a little younger than he. He was not gaining on him yet but he knew that he would. When he came to the slippery bank he kept running. His feet were swept from under him and he went into the air to crash on his back. The gnarled knob on the tree trunk smacked into the back of his head and, for a few moments he lay there, blacked out. When he came to he gingerly stood and came down the bank holding onto the branches and bushes to the side. He set off once more in pursuit but the energy had been knocked from his legs by his fall.

As night began to fall Aed began to believe he had escaped. He had seen no lights of any buildings and he knew he had to find somewhere to rest. They would be following down the path and he took a bold decision, he would cross the river. They could not follow him across water. He made his way down the bank to the river. Many trees and branches had been washed along in the floodwaters and were caught up at the bank. There was still enough light to see across the river and, selecting a broken branch big enough to move and, hopefully, support his weight he pushed out into the icy waters. The chill took his breath away and the current began to carry him downstream, towards his pursuers. He kicked hard and the tree began to drift across the river. His leg action directed the floating lifeline and he suddenly felt mud beneath his feet. He scrambled up the bank and rolled into the bush which afforded him a hiding place. He watched the path on the opposite bank and saw his pursuer, now just a single boy who ran along the path. Aed held his breath as the boy paused where he had plunged off the path but then relaxed as he carried on. He waited a few moments and then, leaving his lair headed south, away from the river.

Snorri and his two scouts looked shamefaced when they reported that a boy had escaped them. Sigurd's face showed the marks of the blow but he would not boast of it as it came from a woman. Trygg's face hid the anger he felt but it would do no good to berate his scouts in front of the others. It was but a boy and they had achieved much already. The valley was now ripe for their plunder; the sleepy settlements would soon feel the wrath of the men from the east.

Chapter 17

The raiders found the small farmhouse soon after they gave up the search for the boy. The palisade which they found was to keep their animals enclosed rather than intruders out. The extended family of the grandmother, son, wife and five children made a good living close to the river. The regular flooding of their river side field fertilised the earth and it yielded a healthy crop. They had managed to keep alive many of their animals through the harsh winter and the farmer was already anticipating an increase in their numbers. Sadly all that ended when the hungry and tired warriors exploded into the quiet of their hut. Trygg left his men to it and he wandered to view the land to the west. Inside the females, regardless of age were all ravaged and then killed. The males all died mercifully quickly. Even as Trygg watched the sunset and the river snaking along westward to its source high in the hills, vaguely visible in the distance, the animals were being slaughtered to provide sustenance for the victorious easterners.

Gurt joined Trygg, "We have had a successful day. Are all your raids as successful?"

"I think that in all my visits to this land I have lost but ten warriors. I plan well and my men know what they are doing." In another man Trygg's words would have sounded boastful but Gurt had come to realise that this chief was very careful and he was learning a great deal.

"Snorri tells me that this is new territory for you."

"Aye. "He pointed to the river glistening red in the setting sun. "But the river flows from the west, you can see it shining in the distance. If we follow it up then we can make our escape easily."

"The ships could get as far as this place easily."

"True and tomorrow we will send some warriors back to bring up another two ships but remember that the men we use to bring the boats cannot fight and we do not know yet who or how many we face."

Behind them, his warriors had lit a fire and the smell of roasting meat began to fill the air. Gurt glanced at the numbers of warriors. Perhaps Trygg was being over cautious. To his eye, they had plenty of men and the opposition thus far had been pathetic; one boatload could have taken both villages. He sniffed the air appreciatively. This might be a land to visit regularly, without his allies. Now that he had one visit he would no longer need the Tencteri.

The recruits found muscles they had never used before as they stiffly climbed out of their tents. Many sported healthy blue bruises, marks of honour from their falls and their blows. The crisply frozen ground cracked underfoot as they began to saddle their horses. Marcus was already in the gyrus mounted and surveying the young recruits as they struggled to mount.

When they were all before him in their temporary turmae the decurion addressed them. "Yesterday we learned to charge, halt and withdraw; all necessary and useful skills. Today we learn vital skills." He took a javelin in his right hand and galloped hard at the man-sized target erected at the far end. He rode to within thirty paces, hurled the missile and spun around to return to the awestruck recruits. He did not need to turn around to see that he had hit the target, it had only been thirty paces and it had not been a difficult throw. He had wanted his men to have an attainable target and he hoped that they would all achieve some success to give them confidence.

"The vital skill we will learn is to charge, throw and retreat. Firstly we will just charge in turn and throw. Once we have achieved the feat of hitting the target every time we will learn how to do it effectively"

One recruit raised his hand. "Sir, don't we use swords?"

"Good question and yes we do but the enemy you will be fighting will always outnumber us, they are, generally skilful swordsmen and we need to whittle them down and demoralise them before it comes to swordplay. When we ride we have three javelins each. Two of them are to throw in controlled volleys, the third you use as an offensive weapon; you stab down with it like a spear. Only when you have used that do you draw your blade." The recruit with the question started to raise his hand again, "The javelin gives us an advantage as it is longer than the swords of our enemies. By the time we use the sword we would hope that they would be ready to flee. When you chase a routed barbarian warband your sword comes in to its own. The only way they can escape is by lying on the ground and, eventually, we will train your horses to trample men lying prone. That is for the future. Each turma has ten targets each. I will be watching."

Inevitably some of the more enthusiastic riders fell off as they attempted to emulate Marcus. Others totally missed the target but the ones who were successful were spotted by Marcus who made a mental note of them; they were the potential leaders. By the noontime break their horses were ready for a rest and after their bread and the remains of the previous day's ham and cheese Marcus lined them up again.

"Before we attempt this manoeuvre on horseback we will practise it on foot." He walked up to two of the more successful troopers from turma one. "What are your names?"

"Marius sir."

"Livius sir."

"You two will be the acting chosen men of this turma. Marius, stand here and Livius behind him." He turned to the rest of the turma. "Form two lines alongside your chosen men." When they were ready the rest of the recruits watched in eager anticipation at this strange looking drill. "Right turma one you are going to trot forwards when I have given the command to throw then you will turn to your left and form a line behind the other line which will advance." They looked confused. Marcus laughed. "You will find it much easier with the commands. Just listen and obey." Livius and Marius nodded. "Turma one, trot, Marius' rank throw and turn, Livius throw and turn."

Surprisingly they all managed to turn the right way and many of the javelins actually fell close to the targets. "You have now completed a manoeuvre which always brings us victory. Now later, when the horses are rested we will do this on horseback. Not as easy on a horse but you will learn. In battle, of course, we just say front rank throw and we don't say turn. You will all do that yourselves, instinctively. Now turma two; let's see how well you do."

By the end of a tiring afternoon, Marcus was pleased with their progress and they could all perform the charge and volley.

The Legate would be pleased. He would be able to return to Rocky Point in eight days with four well-trained turmae.

The warband set off before dawn. Eight men had returned for the ships and the depleted raiders trotted down the path. By noon they had reached signs of life, there was a large village atop a small mound. The smoke which drifted from its huts identified its occupation by large numbers of villagers. The river looped around the settlement giving it a sense of security which was not justified. Trygg sent Snorri around one side whilst he and Gurt approached from the front gate. The peaceful villagers were all going about their daily business. Even in the incursions from the north by the Caledonii and the Hibernian raids they had escaped notice as they were tucked away in a quiet part of the valley, far enough from the roads and trails to be ignored. They felt immune to attack. Trygg was about to change that. He had ordered Snorri to take some prisoners. What he needed, this far from familiar territory, was intelligence. He had no intention of blundering into a Roman fort and he felt certain that one would be close by. Once again the assault proved remarkably easy and followed the same pattern as the others. The difference this time was they had four prisoners, one woman, one old man and two young men. Snorri brought them to Trygg bound and petrified.

His time with Marcus and Frann had given Trygg enough of the language for him to question the prisoners. As Gurt heard him he resolved to learn to speak languages for he saw that it brought knowledge and power.

Trygg took a stick and drew the river in the muddy soil. He made a mark. "We are here." He made another mark, "Here is the sea." He handed the stick to one of the young men. "Where are Romans?"

In answer the young man spat in Trygg's face. His warriors began to surge forwards but Trygg held up his hand. He took out his knife and cut the cord holding the young man's breeks up. They fell to the floor revealing thin white legs and a trickle of urine running down them. In one motion Trygg took his knife and sliced off the man's manhood. He screamed and fell to the floor, bleeding heavily, although not mortally, from the wound.

Trygg gave the stick to the second man, the bloodied knife still in his hand. "Where are the Romans?"

The young man looked from the old man to the woman, panic spreading over his face. Trygg gave a cruel smile and moved the blade towards the man. The terrified Brigante quickly put a cross quite close to the river. "That's better." He looked at the cross. If the man was telling the truth then they were on the same side of the river as the Roman fort. The problem was he didn't know the scale of the man's cross. "How far to Romans?"

The man shook his head, the terror apparent and Trygg realised he would not have the same concept of distance. "How long to walk there?"

The man looked to the west and then back. "You leave now and you will be there when the sun is high."

That was too close for comfort. They would need to cross the river. He turned to the old man and gave him the stick. "Where is the place of the Sword?" The old man shrugged. "Where is the Sword of Cartimandua?" The old man shrugged again and Trygg moved towards him threateningly with the knife.

The old man laughed. "You are going to kill me anyway so why should I tell you anything?"

Trygg nodded and walked to the girl. He ripped down and her tunic came off, ripped along the back. She stood there naked, shivering in the cold and trying to cover herself with her bound hands. "There is dying, old man, and there is dying painfully. Where is the Sword?" The old man stood defiantly but less sure. Trygg walked to the woman and held her breast in his hand he moved the blade towards the thin white skin and the old man shouted, "No! Just kill us and leave. The sword is across the river, south of the Roman fort." Trygg looked at the girl and she nodded. The young man also nodded. "Thank you. Now kill them."

While his men ransacked the village Trygg called Snorri and Gurt to his side. "It is fortunate that we came here or we would have blundered into the Romans. We need to cross the river here."

Gurt looked at the dark waters which were flowing strongly to the sea. "How? Do we walk on water?"

"No Gurt, we pull down the palisade and use it to make a temporary bridge."

"The river will wash it away."

"Eventually but not before we have crossed. We will put it there." He pointed to a narrow part of the river close to the bend where the river slowed.

Snorri quickly organised the men and they pulled down the palisade, keeping it as intact as possible. They knew that they would have to be quick and all the warriors gathered on the bank as they threw the four sides of the village walls into the black water. One of the walls actually breached the river and caught on some branches on the other side. Trygg roared for his men to cross and, one by one they ran across the four temporary bridges. Some of them fell in the river but they were close enough to the bank by then to wade across. The chief of the Tencteri was pleased. He was within a few hours of his destination and he would soon have the sword and be back aboard his ships heading home.

Aed had watched in terror from his place of hiding as the raiders had ravaged the village. He had arrived shortly before the pirates and had been hiding in the trees when he saw them arrive. He was shaking in fear as they killed their prisoners and he waited for his own death when they continued along their path. He was relieved when he saw them cross the river, away from his concealed nest. He could continue along the path and find the next settlement. He was tired and he was hungry but he was alive and he would carry out his mother's dying instructions; the rest of the valley would know of the raid.

The sentry at Morbium thought he saw some movement from the trail which led east but it stopped the moment he looked at it. He was sure that it was a trick of the light but he knew that he would have to report to someone. "Sir?"

The optio turned. "Yes, soldier. What is it?"

"I think I saw a movement in the tree line over there."

As the optio followed the line of the sentry's arm they both saw the boy race from the cover and sprint towards the open gate. He almost fell into the sentry's surprised arms and he burst into tears. "Barbarians are in the valley. They have killed all my family and they are coming down the valley."

Taking the boy in his arms the optio shouted, "Sound the alarm and close the gates."

Later when the Prefect and First Spear had finished questioning the boy they decided what they ought to do. Both remembered the raids the previous year but, as infantry they were in no position to cover and search a large area. "I want a rider to go to Coriosopitum, another to go to Gaius' farm and warn them and another to ride down to Eboracum and warn the settlements there. Then I want you to take half a cohort east. If the young lad is correct then they are south of the river and that gives them the chance to raid in almost any direction they choose."

First Spear nodded. "Think it is the same ones as came last year?"

"It is either the same men or they have spread the word and their cousins are joining in."

The rider's rapid entry into the yard told Decius and the family that there was imminent danger. "There are barbarian raiders from the sea. They are heading down the valley. First Spear is heading to find them. The Prefect has asked if you wish to come into the fort for protection?"

Decius looked at his mother who defiantly shook her head. "Thank the Prefect and, if you warn any of our neighbours tell them they are welcome here."

Frann's fearful face showed the terror she felt. Ailis comforted her. "They will not find this place such an easy nut to crack. We have hardy men who will defend it to the death and the Prefect has despatched men to help." She looked over at Nanna. "You will stay here?"

Nanna shook her head. "I will bring my people here. I could not let them be taken. "She gave a harsh smile, "Fear not Ailis, they will not have me a captive. I will return within an hour."

As Nanna galloped off, Decius sent one of his men with her as protection. "She is a tough lady but these barbarians are determined. I will go to find Drugi. It would not do to lose him again so quickly."

As his men began to prepare for the defence of the hamlet Decius rode off through the woods to the hut which lay some miles to the south. When he reached the hut he could see no sign of Drugi. He knew he could not be far for the ex-slave did not ride. "Drugi!"

The huge man appeared silently at Decius' side making the Brigante jump. "You are as silent as Uncle Gaelwyn was. Your friends from across the sea are back. We need to defend the farm."

"You go and I will follow."

When Decius looked at him questioningly the big man grinned. "I can move through the woods where your horse cannot. I will be there soon."

The fifty warriors moved swiftly through the sparsely populated and almost empty lands on the southern bank of the Dunum. The dead villagers had given him an idea of where to find the family of the sword but he had ten warriors scout south in a semi-circle, like beaters flushing birds. As they moved deeper into the land to the west Trygg could not help but glance north to where he now knew there was a Roman fort. He knew it was north of him, across the river and he hoped that meant that he was safe. As a Tencteri he had not encountered bridges much for the rivers in his land were not mighty ones like the Dunum and the Tinea. For Trygg a bridge was a boat; that was how you crossed a river.

Sigurd was the scout who had the first success. Buoyed by his first scouting ventures he had embraced the opportunity to impress the leader again. "I have found it, Chief Trygg. There is a mighty stone dwelling and there are many horses."

"You have done well Sigurd. When we next raid you shall do so as a warrior. How far is it?"

Sigurd had little concept of distance. He knew that it had not taken him long to trot back. "Not far. Just over the rise."

The other scouts returned, having been told to just scout a short way ahead. They all prepared for battle. Trygg knew from his conversations with Marcus that the farm had defenders and he was in no doubt that this time they would have to fight to get what they wanted. He relished the opportunity. Hitherto it had been too easy and the combat not worthy of a warrior. The band trotted behind Sigurd and Trygg in a loose wedge formation. It afforded both speed and defence. As they crested the rise, they saw on the hollow below them a fine stone villa but as soon as he spied it Trygg knew that this was not the place they sought for it had neither exterior wall nor ditches but it was somewhere which promised wealth.

Sigurd pointed, his sharp eyes spotting movement. "Look!" As Trygg peered at the Roman dwelling he saw a cart and six riders galloping away westwards. They had been warned. All need for deception was now gone and the warband raced towards the villa. Nanna and her riders had finished packing when they saw the warband and Nanna did not need to urge her servants to make all haste. The Brigante horsewoman wondered what she would return to. All her hard work in making a beautiful home for her man would have come to naught. She shrugged as she urged her horse on; her incarceration with the Irish had taught her that freedom was worth any price. She could rebuild a house and buy new belongings but people were harder to replace.

Gurt was disappointed when they entered the villa. He had hoped from the grand exterior that the inside would be filled with treasures. All that they found were paintings on the wall, a fine floor and statues. None of them was portable and none valuable to the Eudose. "I have found where they had their treasure."

Snorri's voice brought Trygg and Gurt to the master bedroom where the empty hole in the floor showed where the valuables of the house had been kept. "The wagon, that is why they took one, to keep their valuables safe."

Gurt's eyes became excited. "Then we follow the wagon and we find the treasure."

Trygg nodded, "Odin is with us for we find my treasure, the sword. They will be heading to a place of safety; the farm which is the home of the sword."

Even though the afternoon light was fading the warband set off quickly. They had seen their prize and knew that it was almost in their grasp. Every warrior felt that they were charmed for they had come further into Britannia and were, as yet, unharmed and undetected. With the sword and the treasure in their grasp they would soon be back aboard their ships and sailing home with more plunder than any other raiders. When they returned to Uiteland they would only become stronger and more powerful.

Nanna felt relieved that she had saved her people and reached them before the raiders. She knew that it had been close when she had viewed them on the skyline above the farm. "They are coming. I saw them close to my farm." Decius thanked the Allfather that they had begun their preparations so early.

"Find somewhere safe for your people. Drugi, Tadgh, come and help me to unhitch the wagon."

Once the wagon was emptied and unhitched the three men moved it behind the gate. Shouting for the rest of the men they heaved it behind the gate to make it even more impenetrable. Drugi looked around the wooden walls and felt uncomfortable. "I would prefer to be in the open."

Decius smiled, Gaelwyn had said the same. "These walls are safer for such small numbers as we. How many will be in this warband?"

"If it is the same as the ones who sailed from Hjarno-By then there would be five ships, each with thirty men. There could be a hundred warriors here."

Decius bit his lip. One hundred warriors could hurt them. He wished that he had sent a messenger to his brother but he had assumed that the Prefect would have done so. Unfortunately, the training facility had been forgotten in the panic surrounding the raid. Marcus and his men were ten miles away, happily training and unaware of the danger to the family.

By the time that Trygg and his men had reached the farm, the sun had finally set in the west. While scouts watched the walls, Trygg, Gurt and Snorri held a council of war. "I say we attack now! They will not expect it."

Trygg looked at Gurt and shook his head. "They know we are coming. Those people who fled the farm are here. We have seen their tracks. They will be alert and expecting us. Even now they will be behind their walls with weapons ready. Do you know where their traps are? Have you inspected their ditches?"

Gurt shook his head. Snorri spoke up. "The scouts will be back soon. When the moon rises we may be able to attack then."

"No Snorri. The men have travelled far today. Let us rest and let those in the farm wait all night for the attack which doesn't come. In the morning, before the sun rises they will be tired and we will be fresh. Then we will attack." Gurt still looked sceptical. "When the Suebi attacked the citadel it was the Roman who led the defence. He and Drugi helped to defeat and drive off a warband that was bigger than this. Had the Suebi waited, then their guard might have dropped. We will rest and when they are tired then we will attack."

Gurt was not convinced but he knew that the two warriors with him had made wise decisions up to now. He just wanted the treasure that had been in the wagon. The ship they had captured was a rich prize but, looking at the deserted farmhouse, there would be greater prizes beyond the walls. When the scouts returned Gurt decided that Trygg had been right. "There is a deep ditch running all the way around the walls. At the back of the farm is a stream. The trees are forty paces from the walls and there are men on the gates and walls. Anyone attacking would be seen."

Trygg gave a quick knowing look towards Gurt who now saw the wisdom in caution. "How high is the wall?"

"Twice as high as a man and there is stone at the bottom below the wooden stakes."

"Then we cannot burn it and we have no ladders." Trygg had had an idea of attacking on two sides at once to distract the enemy's fire but that was out of the question as he did not have enough men and there was a river there. "The gate, it is wooden? There is no metal on it?"

"It is mighty but it is made of wood."

"Good. You have done well now return to the walls and watch them." When the scouts had trotted back Trygg outlined his plan to his confederates. "We will use torches and brushwood to place against the gate and burn it."

"How will be get close? The scout told us that they can see us and will shoot at us when we advance."

"We use our shields to make a barrier. We advance behind the shields, fire the gate and then wait in the tree line."

Gurt thought that it sounded too simple, but he could not think of a better way. "Why not do that now?"

"I told you before I want the men rested. Have them collect the brushwood and then tell them to rest. We attack before dawn."

Marcus' sleep was disturbed and he knew not why. He and his men had had a particularly good day training with his men and gone to sleep happier than in a long time. They had eaten well so why had he woken? He could not remember the dream he had dreamt but it had frightened him. He stepped out of his tent. It was a cold night and the sentries were huddled in their cloaks trying to get warm. He wandered over to them. "Have you heard anything?"

Pleased that they had not been caught sleeping and wondering why their officer had left the comfort of his bed to freeze with them they shook their heads."

"Quiet as the grave."

The other one said, "Yes sir so quiet that when we heard the hawk it made me jump."

"Jump? I thought you had shit yourself."

Marcus suddenly felt the hairs on the back of his neck prickle. "A hawk you say? In the middle of the night?"

The incongruity struck them both. "Well sir, now you mention it. I suppose…"

"Are you sure it wasn't an owl?"

They both shook their heads. "No sir, definitely a hawk." Owls, the bird of the night was considered an ill omen and warriors on sentry duty always made the sign against evil when they heard one.

Marcus looked to the skies. It was his brother and it was a warning but a warning of what? "How long until dawn?"

One of them pointed to the sliver of light on the eastern horizon. "Right wake the men. We have action today."

As Marcus went back to his tent the two sentries wondered if he had gone mad. Action? They were only recruits. Marcus' head reappeared at his tent. "Now!"

They quickly went around the camp waking the sleepy recruits who wondered why they were being thrown out of their beds. When they saw their decurion with sword at his side saddling his horse they knew that it would not be an ordinary day.

Chapter 18

The guards on the wall were tired. Although they had been relieved in the early hours of the morning they had not had time to prepare for a night standing and their eyes were drooping. With only ten others to share the watch keeping, the six men spread along the walls were looking forward to their relief at dawn. Perhaps they were not the target of a raid but if any barbarian came close they would pay a hefty price. The huge warrior who now lived in Gaelwyn's hut had stalked the walls until the middle of the watch, his nose twitching as he smelled the familiar smell of his home in Uiteland. The last thing he had said, before he slipped away for a couple of hours sleep was, "They are out there. I can smell them." That had been an hour since and, with the first sliver of dawn cracking the night sky they thought that they had escaped.

Trygg did not have many archers but the four he had were in the woods and the sentries had been targeted. The forty paces which separated them were not an obstacle and they were all sure that they could accurately hit their marks. Trygg's assault force was waiting for the first four men to drop and then they would race towards the walls while the archers finished off any who remained at the wooden ramparts. His men were rested and eager to fight a foe who had taken such strenuous efforts to deny them their prize. The light was not perfect but Trygg nodded and three men fell to the yard at the farmyard each one struck by a Tencteri arrow. One of the remaining guards managed to shout a warning before he too was plucked from the walls. The last sentry held up his buckler which took the arrow and he hurled his spear at the men racing towards the gate. He had the satisfaction of seeing a warrior fall to the ground, impaled by the javelin. He heard footsteps behind him and knew that the rest of the erstwhile garrison was arriving.

By the time they made the walls the damage was done and the fire party, nestled near to the gate were already setting fire to the brushwood they had brought. They had kept the kindling dry and had brought spare flints. Within a few moments, there were the first flickers of flames and, as the brushwood caught, the flames quickly spread. The water that the defenders had ready close to the gates could not stop the conflagration, but it did at least slow it down. Decius and Drugi stood next to each other safely protected in the small tower which Decius had built adjacent to the main and solid gate; they exchanged a look which did not bode well for the others inside; the two men knew that they could not hold against an enemy with no gate to protect them. "We have lost too many men already." Decius was shaken. The men who had fallen were not only friends and co-workers, they had been good warriors.

"I know Roman. All we can do now is to slow them down. At least the cart will take longer to burn."

Decius turned to shout an instruction to the women. "Soak the cart in water and prepare yourselves. They will break through. "

Frann looked petrified but Nanna and Ailis comforted her. "We have been through worse than this sister. We fight until there is no hope and then we fight a little longer. We were given this life for a purpose and that was not to die at a barbarian's hand."

As Drugi shot an arrow through the shields, now at the edge of the wood he had the satisfaction of seeing a warrior fall. He aimed again and the warriors withdrew a little more into the safety of the woods. Drugi's prowess with a bow was legendary. Decius took heart and he aimed his bow looking for a chink in the shield wall. Ailis' voice sounded through the crackling of the fire, "Drugi, sound Gaelwyn's horn. Let them know that Brigante still fight here."

Drugi took the bow from his neck and blew a mighty fanfare. The Tencteri heard it and wondered how such a noise could come from within the farm for it sounded like the horn of a mighty army. The defenders took heart and roared their defiance. Trygg turned to his men, "Are you warriors or women that you quake at a horn. Look the gate is burning and we will be amongst them before dawn has broken. There is no answering horn, no-one is coming to save them."

Decius and his men stood alongside Drugi with bows drawn. As soon as the flames died down then the barbarians would attack. Decius had to admire the cunning of the raiders.

Had this been daylight then the pall of smoke would have alerted the garrison at Morbium. The early dawn meant it was just a glow to the south, an early sunrise. Some of the barbarians were struck by arrows when they peered out to see if the gate had finally succumbed to the flames. The archers on the walls were all experts and had a clear line of sight. Trygg roared out, "Stay behind your shields until I give the command!"

His men were eager and did not like this waiting. They could now count those on the wall, as the first rays of the new day sparkled along the wooden stakes atop the rampart, and knew that they outnumbered the defenders. The Tencteri would rip through them. Trygg watched as the flames grew higher, forcing the defenders from the towers and the gate to the two sides of the walls. When he saw part of the top of the wall begin to burn, then he knew that they would not have long to wait. He turned to the men around him, his face filled with the pride and the passion of a warrior leading his men into battle. He nodded to Snorri who grinned. "We go in behind me! I want a shield wall with not a gap between us. The flames cannot hurt us and, once we are through kill all but the slaves!" He looked at each of his handpicked warriors to see that they understood.

Gurt and his warriors were largely ignored. Today was about the Tencteri and the warriors fulfilling their chief's oath that he would retrieve the sword. Today they would honour that oath. Straining like hounds on the leash they awaited Trygg's command. All of them would have run through the flames, such was their zeal but they waited for the command. Trygg saw more of the timbers collapse and he yelled, "Tencteri!"

Drugi knew what was coming and his first arrow took the warrior whose shield did not quite cover his leg. The arrow plunged through his shin and as his shoulder dropped Drugi sent a second one through his neck. Other warriors began to flood from the trees eager to be part of this attack. The defenders fired as fast as they could string their bows. Decius shouted to four of his defenders to wait behind the cart. To Drugi he shouted. "You keep firing; when they are through I will take my men and fight them on foot. Thank you for honouring us today. Marcus would have been proud of you, you are a true warrior."

Drugi just nodded, never taking his eyes off targets which were now increasing as Gurt's warriors joined the others. They were easier targets, with fewer shields and armour but Drugi knew that he was merely slowing the burst dam of humanity. Only a miracle could halt them. He risked a glance in the sky but the hawk was not there, had it deserted them?

The momentum of Trygg and his wedge burst through the gate but the cart behind the gate was a much more immovable barrier and they crashed into it. Two of Decius' men plunged spears into the surprised faces of two of Trygg's warriors. He knew that they needed momentum. "Back!"

The warband moved back a few paces from the gate, the air filled with the smell of blood, singed hair and burning timbers. "Behind me! Shield wall!"

They raced forwards again, their shields and bodies crashing into the cart, knocking it back ten paces and giving them space to flood around the side. As Trygg and Snorri prepared to fight the defenders they saw the grim faced warriors next to Brigante women, all of them with a weapon in their hand, determined to sell their lives dearly. Frann's face was a mask of hate and Trygg shouted, "Today you return to Hjarno-By and every one of my warriors will have you and I will cut out the heart of your Roman lover when I meet him man to man!"

Before they could race forward and carry out the grim threat they heard a wail behind them. Snorri glanced over his shoulder and saw to his horror, racing towards them in the cold bright rays of the new sun, over a hundred Roman horsemen led by the Roman slave, Marcus, and wielding the Sword of Cartimandua. Gurt and his men had already been surprised by a volley of javelins and they were streaking eastwards, their dreams of conquest shattered and replaced with the hope of an escape to their ships.

Snorri grabbed Trygg by the shoulder, "We are surrounded! We must flee!"

Drugi yelled down to Decius, "It is your brother! Hold on!"

The defenders took heart from the news that they were reinforced and pushed hard against the warriors who had broken into the open space. When Drugi added his marksmanship to the assault from in front they started to pull back.

Chief Trygg knew that it was all up for he had begun with under fifty warriors. He was caught between two forces and they were many miles from safety. "Fall back! To the river!" He had been thwarted again in his attempt to get the sword but they would not be leaving empty handed; there was a fine trading ship which would yield them a greater profit than any previous visit.

Marcus had headed for his home the moment he heard Drugi's horn. He knew that he might be reprimanded for throwing his young recruits into combat but the alternative was to lose more captives to the Tencteri and this time it would be his family. He had been proud of their first volley which had thinned the ranks of the barbarians. He now had to control them. He turned and yelled. "Recruits! Turma one and two reform and hold them. Turma three and four follow me!" He dared not risk all the recruits and he knew that he could only control and manage two turmae. The other two would have to wait as a visual threat to the Tencteri.

The fifty recruits formed a solid barrier of men and horses and the retreating barbarians assiduously avoided the bristling spears and armoured horsemen. Marcus was keen to ride down as many of those who had first fled before they got too far. "Use your javelins. If any of them fall then two of you take them. Don't try to fight them one on one!" He had no idea how they would fare in hand to hand combat and he preferred them just to deter his enemies.

He hated to endanger his young men but he had to kill as many of the enemy as possible. One of the barbarians halted before Marcus and swung an axe at his horse's head. Marcus jinked to one side and threw the javelin into the man's throat. At three paces he could not miss. He drew the sword and impulsively shouted, "The Sword of Cartimandua!"

As Snorri and Trygg pushed their way through the burning gate they heard the shout and Trygg cursed the hawk which had protected the Roman. "Take the men to the boat. I will join you." Chief Trygg had been given one last throw of the bones. He could still win the blade and if he did not at least try, then he would spend his days in regret.

Snorri knew what his chief intended but he could do nothing but obey. He saluted and led his men off. Chief Trygg ran down the trail and he bore a charmed life as the arrows and javelins hurled at him missed. He had seen the departing horses and he ran after them. He was able to move almost as swiftly through the woods as the horses. The recruits who had been ordered to hold the line watched impotently as the survivors could be seen barely thirty paces away. They had been given their orders and they waited.

Sigurd and Ormsson had watched in horror as the attack had faltered and then crumbled, now they saw their leader running through the woods and they followed. They might only be armed with a slingshot but if they could defend their chief then they would be warriors.

The woods were filled with the fleeing warriors and the young recruits elated by their apparent victory. Their inexperience was the undoing of some of them. As they recklessly charged after the warriors they were surprised when some of them stopped, and whirling axes, struck their horses. The ones who had remembered Marcus' lesson survived others were not so lucky and, as they lay winded were killed where they lay.

Marcus saw two more of his boys die and knew that enough was enough. He had saved his family; he would not lose his men. "Recruits recall!" He repeated the call and was pleased when he heard others sound the same command. A buccina would have been quicker but at least his men stopped. He watched as the survivors of the Tencteri hurtled northwards towards the river.

"Roman that is my sword!"

Marcus wheeled his horse as he heard the familiar voice of Trygg of the Tencteri. The chief had a shield already burned at the edges and studded with arrows and a blade which dripped blood but in his eyes was cold white anger. Marcus was not in a merciful mood and he rode his horse straight at Trygg. He hoped that he would not know what to do and this would be a swift but deadly encounter. It was Sigurd whose slingshot did the most damage and it smacked into Marcus' mount's head making him rear away from the threat. Marcus was thrown from his horse but he rolled away from the danger. Ormsson threw his slingshot and it cracked into Marcus' helmet. Before Trygg could run the twenty paces to the recumbent decurion the recruits had seen the danger to their leader and were also racing to the scene. Sigurd fell to a javelin in the chest, falling at his leader's feet. Ormsson threw another missile at a horseman but missed and he too paid the price as a recruit took off his head. Trygg could see that he was outnumbered and five recruits dismounted between him and Marcus' body. He swung his sword at the recruit who galloped towards him, making the young man veer to the side and then ran off through the woods to follow the last of his men.

Marcus was only stunned, and when he regained his senses he looked around the scene. The sight of the two dead barbarian boys upset him and he applauded their courage. He remembered when he and Macro had behaved in a similar way, they had survived. "Where did the chief go?"

His men pointed north. Marcus would dearly have loved to follow and finish off the raider but he knew that the blow and the fall had taken much from him. They had done enough. It would now be up to others to stop the Tencteri. "Back to the farm. You have done well. I am proud of you."

When the Romans had left the glade, it seemed somehow quiet and peaceful. The two bodies looked ungainly, especially Ormsson for the head seemed to stare at its own body. Orm had been wounded in the leg and, having hidden to bind his wound was now heading north. When he came to the glade and saw the body of his son, silent tears coursed down his bloodied cheeks. His son had died with honour whilst he still lived. He took the two bodies and began to prepare a grave. They would have honour together in death.

When Marcus reached the farm there was a collective cheer from both the defenders and the recruits. Ailis and Decius rushed to embrace him. Decius whispered in his ear, "Thank you, my brother. I knew that you would come."

Suddenly Frann's authoritative voice rang out. "He is wounded. Let me see to him." Ailis smiled, her son had picked a good woman.

Marcus kissed her. "Later my wife." Turning to Decius he asked, "Does the Prefect know about the raiders?"

"Aye, there are five hundred men heading down the river."

Marcus nodded and regretted the action instantly; his head was hurting. "He should catch them. He looked to his men and sought a face. "Livius ride to Morbium and report to the Prefect. Tell him that we have turned the raiders away from Decius' farm." The recruit rode off hard. "Marius, yours is a harder task. Ride north but avoid the woods, and then along the northern bank of the Dunum. Find First Spear and the infantry; tell them of the action. The raiders will be coming their way along the river. They will know what to do."

As the two recruits disappeared Ailis took charge. "You boys dismount and we'll get you fed. Drugi, organise the men to get rid of these bodies. Mara let us get some food while Frann sees to my son."

By the time that Snorri and the men reached the temporary bridge they had constructed, they were exhausted. Snorri gathered them together to count the cost. He would not abandon his chief even though he had been ordered to leave. He would wait. He counted and found but twenty-five of the warband remained. He peered around and could see nothing of Gurt or any of Gurt's men. "Where is the fat one?"

His men laughed at the nickname they had given to Gurt, a man who liked his food.

"When I reached here there were some of them crossing the bridge. I think he was with them."

"Good riddance. We will wait on the other side in the village. You four into the woods and keep watch." Even as he took the men across the river, Snorri wondered if Gurt would reach the trader and the other ships. If he did then they would be left without anything to show for their raid, just empty oars on the way back. Snorri was just pleased that they had sent their own men for their boat. At least they would have less far to walk.

"Someone coming!"

Everyone grabbed their weapons and then breathed a sigh of relief as their chief and three wounded men hobbled in. Trygg looked at the remnants of his men. "This is all?"

"Aye, Gurt has gone on."

Trygg shrugged. "It was to be expected. Now we had better move swiftly and see if we can find our ship before the Romans find us."

First Spear and his men had spent the night at the ransacked settlement on the hill above the Dunum. They had seen no sign of the raiders but they could see the devastation they had left in their wake. They had missed the ships which were now waiting closer up stream in the twilight hours. What they could not see was any sign that the raiders had returned. Centurion Marius Pompeius turned to his friend, the Centurion of the second century. "Appius I think that they are somewhere between here and Morbium. They must have been south of the river."

"Do we go back to find them then?" Appius had served for ten years along the Dunum and knew that the only way to cross the river was back at the fort.

"No. They must have some way of crossing the river because they definitely came through here. I think we will stay here and give them a little surprise when they return. Place pickets along the path and then rebuild the gate. If we put the third century by the river then they will be trapped against the walls of the village. Send the fourth century up the river to Eabrycg. They can catch any who manage to get by us here." Appius went quite happily to give the instructions; this way they would be rested when the raiders came along the path. First Spear was quite right, they would get a surprise.

Gurt and his men were running along the trail as fast as they could. When they had reached the temporary bridge they knew that they had survived. With twenty of his men with him, and another fifteen aboard his ships Gurt had fared better than the Tencteri. At least he would have the iron aboard the trader as his reward. Trygg had overreached himself but Gurt would return. This was a rich land and he could harvest it annually. They had been unlucky when the horsemen stumbled upon them but the Eudose knew that they could find many unguarded places in this rich province of Britannia.

"Look the ships!"

One of his sharp-eyed sentries saw the two ships just as they turned the bend upstream. Gurt was a little worried. He had thought they would be waiting for them at Oegels-Dun. Had Trygg somehow tricked him? "Was the trading ship with them?"

"No Chief Gurt, just two of the Tencteri ships." Gurt's treachery was matched by Trygg's but at least they would have their own ship and the trader once they reached Eabrycg. The muddy conditions by the river had made them take this higher path and Gurt wondered about the Norns who had forced them this way. Had they been by the river then they might be aboard Trygg's ships instead of still trying to find their own.

"First Spear. There are barbarians heading down the path."

"Stand to!" The three centuries who were close to the path formed three ranks with First Spear on the right. His left flank was secured by the river and the Third Century. He would have liked to know how many men he faced but he was confident that even if he was outnumbered he could defeat them. He had fought barbarian raiders before and they could not fight against the discipline of his men. "No one throws a javelin until I give the command." He glared at the men who knew better than to disobey this twenty-five year veteran. No one would escape this trap.

When Gurt and his men reached the top of the bank they were met by a steel wall of shields, armour and bristling spears. One or two of the braver warriors hurled themselves at the wall but Gurt and the remainder plunged down the bank to the river. The men of the Third Century heard the clash of arms above them and were waiting with javelins at the ready. The Centurion had placed his men at an oblique angle to maximise the effect of the eighty men. In the event, the twenty warriors who tumbled and crashed through the bushes, mud and tangled grass were in no condition to give the auxiliaries any resistance.

Gurt knew that his raiding days were over but he determined to go out like a warrior, sword in hand. He watched the man before him plunge to the ground, pierced by the javelin and he took the opportunity to stab the auxiliary in the throat. Emboldened by his success he punched the next man in line who was struck in the thigh by the axe of the warrior following Gurt. Gurt could see the river just a few paces away. If he could make the river there was a chance he could either float to the other bank or further downstream, beyond this wall of steel. He thrust his long sword forward and although the auxiliary deflected the blow it enabled Gurt to slip through the gap and stab another auxiliary in the side. Behind him the survivors were following Gurt through the gap.

The Centurion saw the breach. "Fuck this! Third Century! On me!" The whole line wheeled as one and the survivors were hacked down where they stood.

Alone out of all his men, Gurt managed to reach the water and, throwing his shield at the auxiliaries trying to catch him, began to wade out into the water. Fortune favoured him as a log, displaced by the fighting drifted by. Still clutching his sword the chief grasped the life-saving tree trunk for all that he was worth. He kicked and quickly reached the middle. He was safe. The Centurion saw the single survivor; he had other ideas and, taking a javelin from one of his men he hurled it towards the log. Its arc took it into the air and then plummet down to pin Gurt's right arm to the log. He was trapped. He could not free the javelin which had firmly stuck in the wood and, with the blood seeping behind him Gurt drifted towards the sea.

The Fourth Century took two hours to reach Eabrycg. They would have covered the ground faster if it had not been for the mud which slowed them down but, as they turned the bend in the river, they saw the masts of the ships. The Centurion had expected to find the settlement deserted and he was delighted. There were some of the raiders close by and they had the element of surprise. He led his men away from the river to approach the moored ships from the north. He knew the port well and the settlement would hide them from view. The stench of death hung over the ransacked town for the raiders had left the bodies where they lay, unconcerned with the smell and the animals who chewed on the carcasses at night. Sending his optio with half the men to the east, the Centurion took the rest to the west. He halted close by the wall of the settlement and peered around. There were two ships, a dragon ship and a trader. A quick glance told him that there were less than ten warriors left with the ships. As long as they did not slip their cables they would have them. His optio had been told to wait until the

Centurion struck and when he saw that the warrior's attention was on some dice game on the deck he raced forwards. Had the warriors kept the gangplank aboard they might have escaped but the Centurion, young and newly promoted, sprinted up the wooden board and leapt amongst the warriors. His men flooded behind and the unarmed raiders died to a man; their game of dice still unfinished before them.

Chapter 19

Marius had easily spotted and then avoided Trygg and his men as they crashed about in the woods heading for the river trail. Once he knew they were behind him he kicked on hard, eager to report the success of his fellow recruits to the man who had first trained them. He was slightly disappointed when he saw the auxiliaries piling up the bodies of the raiders. He had thought that he and his fellows had disposed of a greater number.

The Centurion watched as the keen young rider brought his horse smartly to a halt. "Sir. Decurion Marcus Gaius Aurelius sent me to tell you that the warband attacked his brother's farm but we managed to defeat them."

He looked so proud that First Spear couldn't help but smile. "You and the Decurion all on your own defeated a warband?" He gave a mock bow and turned to his men. "We are truly among the gods."

As his men laughed the chosen man blushed. "No sir. It was the recruits the Decurion was training. And I was told to tell you that they are heading this way."

First Spear was more impressed that Marcus had taken them on with recruits. "Are these not the raiders then?"

"No sir. This was a band which fled first. The others are further upstream. I passed them a while ago."

"Thank you and forgive me for having fun at your expense. You and your comrades have done well. Now ride to Eabrycg and tell my Centurion there to watch for the raiders in case they slip by here."

Disappointed that he would not be fighting by the side of the auxiliaries he smartly saluted and galloped off. "There will be more of them coming soon. Scouts out again." He turned to Appius. "This is my kind of fighting. Wait in one spot and they come to us."

Trygg had worried that something had happened to his ships but, as they waded through a particularly flooded part of the path they saw, hidden in the willows, two of them moored and guarded by his ten worried-looking warriors. Once they had boarded the ships the warrior responsible for the ships came over to Trygg. "We heard some Roman infantry go by last evening. It sounded like many men."

"You did not see them?"

"No we saw their standard and their red crests but we could not count them. "

"It matters not. We will be aboard our ships soon and they cannot touch us." Trygg sounded confident when talking to his men but in his heart, he worried that there might yet be the problem of the Roman ships in the estuary. They had sneaked through but if they had returned then they would be trapped. There was little point worrying. He waved to Snorri in the second, slightly smaller boat and then he went to the stern to steer. The two boats had barely fourteen men each to row and their progress would perforce, be slow. When they reached the trader at Eabrycg then he would have to make a decision. There would be men there and it might be expedient to burn all except for his own boat and crew the trader. It would be sad to lose such fine boats but it could be there was no alternative. "Lower the sails."

Snorri shouted over, "There is little breeze."

"We need all the help that Odin can give us. As long as the wind is not against us we will use the sails and whatever wind he sends us."

The two scouts came racing back to tell First Spear that they could see the masts of two ships. First Spear had not seen the ships when coming down the river and wondered where they had been hidden. It made his task almost impossible but he would do what he could. He was fortunate that the river was relatively narrow close to Oegels-Dun. Further upstream it widened but a bend in the river narrowed it to sixty paces close to the settlement. The ships would have to go down in single file. He could see some debris close in to the bank and he shouted to the Centurion of the Third Century, "Throw those logs and branches as far out as you can into the stream." He turned to the rest. "I want every man lining the bank. When these boats come by I want us to hit them with as many javelins as we can. There will be men pulling oars and a man steering. Aim for them."

Trygg had hoped that his fighting was over for the day but, as his boat edged around the bend he saw the red crests and shields which told him that there were Romans. "Up oars! Protect yourselves!" With his left arm he held his shield whilst he gripped the tiller. There was little breeze but the current was taking them towards the sea; it was already a little faster here where it narrowed.

He peered over the shield. He could see what would happen next as he saw the auxiliaries holding their javelins and preparing to throw them. He wondered how many volleys they would get off before both ships had escaped. The first six javelins were all aimed at Trygg's boat and one of them managed to beat the shields and strike a rower. They found that the javelins began to pull their shields down and they had to fight to keep them upright. The Chief thought that they might escape if only one wound resulted from a volley. Suddenly he heard cries from Snorri's boat. They had just come under attack and two men had been struck but even worse the debris from the river had drifted in front of the bows and the ship was drifting towards the other bank; it was no longer pointing down stream. One man tried to free it but was pierced by three javelins. As Snorri's boat grounded next to the grassy bank the javelins targeted his ship.

"Snorri! Abandon ship and run down the other bank. We will pick you up!"

The survivors needed no further urging and they scrambled down the side, mercifully safe from attack as the ship afforded some protection and then clambered up the bank. The bushes lining the bank afforded them further protection and they ran as hard as they could. The slow progress of the boat meant that they soon outstripped both Trygg and the Roman javelins but Snorri knew that only eight of his men remained and the dragon boat he had left seemed to be shaking its head as the water rocked it back and forth. Trygg's men had suffered another wound but they were moving away from the Romans. He heard the Roman officer shout a command and when he risked a glance he saw that they were forming up to follow him. "Oars out!" Once they began rowing they made much better progress and Trygg steered the ship towards Snorri and his men. They needed no urging to make all haste and once on board, they joined Trygg's men at the oars.

They were just about to begin rowing when they heard a weak voice cry out. Snorri looked over the side and saw, entangled in the overhanging trees, Gurt, his arm still pinned to the log."It is Gurt! He is wounded."

Trygg contemplated leaving the treacherous Gurt to his fate but then he thought better of it. This would improve his standing once he reached home, that he had risked his crew for a dishonourable man. "Help him aboard but be quick about it."

Snorri jumped over the side and, putting his foot on Gurt's arm pulled the javelin for all he was worth. It popped out spraying blood on Gurt's face. Snorri and the other crewman helped him aboard and then, after unceremoniously dumping him to the deck they grabbed their oars as they began rowing again. It was now a race down the river. The bends and loops slowed down the ship and every time Trygg looked to his left the Romans were keeping pace with them as they trotted down the river trail. If they slowed up then they would be in danger of another volley of missiles.

Marius had made excellent time to reach the detached Century and the Centurion knew exactly what to do. He lined the trader and the dragon boat with his men. Although the river was much wider here he still hoped that his men could inflict casualties. Marius eagerly joined them on the ship and the Centurion smiled at the youthful enthusiasm. "Any good with that?" He pointed at the javelin.

Marius grinned sheepishly, "We'll find out soon enough won't we sir?"

"Good lad. Now everyone down and hide. If they see us they will steer to the middle."

Trygg was delighted that the two ships were where they had been left and he began to steer towards them. There was, however, a nagging doubt in his mind; where were the guards who had been left. They were not his men he knew that but he hoped they had stayed with their ship. He shouted, "Ho! Jackdaw! Show yourselves." The silence seemed to be deafening. They were not within hearing; perhaps they were drunk. The fat little trader seemed a very tempting prize. Snorri had told him of the iron it held and he could almost smell the profits but there was something about this he did not like.

"Snorri. Get that javelin that was stuck in Gurt." The unfortunate Gurt had passed out shortly after he had been dropped to the floor but the javelin remained where Snorri had left it. "Throw it at The Jackdaw."

Snorri did not argue but bent his arm and hurled the missile across the thirty paces which separated them. As it thudded into the mast the Century all stood up and hurled their javelins. "Shields up!"

Snorri barely had time to roll into the guardrail before the deck was peppered with the javelins from the Roman-occupied ships. One man was too slow to react and lay pinioned to the bench. Gurt would not return to his home for exposed as he was hit by three javelins and silently expired. Trygg pushed the tiller hard over and the second volley fell harmlessly into the water. By the time they had reached their last two ships their nerves were in tatters. Trygg pulled over to collect the eight men who had been left and putting Gurt in one dragon ship and the dead rower in the other they towed the boats into the middle of the stream and set fire to them. It was a warrior's death and a warrior's funeral; it was more than Gurt deserved but Trygg knew that this tale would be told around fires for winters to come and he wanted men to think well of Trygg Tryggvasson, Chief of the Tencteri who had risked all to give two warriors safe passage to Odin.

"Well, horseman, that was a good shot. My men hit the body and you killed the rower. Well done." Marius took the plaudits but knew that he had thrown more in hope than expectation.

Marcus did not have much time to spend with his family. Once Marius had returned with the news of the departure of Trygg he had to finish off the training of his recruits. They had lost eight men in the skirmish but, as the Prefect at Morbium said when they passed through, that was a small price to pay in the scheme of things. First Spear had lost three men but the barbarians had lost all but one ship and, so far, forty bodies had been found. It had been a victory.

His farewell with Frann was brief but poignant. "I will return when I can but this is the season for fighting on the wall. Just let me know that you and the child are well when he is born."

Frann was too upset to speak but Ailis put her arm around her son's wife. "She will be cared for here so do not worry." She smiled a nod at Drugi, "And we have our giant to protect us now."

Drugi grinned. "It will be an honour!"

The return to the northern frontier was something of an anti-climax for it was incident-free. The Prefect at Coriosopitum merely inclined his head when Marcus gave him his report. "You horse warriors seem to do things the hardest way but the Legate and your Prefect will be glad to see the recruits and at least we know that they are blooded."

The recruits were all keen to see Rocky Point having heard so much about it. Once they reached the wooden fort it seemed to be smaller than they had imagined it. Marcus had laughed at their reaction. "Compared with your new homes this is a palace. But I would like to thank you, gentlemen. I am in your debt. You helped to save my family."

Marius rode forwards. He had become the one who spoke for the recruits since returning from his patrol. "No sir we would like to thank you for having the confidence in us and we too will swear allegiance to the Sword of Cartimandua."

Drugi saw the hawk as it circled the farm. He had seen it every day for a week since the battle. Each day it had come closer. He decided to speak with Ailis about it. When he reached the farm he could see that Frann was even bigger. In another two moons, she would give birth. Drugi had seen many animals give birth and he had a sense about that sort of thing. Frann's face always lit up when he entered for he was at once familiar to her and a close connection to her husband. As he sat in the kitchen drinking the weak beer he looked seriously at Ailis.

"The hawk is the spirit of your son."

"My adopted son, yes."

"Would your heart be sad if it was tamed?"

Ailis thought about that for she too had seen the hawk flying over the farm and wondered why it was not watching over Marcus. "I believe that Macro's spirit is in the bird but if it came to you and allowed you to train it then it would not be tame for taming suggests control and Macro could never be controlled. If he comes to your hand then it is his choice. You have, for what it is worth, my blessing."

"I have wondered why it has not flown north with your son and I believe it watches for his child. It means Marcus is not in danger if the hawk stays here. I will make a glove and see if it chooses me."

A week later and the glove was ready. Drugi had killed a dove and held the piece of choice meat in his hand. The hawk circled above, lazily and then swooped down to sit astride the glove. It picked lazily at the meat as though that was not its main concern. Now that he was this close to the bird he saw what a magnificent creature it was. The bright yellow eyes were sharp with interest, the head constantly turning to take in all that it saw. Its plumage was magnificent and its claws, razor-sharp. When the head swivelled and the yellow eyes bored into him Drugi felt a connection and he smiled. "Your brother has told me much about you and we shall hunt together. I know that I can learn much from you and, hopefully, you will learn a little from me."

Epilogue

On the wall, the legionaries were feeling marginally safer. They now had at least one fort on the wall and they could sleep easier at night without the worry of having their throats slit. They were less happy about the order they had just received from the Emperor. They were to paint the plaster running along the face of the wall, white. They understood that it was to make a statement to the barbarians that this was a line they could not cross but as First Spear Vibius said, "There is no reason to totally piss them off is there? They don't like it at all but to make it stand out… I think we are in for more fighting here lads not less."

The defenders of the workers, the ala and the auxiliaries knew that their summer would be a hard one as the massive construction spread like a white snake westwards. Although not a continuous barrier, large sections had been built and, even now, Emperor Hadrian was making subtle changes. His experience on the frontier had shown him that this was not an easy place to defend and, unless he was prepared to keep a massive standing army then he would need to make the wall a real barrier to the barbarians. If that meant more money now then, in the long run, it would be worth it. The plans made so long ago in Rome were now being changed and altered to suit the circumstance. He would have to delay his departure a little longer.

The huge villa at Capua was surrounded by guards. As the brother in law of the Emperor, Lucius Julius Ursus Servianus demanded such protection but they were also there to protect the meeting. The Senators, who had arrived clandestinely, hooded and with no sign or rank were there to sound out a possible new Emperor. The fact that Hadrian's brother in law had agreed to see them went some way to allaying their fears that this might be a devious trap created by Hadrian. During the meal, they had dropped vague hints about what they wanted without committing themselves and, perhaps, incurring a sojourn in the Praetorian prison.

"Gentlemen," Servianus had a deep and rich voice which sounded as though it had been drenched in honey. "The Emperor is performing a fine job in Britannia defending that province from raiders, renegades and rebels. I fail to see why you need to meet with me." He knew, of course, precisely why they were there but he was intrigued to discover how they would persuade him.

"We understand the valuable work your brother in law is carrying out but the expense is exorbitant. The taxes in Britannia will not cover the cost of the building of his limes. If you could persuade him to cut back on some of his ideas…"

Spreading his hands he said, sympathetically, "By the time a letter reaches him in that forsaken frontier he may well have finished his wall or moved on. I am not sure how I can help you. It isn't as though I have any power myself."

"But if you did have power…"

"Then things might be different. I will do as you suggest and write to my brother in law but until I have real power my hands are tied." The smile which spread across Servianus' face reminded one of the Senators of a Nile crocodile.

"It may be that the Senate can use your skills, perhaps in Egypt?"

Servianus' eyes lit up. Egypt was somewhere where he could become even richer and more powerful for corruption was rife. All he needed was a power base and then? Who knew? "Thank you kind sirs, I will sleep on that." As long as his brother in law stayed away from Rome then Servianus would continue to build up both his power and his riches. When he did return…

There was a stunned silence as the solitary boat pulled into Hjarno-By. Women looked beyond the ship to see other slower boats who they hoped would be following; there were none. As the handful of survivors trudged from the dragon ship they wondered what disaster had befallen their men. Women and children began to wail and to weep as they saw that their man was not amongst those weary-eyed and haunted men who stepped gratefully on to dry land.

Finally, Trygg stepped on to the jetty. He did not need to hold his hand for silence as there was only the gentle keening of crying women. "Odin was not with us on this journey. My pride was too great and we have all paid the price but I tell you this, people of the Tencteri, we will emerge stronger from this. We have seen weapons of such power that to own one would be to be as a god. When we have perfected such weapons and learned to fight as the Romans do then we will conquer the whole of Uiteland and drive the Suebi from our land."

The cheer from his men did nothing to disguise the silence from the people. He had lost, in a few short weeks all the power and honour he had spent years building. He cursed the day that he had seen the sword, found the Roman and heard the hawk.

Orm had spent the last three months surviving in the woods and forests. Since he had buried his son he had little left to live for. He had tried to get back to the sea but the increased Roman patrols along the road had forced him to constantly hide and change his direction of travel. He had become a bandit, preying on those who travelled alone. He hated himself for it but his heart burned with a desire for revenge. Either the Roman with the sword or the slave who helped them to escape would die and then Orm would be content; he would have avenged his own dishonour and made up a little for his failure to protect his son. Now two months after the death of his heir he was back in the place of the battle. The cairn of rocks above the grave of Ormsson and Sigurd was undisturbed. If he could have seen himself he would have been shocked at the sight, a thin, emaciated scarecrow of a man with a short seax, a bow and handful of arrows. He ate his food raw, when he could get it and slept under the trees. He was no longer a warrior, he was barely a man, and he was a carrion creature, feeding off the dead. Now he was back seeking revenge once more.

Drugi and the hawk were close by the river. The hawk appeared to enjoy the taste of wild ducks and, when he could get one, a goose. A brave bird, he would attack the bigger goose but if there was a pair then he would always have to beat a hasty although still dignified retreat. Still, he always looked for another chance to get the bird he relished eating. Drugi could speak Brigante like a native and all of his conversations with the hawk were in Brigante. "Well Macro, I have seen your brother's wife this morning and her waters have broken. By the setting sun he will have a son." The hawk fluttered its wings and half raised itself up. "Soon you will have to find a mate and have chicks of your own. Come we will see if we can catch a squirrel for supper." Drugi contentedly led the bird up the trail through the forest to the farm.

Orm heard the voices and hid in the bushes. He fitted an arrow. He had learned over the past two months that every man he met was his enemy; it made life easier. When he saw the huge figure of Drugi wander into the clearing he knew that his prayers had been answered. He pulled the bow back and sighted along the arrow. He would need two to kill such a big man but, as Drugi was fifty paces away he would easily have time for three shots and then he could finish him with his knife. He sighed with the joy of an end to a journey as he released the arrow.

Drugi sensed the movement as did the hawk; suddenly before Drugi could react the bird had spread its wings, taken flight towards the hidden man and taken the arrow to the chest. With a roar of rage Drugi ran towards the spot from whence the arrow had come. Orm hurriedly fired a second which thudded into Drugi's leg. The giant merely snapped it off with his left hand, his right drawing the Roman sword he used as a knife. Orm had no chance for a third shot as Drugi plunged the blade up through his stomach, twisting as the blade went on to pierce the heart of Orm. As he withdrew the blade, shiny with blood and entrails he saw the strange smile of happiness on the dead Tencteri. Racing back to the hawk he picked it up. Its heart was still beating weakly and there was defiance in its eyes. He began to head back to the farm as quickly as he could. When he was within sight of the buildings he heard a loud cry from inside and then the unmistakeable wailing of a new born baby. He glanced down at the hawk and saw the light of life pass from its eyes. The Spirit of Macro had gone to reside elsewhere.

Roman Hawk

The End

Author's Notes

The idea for this book came when I was researching Hadrian's Wall. I discovered that whilst the wall was being constructed there were barbarian raids from across the sea. I also watched the Neil Oliver television programme, "The Vikings" and discovered that the lives of the people of Scandinavia were the same in the Iron Age as in the medieval period. As the Vikings, as they became known, did not colonise the lands they raided until the seventh and eighth century it seemed likely that they would just plunder. The Eudose tribe, of which the Tencteri were a clan, did indeed live in what is now Jutland but they had come from Norway originally. As the Scandinavians had an oral rather than a written tradition then I have had to make many assumptions to create the world of Trygg Tryggvasson. At the end of the day it is a world out of my own head but I have tried to make it as realistic as possible.

I have used the generic name for the bird as a hawk rather than a specific type. This is partly because it is a better title but also the people of the time would all have had a different name for each species of bird. The days of falconry were still to come. The evidence for ports and buildings in Denmark is sketchy, mainly because Iron Age people did not build in stone and wood rots away. The places I describe are from my imagination and the research into Iron Age peoples.

The Emperor did indeed modify his plans for the wall when he was in Britannia and saw the difficulties with both the terrain and the natives. Even after he left the concept of the wall was still his but the later modifications came as a result of the Governors and Legates in the Province. The wall was painted white as it was plastered and this was deliberate to show the native population that this was Rome. Needless to say the natives did not like it. While the wall was being built there were constant raids both from north of the wall and the east and west. The Brigante also began to rebel more frequently.

There will be more books to follow, mainly because I like the people who inhabit the world of Northern Britannia at this time. I thoroughly enjoy the research and talking to others who, like me, love Hadrian's Wall and the country which surround it.

Griff Hosker
October 2012

Roman Hawk

People and places mentioned in the story.

Fictional characters are in italics
Ailis-Gaius' wife
Alavna-Ardoch in Perthshire
Alro -Eudose island
Angus-Manavian warrior
Appius Sabinus-Quartermaster of the ala
aureus (plural aurei)-A gold coin worth 25 denarii
bairns-children
breeks-Brigante trousers
Bremenium-High Rochester Northumberland
Brocavum-Brougham
Brynna-daughter of Morwenna
Capreae-Capri
capsarius-medical orderly
Caronwyn-daughter of Morwenna
Cassius-Decurion Princeps
Castra Vetera-Fortress of the 1st Germanica
Clota Fluvium -River Clyde
Coriosopitum (Corio)-Corbridge
corvus-a ramp lowered from a Roman ship
Decius Lucullus Sallustius-Brother of Livius Sallustius
Derventio-Malton
Deva-Chester
Din Eidyn-Edinburgh
domina-The mistress of a house
dominus-The master of a house
Dumnonii-Scottish tribe
Dunum Fluvius-River Tees
Eabrycg-Stockton on Tees
Eboracum-York
Eilwen-daughter of Morwenna

Eudoses-Germanic tribe living in Jutland
First Spear-The senior centurion in any unit
frumentarii-Roman Secret Service
Furax-Street urchin
Gaius Brutus-Son of Antoninus
Gaius Saturninus -Regular Roman Decurion
Glanibanta-Ambleside
Gnaeus Turpius-Camp Prefect Corio
groma-surveying equipment
Gudrun Gudrunsson -Headman of a port in Uiteland.
Gurt-Pirate from East Uiteland
Habitancum-Risingham Northumberland
Hadrian-Roman Emperor
Hercules-Captain of The Swan
Hjarno-Trygg's capital
Hjarno-Eudose island
Hjarno-By-Settlement of the Eudose
Itunocelum-Ravenglass
Julius Demetrius-Senator and Legate
Julius Longinus -ala clerk
Keltoi-Irish tribes
liburnian-small Roman ship
limes-Roman frontier defences
Livius Lucullus Sallustius-Prefect of the ala
Luguvalium -Carlisle
Lupanar-The red-light district (in Rome)
Mamucium -Manchester
Manavia-Isle of Man
Marcus Gaius Aurelius-Decurion
Marius Arvina-Camp Prefect Morbium.
Marius Pompeius-First Spear- Morbium
Mediobogdum-Hardknott Fort
Metellus-Decurion
Mona-Anglesey
Moray-Selgovae Chieftain
Morbium-Piercebridge
Neapolis-Naples
Norns-Scandinavian Fates
Octavius Saturninus-Camp Prefect Eboracum

Oegels-Dun-Egglescliffe on the River Tees
oppidum-hill fort
Orsen-Port of the Eudose in Jutland
Parcae-Roman Fates
phalerae-Roman award for bravery
Porta Decumana-The rear gate of a fort or camp
promagistrate-Local official in charge of a vicus
pugeo -Roman soldier's dagger
Quintus Licinius Brocchus-Centurion Vexillation of the 6th
Quintus Pompeius Falco-Governor of Britannia
Radha-Queen of the Votadini
Rufius-Decurion
Scipius Porcius-Prefect at Eboracum
Seolh Muba-Seal Sands -River Tees
-

Other books by Griff Hosker

If you enjoyed reading this book, then why not read another one by the author?

Ancient History

The Sword of Cartimandua Series
(Germania and Britannia 50 A.D. – 128 A.D.)
Ulpius Felix- Roman Warrior (prequel)
The Sword of Cartimandua
The Horse Warriors
Invasion Caledonia
Roman Retreat
Revolt of the Red Witch
Druid's Gold
Trajan's Hunters
The Last Frontier
Hero of Rome
Roman Hawk
Roman Treachery
Roman Wall
Roman Courage

The Wolf Warrior series
(Britain in the late 6th Century)
Saxon Dawn
Saxon Revenge
Saxon England
Saxon Blood
Saxon Slayer
Saxon Slaughter
Saxon Bane
Saxon Fall: Rise of the Warlord
Saxon Throne
Saxon Sword

Roman Hawk

Medieval History

The Dragon Heart Series
Viking Slave
Viking Warrior
Viking Jarl
Viking Kingdom
Viking Wolf
Viking War
Viking Sword
Viking Wrath
Viking Raid
Viking Legend
Viking Vengeance
Viking Dragon
Viking Treasure
Viking Enemy
Viking Witch
Viking Blood
Viking Weregeld
Viking Storm
Viking Warband
Viking Shadow
Viking Legacy
Viking Clan
Viking Bravery

The Norman Genesis Series
Hrolf the Viking
Horseman
The Battle for a Home
Revenge of the Franks
The Land of the Northmen
Ragnvald Hrolfsson
Brothers in Blood
Lord of Rouen
Drekar in the Seine
Duke of Normandy
The Duke and the King

Roman Hawk

New World Series
Blood on the Blade
Across the Seas
The Savage Wilderness
The Bear and the Wolf

The Vengeance Trail

The Reconquista Chronicles
Castilian Knight
El Campeador
The Lord of Valencia

The Aelfraed Series
(Britain and Byzantium 1050 A.D. - 1085 A.D.)
Housecarl
Outlaw
Varangian

The Anarchy Series England 1120-1180
English Knight
Knight of the Empress
Northern Knight
Baron of the North
Earl
King Henry's Champion
The King is Dead
Warlord of the North
Enemy at the Gate
The Fallen Crown
Warlord's War
Kingmaker
Henry II
Crusader
The Welsh Marches
Irish War
Poisonous Plots

Roman Hawk

The Princes' Revolt
Earl Marshal

**Border Knight
1182-1300**
Sword for Hire
Return of the Knight
Baron's War
Magna Carta
Welsh Wars
Henry III
The Bloody Border
Baron's Crusade
Sentinel of the North
War in the West

**Sir John Hawkwood Series
France and Italy 1339- 1387**
Crécy: The Age of the Archer

Lord Edward's Archer
Lord Edward's Archer
King in Waiting
An Archer's Crusade (November 2020)

**Struggle for a Crown
1360- 1485**
Blood on the Crown
To Murder A King
The Throne
King Henry IV
The Road to Agincourt
St Crispin's Day

Tales from the Sword

Modern History

The Napoleonic Horseman Series

Roman Hawk

Chasseur à Cheval
Napoleon's Guard
British Light Dragoon
Soldier Spy
1808: The Road to Coruña
Talavera
The Lines of Torres Vedras
Bloody Badajoz
The Road to France

The Lucky Jack American Civil War series
Rebel Raiders
Confederate Rangers
The Road to Gettysburg

The British Ace Series
1914
1915 Fokker Scourge
1916 Angels over the Somme
1917 Eagles Fall
1918 We will remember them
From Arctic Snow to Desert Sand
Wings over Persia

Combined Operations series
1940-1945
Commando
Raider
Behind Enemy Lines
Dieppe
Toehold in Europe
Sword Beach
Breakout
The Battle for Antwerp
King Tiger
Beyond the Rhine
Korea
Korean Winter

Roman Hawk

Other Books
Great Granny's Ghost (Aimed at 9-14-year-old young people)

For more information on all of the books then please visit the author's web site at www.griffhosker.com where there is a link to contact him or visit his Facebook page: GriffHosker at Sword Books

Printed in Great Britain
by Amazon